*Barbara*
*Enjoy!*

# ALIVE
# BY
# DEFAULT

## A Novel

D1569392

*John Shivers*

John Shivers

Printed in the United States of America

ISBN: 979-8-3777969-3-0

BearNekkid
BOOKS & SOME SUCH

# Dedication

In October 1990 I made a trip to Bristol, Connecticut to take part in a writers' retreat. For the first time in my writing career, I was going to be interacting with "real" writers, as well as a bunch of fellow writer wanna-be participants, some of whom already had published books to their credit. I was both excited and apprehensive, and I also hit the big 40 while I was there.

One of those participants was a young woman from Mt. Airy, North Carolina. Her name was Jane Tesh, and she is the only participant I've kept up with. In the 32 years since, we have continued our good friendship from afar, some of it built around the standard catch-phrase of literary agents when turning down a potential client, "I can't manufacture the enthusiasm necessary to successfully represent your work." Much of our relationship has been underwritten with extreme enthusiasm.

In the years since we first met, Jane and I have both begun publishing books on a consistent basis. And Jane has been both enthusiastic and encouraging of my efforts. It's with a great deal of pleasure and honor, that I dedicate **Alive by Default** to Jane. And I enthusiastically encourage you to check out Jane's books on her website: https://www.janetesh.com/.

And after twenty-four books, Elizabeth, my wife and one of my best critics, must be remembered in this dedication. Without her, book one might never have happened.

# Other Books by John Shivers

*Create My Soul Anew* Trilogy
**Hear My Cry**
**Paths of Judgment**
**Lift Up Mine Eyes**

◊

*Renew A Right Spirit* Series
**Broken Spirit**
**Merry Heart**
**His Mercy Endureth**
**Let Not Your Hearts Be Troubled**

◊

**Repossessed**

◊

*Slop Bucket Mystery* Series
**Boat Load of Trouble**
**Out of Thin Heir**
**For Sale... Or Not?**
**Revenge And Gravy**

◊

**Gone Astray**

Colorblind

◊

In Service

◊

The River Rolls On

◊

Mountain Laurell

◊

Unwillingly Amish

◊

*Christmas Collector Series*

Three Gifts For Christmas
Weaving a Family for Christmas
Moonshine for Christmas
A Blessing for Christmas
Rekindling Love for Christmas

# Author's Note

On April 3, 1996, U.S. Commerce Secretary Ron Brown and a load of lesser American VIP's were killed in a plane crash while on a European trade mission. This was in the early days of Bill Clinton's presidency, and early news reports suggested that first lady Hillary Rodham Clinton was supposed to be on that trip, but changed her plans at the last minute.

This news flash precipitated a conversation with my daughter, who asked if we'd ever had a first lady killed while her husband was in office. Later that same day, as I was driving on Interstate 75, the premise for this book, **Alive by Default**, was born at about mile marker 315 in Gordon County, Georgia.

I pulled over to the shoulder, grabbed a big brown grocery bag out of the back seat, the only paper I could find, and wrote for about 45 minutes, until the premise for the book stopped gushing. It's taken me over 25 years to bring the idea to fruition, but it's with a great deal of pleasure that I give you Patti Hobgood's and Mollie Montgomery's story in **Alive by Default**.

2023

## *Think about it…*

When you buy a book from an author,
you're buying more than a story.

You are buying numerous hours of errors and rewrites.

You are buying moments of frustration
and moments of sheer joy.

You are not buying just a book,
you are buying something they delight in sharing –

a piece of their heart, a piece of their soul…
a small piece of someone's life.

# CHAPTER ONE

The aircraft was at 28,000 feet and climbing, its sleek, blue and white fuselage shimmering in the mid-morning sun, like priceless jewels in a coronation crown. The golden seal beside the forward access door proclaimed the craft's identity, although on the air traffic control screen it appeared, at first glance, as just another blip among many.

In the cockpit, Captain Anthony Jenkins confirmed the instrument settings and requested a vector reading that would allow him to set the craft down on the other side of the country in record time. That request, while phrased in the appropriate vernacular of the FAA procedures manual, was actually interpreted as an order. When you piloted official presidential aircraft, few corridors were denied you. In response to the transmitted reply, Jenkins adjusted his controls and aimed the black nose of the jet eastward. Only eighteen minutes earlier their wheels had left the tarmac at Vandenberg Air Force Base in California.

"Next stop, Joint Base Andrews," he said aloud to his flight crew in the cockpit. "Man, it's one more hell of a great day for flying."

"It'll be good to get to the house, though," his navigator, a tall and lanky colonel with a decidedly Virginia accent replied. He pronounced it "hoose," further validating his heritage. "I promised the kids we'd do something special this weekend."

To the rear of the massive flying fortress, his passengers were absorbed in their own agendas, unaware of the high spirits of the flight crew, or of a potentially catastrophic situation rapidly deploying deep in the plane's underbelly.

On board was the wife of the free world's most powerful leader, as well as a number of her staff. The retinue of media, who scrutinized every fart and faction of the first family, were in their quarters in the tail section of the executive aircraft, preparing for the wave of photo opportunities awaiting them once they touched down outside Washington, D.C. These were the grapes of harvest that assured them their high profile careers, and down to the last reporter, each was already mentally jockeying for an advantage over the competition.

The sky was cloudless blue, a weatherman's ideal day, and the reports that continued to issue from the cockpit printer promised that the flight to Joint Base Andrews, where government aircraft were based under tightest security, would be smooth and uneventful. It would be just the latest successful flight in a career of perfect trips, Captain Jenkins promised himself.

In her bedroom mid-ship, Mollie O'Brien Montgomery was engaged in animated conversation on the red bedside phone, just one of the perks afforded her as first lady, along with a private suite aboard all official presidential aircraft. From that most ordinary looking telephone, thanks to the sophisticated communications equipment aboard the Presidential plane, and the clout that her title bestowed, she could, at any given moment, connect with and talk to anyone, anywhere in the world. But on this particular day, Mollie Montgomery viewed the instrument as more curse than convenience.

"You damn bastard," she screamed into the phone, "Nobody screws around with Mollie Montgomery! I'll see you in hell...!"

\* \* \* \* \*

When the impact of the news bulletin hit, I was hung over the john, the rancid aftertaste of puke still coating the inside of my mouth. The newscaster's words unleashed a fresh eruption of soured stomach contents. But the consequences of a tainted batch of chicken salad were nothing compared to hearing that you should be dead. I gripped the rim of the white china bowl until my knuckles ached. To release my hold, I feared, might sever the thin strand of life that allowed me to breathe and feel. I had been sick even before the special announcement interrupted a heated abortion debate on "The View." I never knew when, or how, I got up off the cool, black and white tile floor. I couldn't have known then, how attractive a case of acute food poisoning would become before my life was normal again.

*Exploded in mid-air*, the commentator said. *Everyone on board, including the first lady, is presumed dead.* Suddenly I felt damned lucky to have eaten that generous scoop of chicken and grapes and crème cheese and pecans. It had to have been the crème cheese that had turned.

I attempted to wash away the putrid taste of vomit with a big swallow of club soda and wondered who the paper had sent in my place. *The paper! I've got to call the paper. Oh God, don't let it be one of the guys with a family.* Suddenly consumed with guilt, I prayed even as I punched in the number for Herb Martin's office. I needed to talk to somebody who could assure me that I really was alive.

While I listened to the endless ringing of his phone, I was frantically punching the TV remote buttons – channel surfing. All the major networks had suspended their regular programming in an effort to score one over the competition. America's first lady, her staff-in-waiting and assorted press had been blown out of the American sky. That was big news. Dr. Phil and Steve Harvey would have the luxury of re-runs. A plane load of dead VIP's wouldn't, and the news media was playing it to the hilt.

"Yeah, what is it?" a gruff voice demanded from inside the phone. It was a voice I knew well. Herb's "nice" voice.

"It's Pat… Patti Hobgood," I stammered, my eyes still glued to the TV screen. "What the hell's happening with this plane explosion?"

"Oh, my God, Hobgood," he groaned. I could picture him dancing around his miniscule office like a little boy needing a bathroom. He was always that way whenever things got harried and he had to think on his feet. He was always in a bad mood anyway, but some days were worse than others. "You better be damned glad you weren't on that plane."

*Well, duh!*

"You're telling me? But what happened, exactly? And Herb," I asked, fearfully, "Who'd you send in my place?"

"All hell's breaking loose, Hobgood. They blew that bird clean out of the sky. The rescue crews don't expect to find enough wreckage to identify."

"They who?" I asked. "You mean this wasn't an accident?" I was still trying to digest his latest nugget of information. "Who

14

would have wanted any of them dead badly enough to commit such an act of terrorism?" It hadn't occurred to me that this could have been deliberate.

"No one has claimed responsibility, yet, but from the reports coming in, it was one more hell of a bang that brought that plane down. Everything points to sabotage," he said. "And it'll be one of those damned radical lunatic groups. You wait and see."

I was listening to Herb with one ear, and at the same time doing my hardest to catch what the CNN commentator was saying. Knowing that I had cheated the grim reaper wasn't as comforting as I had always assumed it would be, and I found that I was starved for anything that would explain such a senseless tragedy.

"You still there, Hobgood?"

"Yeah," I told him. "CNN's updating the story. Maybe they have something new."

But the latest details didn't yield any additional hard facts. I still had plenty of questions. Instead, I saw the President, grim-faced and drawn with grief, speaking to reporters as he prepared to leave the south lawn of the White House on his official chopper, Marine One, enroute to Joint Base Andrews. From there, he'd fly to the U.S. Air Force Academy in Colorado, the closest secured landing strip to the wreckage site.

"We will find the animals responsible for this atrocity, and they will suffer the punishment they so richly deserve," he pledged to the sea of microphones grouped near the helicopter's forward steps. His face was ashen and lined, a study in gut-wrenching anguish. I'd never seen our President look so ancient, or so beaten.

"You gonna watch TV or you gonna talk to me," the voice on the phone demanded. "I don't have all day."

"Sorry, Herb. It's just I feel so weird knowing I'm alive, and everyone else on that plane was blown to little bits. It's a hell of a feeling."

"Enough of a feeling to go to work?" he asked. "After all, you are my chief White House reporter."

"Yeah," I told him. "I can handle it. Let me grab a quick shower and I'll be in."

"I'll be waiting," he said. "And bring a change of clothes, too."

I realized then that he planned to send me to the disaster site, and for the first time in my life, I didn't know if I wanted to get on a plane or not. It seemed too much to expect to cheat death twice in the same day.

"I'm on my way," I said. "And Herb, you didn't tell me who went in my place."

There was a long, awkward silence on the other end, before finally, he said, "McEntyre. It was McEntyre."

The name hit home with as much impact as the explosion that had destroyed the first lady's aircraft. *McEntyre. Married, three kids, with number four due in less than a month.* I was sick all over again.

* * * * *

The take-off from Dulles was choppy, thanks to an evening

16

storm that had blown in from the coast. The Delta 747 aircraft was too powerful for the front, however, and we were soon cruising above the unpleasant weather, on our way to Denver, Colorado.

But the turbulence outside the plane was nothing compared to the conflict still raging in my gut. The chicken salad was staging its last hurrah, in the face of stiff competition from a damned good case of nerves. I wondered if my stomach could ever be calm enough to crave food again.

I wasn't totally comfortable to be in the air so soon after missing my appointment with destiny. And it didn't help that I was pissed over my fiancé's apparent lack of concern about whether I was dead or alive. I'd called Lee Stanton's office on Capitol Hill before I left, and, as usual, he wasn't available. When I needed him most, he was "detained elsewhere," the unfeeling voice that answered the phone informed me. Make a note I reminded myself, as I hung up the phone: *Think twice about marrying a senior congressional aide, unless you're willing to always play second fiddle!*

There was no way he didn't know about the tragedy. What's more, there's no way he could have known that I missed the flight, because I'd been too sick to let him know. *So why isn't he calling me? Why isn't he calling somebody?*

Lee's title had been impressive, at first, and being seen on his arm at hundreds of receptions and parties had been a heady experience. Profitable, too, when it came to my job. Lately, however, I'd found myself resenting the constant demands on our already limited time together. When I'm only one plate of chicken salad away from being killed, it's hard for me to accept that he's too busy playing puppet for some senile old senator, to hold my hand

17

for a minute when I need him. As it was, he didn't know if I'd been on that plane or not, and it didn't appear that he was taking any steps to find out.

We landed in Chicago, where I deplaned long enough to visit a real restroom. Once I'd washed my face and put on fresh makeup, I actually began to feel like I might survive.

The information Herb had emailed me showed that once I landed, it would be another two hours' drive to reach the wreckage. I'd need my GPS, because unlike the President, I didn't have the option of flying into the Academy. But first things first. My stomach was finally begging for food, and when the flight attendant offered me a snack shortly after take-off, I ate heartily. The job that confronted me wouldn't get done on an empty stomach. Or a queasy one.

Question was, exactly what was I being sent to get? The news reports I'd read before leaving D.C. had already confirmed that the explosion was so massive, identifiable body parts weren't expected to be recovered.

It must have been one hell of an explosion, all right, was all I could think. My spine tightened from the chill that swept over me, as I was reminded for the umpteenth time that I should have been on the passenger manifest. Realization revisited me in a myriad of ways. I wondered in those first hours if I would ever again know the luxury of forgetting.

It had been a last minute emergency that caused Herb Martin to send McEntyre in my place. I'd been **The Washington Times'** chief White House correspondent from the day James Madison Montgomery gave his November victory speech to supporters crowding into the ballroom of Washington's famous old Willard

18

Hotel. The F.B.I. investigation had been quite an ordeal, but finally the coveted credentials that would admit me to the Executive Mansion were in hand. It was a high I will never forget.

I was still in awe of my permanent assignment, and would have followed the President and first lady into the bowels of hell. Not because I worshipped them, but because I appreciated and respected the magnitude of their positions. And I would have been on that California trip with the first lady, but for my Achilles heel – a gastronomical love affair with good chicken salad. That's why I'd pigged out when I discovered the newest menu item at the little Georgetown bistro where several of us ate lunch at least once a week. And at about the time I should have been leaving for Andrews, to accompany the first lady to comfort California earthquake survivors, right at that moment, I was locked in a life or death embrace with my favorite john.

The west coast disasters were old news, but Molly Montgomery's trip was designed as a relief effort. Both for the victims of the quake, and for the unofficial "Montgomery for President" re-election campaign, which had to have California's electoral votes, if he stood any chance of renewing the lease on 1600 Pennsylvania Avenue.

It was big news, alright, and that's when McEntyre got blasted out of bed to sub for me; the first of two explosive, life-changing events for him and the world.

The White House beat had been the plum assignment of a chaotic but exhilarating career that began while I was still enrolled at Georgetown University. It was a case of having been at the right place at the right time, and there were moments when I still pinched myself to be certain that it was all for real. Washington was worlds removed from the sleepy prairie town of Council Grove, Kansas, where I'd grown up, and later, my days on a small town newspaper there.

I'd been on the **Times** staff for almost five years, long enough to get to know the nation's capital in the ways that only an insider can understand or appreciate. Long enough to watch James and Mollie Montgomery parlay a lifetime of prominent public service into the nation's most prestigious elective positions.

Now this. With elections looming, there were questions in many quarters about whether the President had the support to win a second term. His administration had been wracked with scandal and political faux pas. In many cases, he himself had given his enemies the very ammunition they needed to bring him down. It would be interesting to see how much the sympathy factor would influence next November's voters.

How ironic, I thought. Of all the negatives, it had been the late first lady whose actions had generated the most disturbing press that many predicted would spell the end of the Montgomery dynasty. After all, where do you go after being president, especially a one-term president? Unless your name was James Earl Carter, that is. And President Montgomery was a James cut out of an entirely different piece of cloth.

From a lifetime of what could be described as either triumph or tragedy, depending on which side of the aisle you chose to believe, Mollie Montgomery's track record was dotted with high profile accomplishments and conquests.

Those on the inside, I had discovered early on, knew for

certain that James Montgomery would still be working for his family's banking empire in Mobile, Alabama, if Mollie hadn't been behind him, pushing him, kicking and screaming all the way to Washington.

It had been the unique combination of her iron will and his pasta backbone, financed by his family fortune and her determination to rise above her raising, that had catapulted him into a U.S. Senate seat on his first try for public office.

That had been more than 20 years before, and during almost four terms, Senator and Mrs. Montgomery had become a staple topic of the D.C. cocktail party unofficial speakers' bureau. Perhaps nothing had generated as much conversation or controversy as The Cumberland Group, Mollie's left-wing, political think tank.

It had been near the end of her husband's first term in the Senate that she had established The Group. Without apology or deference to the toes of the powerful, Mollie Montgomery sent the Beltway establishment into a self-protective tailspin. She was a force to be reckoned with, although during all the years the organization dominated the D.C. landscape, no one was ever certain of its exact mission, or its place in the Washington establishment. That's exactly the way Mollie wanted it.

She was, her husband's supporters vowed, going to wreck him politically. But she hadn't, despite many episodes of rough going. In true O'Brien fashion, she had kept the faith; while telling all of those who would have brought her down... to go to hell!

In death, she might be the one factor that could ensure her husband a second stint in the Oval Office.

It was the classic rags to riches success story, with several curves thrown in to make the story all the more intriguing. Washington government's male population was infamous for their risqué jokes about the first lady's background, all of her curves included.

During the first presidential campaign, his wife had been judged as either the strongest attribute James Montgomery had to offer the voters, or she was labeled the one skeleton guaranteed to bring him down. Everyone had strong opinions about the woman who had promised openly, early on in the campaign, to serve as her husband's unpaid chief of staff. And as could have been predicted, the public reaction to her declaration was split along party lines.

I'd done extensive research into her background during that first presidential campaign. The more I discovered, the more I understood and admired her accomplishments. I also came to understand why so many in high places foamed at the mouth at the mere mention of her name. They feared her, I decided, because most of them weren't man enough to acknowledge her talents while ignoring her gender.

She was a southerner by birth, another monumental strike against her inside the cliquish Washington Beltway. Her mother had been the town whore of a small Alabama crossroads, and as Mollie freely admitted, she had never been sure exactly who her father was.

She might have eaten free lunches in the school cafeteria, but in the classroom she had out-shown the children of the community's most elite. Eventually, it paid off. In her senior year of high school, she qualified for enough scholarship money to buy a one-way ticket to the University of Alabama at Tuscaloosa. A part-time job in the college library, along with a frugal lifestyle, had allowed her to graduate magna cum laude with a debt-free degree in history.

James Montgomery, five-generations descended from old Mobile money, was also at the University, majoring in recreation – primarily his own. For where his academic performance was found lacking, his family's influence more than compensated.

Mollie O'Brien first noticed the tall, blond-haired football player when he declined to pay an overdue library fine. It wasn't necessary, he had explained. The Montgomery Fine Arts Center – a gift from his grandfather's estate and the newest building on campus – more than made up for any dollar ninety-five library fine.

But Mollie hadn't bought it, so the story went. And she raised holy hell with him, even going so far as to report his refusal to pay to the library director.

That was the first of many documented occasions when their points of view would clash; often in public, and usually to the embarrassment and discomfort of those around them. But from that first encounter, James Montgomery and Mollie O'Brien were in love. And they didn't give a damn what anyone else thought.

It didn't take long for their relationship to reach a crisis point. When James Montgomery Sr. and Allison Whelchel Montgomery discovered that the crown prince of their dynasty was infatuated with a whore once removed, their salt-air nurtured blue blood topped the boiling point. Only the cunning and ingenuity of the little girl from Sugar Cove, Alabama rescued the engagement. It was a talent she would use to advantage many times over the ensuing years. Some speculated, after the fact, that her sole purpose behind promoting James for the senate seat was to put him -- and her -- a rung above the small-town, high society bankers that were his family heritage.

When their engagement was official, the senior Mrs. Montgomery, so the story went, sent Mollie's mother a haughty note of instruction. From the engraved, curlicued "M" on the front, to the frosty message inside, the note was intended to put the bride's mother – if not the bride herself – in their rightful places at the bottom of the social register. Mollie's future mother-in-law had dictated that the wedding would be in keeping with the Montgomery social reputation, and that the groom's family would underwrite the entire production, which would be staged in Mobile. Mollie and her mother were to spare no expense, Mrs. Montgomery dictated, and were to bill everything to the Montgomery account.

Mollie was pissed as hell. She admitted as much in later years. Revenge would be hers, she had vowed, and spend the money she did. It was a wedding fit for royalty. Her future in-laws had hinted that Mollie's mother might want to "observe" the activities from a distance. In other words, she wasn't good enough to be seen by their friends. And Mollie had let them believe such would be the case.

Once her future mother-in-law had selected her dress for the wedding, Mollie and her mother shopped until they found a dress even more stunning, more expensive, and bought it. Charged it to James Montgomery, Sr. On the day of their wedding, when Allison Whelchel Montgomery was all set to be the star of her son's wedding, the bride's mother stole center stage. It was a position that Mollie had gladly relinquished, if it meant that her future in-laws were finally put in their rightfully deserved places.

When their vows were exchanged, and the four-carat diamond-studded wedding band was securely installed on her left hand, Mollie O'Brien Montgomery put the world on notice that she was a force to be reckoned with. She began with her mother-in-law, and in her wake, down through the years, were strewn the mutilated corpses of all who had attempted, albeit unsuccessfully, to best her.

Mollie Montgomery thumbed her nose at her detractors on the day she married a future president, and she continued to disregard them even into the White House.

Unlike previous first ladies, she had refused to become just the dutiful White House hostess and presidential helpmate. Instead, she had searched for and hired an official mansion hostess with the bloodlines and social acumen guaranteed to assuage the biggest snobs inside the Beltway. She continued in her high-profile position with The Cumberland Group, while still serving as her husband's right hand advisor. This was a move that incited a massive outcry among official Washington, where critics decried her easy access to confidential presidential politics, and charged her with multiple conflicts of interest.

As one of her predecessors, Hillary Rodham Clinton had learned the hard way in the early 1990's, America had a very defined model for first ladies to emulate. But Mollie Montgomery didn't fit that mold; what's more, she made no attempt to try.

Now she was dead. Gone as explosively as she had lived. And I was supposed to be dead along with her!

I needed to check in on reality in the worst sort of way. After the attendant removed my tray, I used the phone in the seat-back ahead of me, and put through a call to Herb Martin.

# CHAPTER TWO

Steam rising from two mugs of fragrant coffee danced a tango of camouflage, alternately shielding and revealing the features of two men at a small, round metal table. The hour was late and the two had arrived at the shabby little cafe from opposite directions. Each had navigated the narrow, winding streets in Sarajevo, in Eastern Europe, without need of directions or a map. Only those who knew the old Bosnian city, before the breakup of the U.S.S.R. and the civil war and destruction that followed, could have moved about so easily.

The older of the two, a short and stocky man of middle-eastern descent, had arrived first, quickly located a table in a secluded corner, and settled in to wait. Patience was a trait he'd cultivated early in his career. Simultaneously juggling two identities that were often at cross purposes to each other required rock-solid stability and minute attention to detail. To his annoyance this night, however, he found it impossible to wait without outwardly betraying his emotions. This had been his most challenging assignment; and it had been flawlessly executed, he told himself, judging from the American news broadcasts he'd been monitoring. Still…?

He ordered cognac coffee, desperate for something to chase the unaccustomed chill he'd felt since hearing the first news bulletin earlier in the day.

His companion, a younger, shorter, dark-haired man of

German descent, judging by his accent, finally arrived. Casual passers-by would have assumed the two men were friends, meeting after an evening of work perhaps, for a final cup of coffee before heading home.

But appearances can be deceptive and often presume facts not in evidence.

"Did you bring it?" the German asked, the timbre of his speech heavy with an accent usually found in the former communist bloc states near the Russian border. He picked up the heavy mug of steaming coffee the waitress had placed before him, and took a sip. "The deed is done," he said. "I assume you've heard the reports. It was exactly as you ordered. The American woman will betray no one."

His companion answered by pulling an envelope from a pocket inside the wine colored jacket he wore and sliding it across the table.

The other man intercepted the bundle midway, tore it open, and when he was satisfied, shoved the contents into his pocket, wadded the envelope and tossed it into the corner.

"You are to speak of this to no one," the delivery man cautioned. "Forget everything you know. Disappear. That was the deal."

"I'm as good as dead," the German laughed. "And dead men don't talk."

He raised the cup to his lips in a mocking, sarcastic salute, but the haste with which he gulped the amber liquid it contained made lie of his cocky demeanor. He banged the mug against the table top, spilling some of the remaining contents, before he patted the jeans pocket where he had stuffed the cash, and rose to leave the cafe.

The older man ignored his companion's flippant response, but concentrated instead on the man's retreating back. His face wore an odd expression the younger German wouldn't have recognized, or understood. Only after the sharp echo of two gunshots from outside ricocheted off the weak coffee-colored stone walls, did the messenger rise from his seat and take leave, making sure to retrieve the discarded envelope on his way out.

The young German's body was sprawled in death across the cobblestone sidewalk near the cafe entrance. Even at that late hour, the streets were busy with passers-by, many of whom had stopped to watch life slip away from the young stranger. The crowd of curious on-lookers that had gathered rag-tag around the victim continued to grow. After too many years of war, the people of Sarijavo had become numb, insulated to the horrors of sudden, violent death. Testimony to their attitude was their lack of compassion or first aid.

One of the men in the crowd dropped to his knees beside the body and began to rifle through the victim's pockets. After he realized that no one objected, he stuffed his own pockets with ill-gotten gains, including a wad of bills, which he hastily hid from view of those standing closest.

When the older man was sure that all was as it should be, and that the victim's death would be classified as simply the latest daily incident of random violence in a city wracked by multiple murders every day, he slipped away, quietly, lest he call undue attention to himself.

\* \* \* \* \*

Herb was in the office, and answered my call on the third ring.

I had landed in Denver amid a late spring snow storm. The TV in the baggage claim area was showing shots of President Montgomery and his staff landing at the Air Force Academy earlier in the day. The Chief Executive had, the newscaster said, traveled by Air Force chopper to the mountain top where most of the debris was concentrated. News crews, he added, were being restrained some distance away. Following my talk with Herb, and after the latest of several unsuccessful calls to my fiancé's personal cell number, I had headed my rental car north through the heavy, falling snow.

"It's me, Herb. Patti," I had said, when he answered.

"Thank God," Martin said. "You forget how to use the phone or something?"

"Don't hassle me, Herb. I'm still not comfortable knowing that I was supposed to be on that plane, and I feel guilty as hell that McEntyre's youngest kid won't ever know him. Besides, this is the first chance I've had. So talk quick. Tell me what's happening?"

"A hell of a lot of rumors; very few facts." he said. "But you're gonna be where you can follow up."

Herb filled me in, while I scribbled in the notebook I always carried in my jacket pocket.

The rescue effort was continuing, he said, but only body parts too small to identify and larger bits and pieces of the plane had been found. "That was one hell of a bomb, Hobgood."

The remote mountain top where most of the debris had fallen, he explained, lay in rugged terrain. They don't expect to be able to recover much. "The cherry trees may be blooming here in Washington, but it's still winter in the Rocky Mountains!"

"So it was a bomb?" I didn't know whether to ask it as a question or as a foregone conclusion.

"No one is sure," Herb said. "All the indicators point that way. But it's still too early. That call belongs to the NTSB boys... and they aren't talking. Especially not in this case."

"But how could a bomb have gotten on board?" I asked. "Security on a presidential aircraft is tighter even than Fort Knox."

"They don't know the answer to that. At least, not yet. But the grapevine says it has to have happened at Vandenberg. Which doesn't say a whole lot for the security of our bases on the home front," he added.

"Are they certain of that?"

"They aren't certain of anything," Herb cautioned. "But since the plane was overnight at the base, it seems to be the most likely scenario. How they did it is another question entirely."

"So what's my assignment?"

Covering the President's White House was one thing. Making sense of all that had happened in the past eight hours was something else. I was a hard news reporter, comfortably at home covering international personalities, government crises, and every aspect of the American political process, from convention floor to the Senate floor. But this was the first time I had ever covered the death of a first lady, let alone a first lady who died under questionable circumstances.

"Just keep your eyes and your ears open, Hobgood." Martin said, giving me directions. "Leave the emotional hoopla to the others – I want you to examine everything closely, ask questions, and give me some copy that no one else will have. Stick to President Montgomery like glue. There's more to this story than meets the eye."

"You make it sound like the President killed his own wife," I joked. "Surely you don't believe that?" I couldn't conceive that the nation's Chief Executive could be so cruel or callous, or desperate for re-election.

"They were always at each other's throats, usually in public. It's common knowledge. He could've had enough. Who knows?"

"You don't really believe that, Herb," I charged. "They were also very much in love; I've been with them enough to know. They felt free to attack each other in public, because they are... I mean, were, totally devoted. They were safe with each other, and they knew it.

"It looks like to me it would be more productive if I went to Vandenberg to explore that angle."

"Right, Hobgood," he answered sarcastically. "Security may have been lax last night on that base, but you can bet the Pope himself wouldn't get in tonight."

"I'm just not sure how much information I can accumulate here, after the fact. The plane's blown to bits, and everyone is dead. Dead men don't talk, Herb."

"Maybe not," Herb answered, "but the way other people react and respond can speak louder than words. That's what I want to read about. Hell, Hobgood, you're a damned good reporter. Do I have to tell you how to do your job?"

"Not on your life, Herb! I know how to do my job. I just wasn't certain you knew it!"

\* \* \* \* \*

The embassy official twisted the knob on his office door, ensuring that it was locked. He returned to his desk, lifted the telephone, and punched in an international long distance code followed by the number. Two rings later, half way around the world, a woman's voice answered.

"Is he in?" the official asked.

"Hold please."

In only micro-seconds, he was connected with the only person he feared more than God Himself.

A man's voice, gruff and mercenary, jumped through the phone. "You have something for me?"

"The job is done," the embassy employee reported. "He won't talk. That's guaranteed."

"Good," the man on the other end replied. "Now if I can be equally certain of your silence, neither of us has anything to worry about."

"Have I ever betrayed you?" the official asked.

His question was ignored.

33

"I don't have to remind you," the unseen voice replied, "what will happen should you betray us. People in high places have gone to great lengths to insulate themselves. At this point they are totally protected. They will be very unhappy if any of this is laid at their doorstep."

"But sir," the embassy official protested, "You know you can depend on my discretion."

"You know what to do." The click of a vacated phone line, and the silence that followed, was the response that echoed around the globe.

# ALIVE BY DEFAULT

# CHAPTER THREE

Men in the flowing robes and head garb of the Middle East stood out in razor sharp contrast to the elderly couples nearby, decked out in their finest polyester hounds-tooth checks from the 1970's. A smattering of business suits, from rack sale quality to hand-tailored, bridged the gap between the important and the obscurely impotent. They were a Heinz 57 assortment, waiting in various stages of impatience outside the office of one of the nation's senators. But as diverse as they all were, each was there in pursuit of a common goal: political intervention.

In the ornate halls of the Capitol Complex, the magnificence of the real estate gave mute testimony to the raw power that the ordinary mortal who occupied these quarters could wield.

This assortment of ambassadors, lobbyists, and even the back-home constituents, naively certain that the man behind the massive mahogany door was their own personally-elected representative, couldn't begin to grasp the extent of his power. They were convinced that their personal cause was paramount, much more critical than anything else. Even these bit players in a greater drama could never have imagined the depth nor degree to which this politician's iron-fisted treachery would reach.

They could never have understood how little he relished the thousands of visitors "from back home" who stopped by to visit him each year. That's what underlings were for, he had dictated. Rare was the voter who earned a personal audience. Equally amusing, the Senator often remarked, was how easily the little people actually bought the aides' standard line of BS, delivered in tones of hushed reverence. The Senator wouldn't be able to meet with them, they were always told in somber tones, because, "He's tending to your business in the Senate." They heard, and left disappointed, but doubly convinced that their business in Washington was in good hands.

"The Senator will see you now."

The voice was male, totally lacking in personality or warmth. It belonged to an aide, a drone of a fellow. In response, a short, stooped man wearing the robes of one of the many Islamic cultures represented in the Washington Diplomatic community, stood, then moved toward the door leading into the inner sanctum; a political holy of holies.

He paused in the entrance way, and bowed slightly from the waist, paying homage to the gatekeeper. The culture of his homeland was thousands of years old, and he himself was closely connected with the royal family in power at the moment. But in Washington, those who needed passports into the halls of the mighty, learned one lesson quickly: Locks click open fastest when lubrication is applied liberally from the bottom up. To have slighted this no-name of a man, more the political eunuch, could have ultimately proven disastrous.

The Senator was a barrel-chested man, more than seventy-six inches tall, and sporting a forty-four inch waist. He didn't look his fifty-five years, an accomplishment attributed to the pickling quality of all the piss and vinegar in his system. Mostly vinegar. The Senator stood as a giant in more ways than one among most of his colleagues, and many was the adversary who had fatally assumed that the man's gentle giant facade was also a measure of his testicular veracity. In reality, the senator operated with a no-holds barred fighting style. He would, his detractors mumbled behind the scenes, be the first to sacrifice his own virgin daughter to appease a killer volcano. He was equally comfortable using all of his attributes to achieve any end he selected.

Few chose to oppose him, and those who did usually lived to regret their hasty, ill-conceived actions.

"Sit down. Sit down!" the senator barked, waving his hand impatiently as the purple-robed Turk was ushered into his office. The senator was on the phone, his voice both belligerent and belittling. "I'm just getting an update," he said aloud to the air space between them.

The little man sat quietly, his hands folded neatly in his lap. He would wait for permission before speaking. It was only right; after all, this was America's highest ranking senator. And when one was summoned, he came. Quickly, and without question, although not always without trepidation.

"There are still too many people who could queer this whole deal," the Senator was complaining to the person on the other end of the phone connection. "I've come too far to lose now because some flunky with loose lips can't follow directions. The fewer people who can talk, the better the insurance." The Senator was twisting impatiently in his high-backed chair. "You know what to do," he thundered into the phone, and without waiting for a reply, slammed the hand piece back into its cradle of termination.

"It was good of you to come on such short notice," he said

to his visitor. "Things are rapidly coming together." And with the same degree of speed that his chair swiveled to face the little man, the Senator's expression assumed the facade of still another of his multiple personalities, ready for the next opportunity, already scheming his next conquest. It was a trait that his contemporaries had labeled as visionary. His detractors also had a description for his range of interactive skills. They compared him to large, filthy, disease-ridden vermin.

"Our government is in your debt, Senator, for the financial aid package you arranged for us," the visitor responded. His hands spoke as eloquently as his mouth. "I could do nothing else when your assistant called. We were honored to have a role in the success of your operation."

The visitor bowed again, in deference to the man he considered his superior. "And may I officially express our shock and sorrow at the unfortunate tragedy which has struck your President Montgomery. It is a most difficult time for him, I am certain."

"I'm equally certain that it is," the senator agreed. "You know, this may be the catalyst that takes him out of the Presidential race next year. And who could blame the poor man?"

* * * * *

Across Capitol Hill from the Richard B. Russell Senate Office Building, and within sight of the magnificent Capitol dome, in the office of The Cumberland Group, a somber late afternoon gathering of the senior executives echoed the mood that had, by now, descended over most of the nation. Political leanings diminished in priority in the face of such a tragedy. And terrorism was something to fear –especially when it invaded the home shores.

40

"It was a deliberate action," Hal Warren, the second in command at The Group was saying to his colleagues. "And from what we've been able to determine from our sources, the first lady was definitely their target."

"She was more aggressive than most Presidential spouses," another member at the table volunteered. "But to murder her? I don't know. Her husband, maybe. But not Mrs. Montgomery. What would it gain them?"

"And who are 'they'?" another voice questioned.

"One of the problems with the liberal-based agenda that we promote here at The Group, is that we often leave our rear flanks unprotected," Warren explained. "Mrs. Montgomery was convinced that this very organization is in danger – and that the enemy is right here at our front door – inside the Beltway. She believed that someone had her marked."

"That's a pretty serious charge. What does – did she base her concerns on?" a voice from the other end of the table asked. "God knows, we've had at least half of Washington nipping at our heels at one time or another since The Group was established."

"She had her suspicions," Warren said, as he struck the tabletop with his clinched fist. "But she hadn't shared the details with me. She said we'd talk about it when she got back from California. She had to take care of that chore, so those bastards at the DNC could stop peeing their pants for fear that California will go Republican next year.

"I don't know anything specific," he added. "But I do know that Mollie Montgomery had a sixth sense about such things. She should have been the President, not him. God knows what he'll do without her. But in the meantime, if she thought someone was out to get us, then I don't have any choice but to believe her."

"So say she was right?" McCallum Kennedy, Vice President of Communications asked. "What do we do now? What can we do? All we have to go on is a dead woman's intuition."

"Tonight, I'm going to take her office apart piece by piece, Hal Warren vowed. "We need to know what all is hidden there, for our own wellbeing."

"Is it wise to invade her private papers?" another member of the group asked. "After all, she was the first lady. Won't the Secret Service object?"

"They probably will," Warren agreed, "and if we wait, they'll seize all her files and we'll never find what we need.

"Remember," he cautioned, "if Mrs. Montgomery was right, we have no reason to trust that the killer will stop with her. Any one of us could be next on the list!"

\* \* \* \* \*

The President walked aimlessly about the mountain slope, where a late falling of fresh snow had transformed the disaster scene into a surreal winter wonderland. I had zeroed in on the Chief Executive with my binoculars. And I watched as he stopped frequently, picking up first one piece of debris, and then another. He would brush away the snow, hold the fragment in his hands, turning it and examining it, before finally laying it aside and moving on to another pile.

It was one of the most heart-breaking vignettes I had ever witnessed, and my heart broke for him. As President, his own private grief would take second place to the communal grief the nation would expect him to endure. I felt like a voyeur.

Evidently the Secret Service agents shared my guilt, because they had abandoned their traditional, almost anal appendage role, I was relieved to see. Instead, they were huddled nearby, a respectful distance away, but still close enough to perform their sworn duties.

What hours earlier had been piles of twisted, mangled wreckage and pieces of luggage and fuselage, had been neutralized by the blanket of freezing, numbing white. Only the bright yellow disaster ribbons gave a clue to the depth of one of the world's worst aircraft disasters.

From the western lip of an adjacent mountain peak, across from the disaster scene, a kaleidoscope of shapes and colors created a crazy quilt panorama of frantic activity. The rescue squad, bundled in their orange garb against the harsh elements on the exposed mountain top, was easy to identify through the light snow showers which continued to swirl across the craggy mountain range.

White House Press Secretary Mart Harris was briefing the milling group of reporters assembled on our side of the mountain, and I pulled my attention away from the President, to concentrate on Harris's remarks. From the sound of things, it was nothing more than a rehash of the now-stale details the networks had been broadcasting for hours. But then, I didn't know why I expected any more from this man who had disgusted me from our very first encounter. He and I had never enjoyed a good relationship, primarily because I have little use for egg-headed Harvard lawyers. From some of the snide comments I'd overheard from colleagues, and the way they purposely mis-pronounced his first name with an "F" instead of an "M," I knew I wasn't alone in my dislike for the tall, lanky, owl-eyed press secretary.

On more than one occasion, when Harris's ego had gotten too inflated, the first lady had bitched openly to the press corps about the man she believed was a political liability to her husband's presidency. I had to wonder how he was coping with the loss of so prominent an adversary. And if, as Herb Martin had speculated, someone had indeed murdered the first lady, Harris would have been at the top of my personal list of likely suspects. That he would have liked to kill her, I have no doubt. Whether he did was another story.

I had edged as close to the action on the other mountain as the mass of press and curious on-lookers would allow. Despite official pleas to the public intended to discourage curiosity-seekers, it was obvious that community rubber-neckers were turning out in force; a wave of humanity that local law enforcement was both ill-equipped to handle and hesitant to restrain. After all, society's morbid fascination with disaster and blood and gore is well documented. When it involves the President of the United States, curiosity would naturally be at an all-time high.

The press briefing hadn't ended, but the ringing of my cell phone gave me a good excuse to withdraw from the crowd.

"What is it, Herb?" I answered, expecting it to be my crusty, impatient editor.

"Patti? Where the hell are you?"

"Contrary to popular rumor, I'm not dead," I snapped in reply. "But it took you long enough to call to verify that little matter." The voice on the other end of the poor connection from D.C. belonged instead to Lee Stanton. "The question is, where in the hell have you been?"

"Covered up here in the office is where I've been. Dealing with all the little people who have to call about the first lady. Like we care," he added haughtily. "God, deliver me from the small minds of the masses."

"Well, you obviously haven't been worried about me," I charged. "You're too busy to call me, and you're too busy to talk when I call you. Don't you realize... I should be dead. I was supposed to be on that plane." I was near tears by now, partially from the exhausting emotions of the day, as well as from anger. "Didn't it occur to you that I might need you?"

"Oh, Patti. Your Kansas roots are showing again. Grow up. It's called life."

"Well evidently it's meant to be a life without you," I screamed into the phone, but the rising evening winds robbed my response of its razor edge. That's when I lost contact with him. Was it the poor connection, or did he hang up on me? Come to think of it, either way, poor connection was the best description of our relationship.

*When I get back to Washington, things are going to change!*

# CHAPTER FOUR

As she surveyed the masses searching for seats in Washington's National Cathedral, Patti couldn't help but pick up on the body language being spoken Tower of Babel fashion, throughout the historic Episcopal house of worship. For certain, there were those whose slumped shoulders and lined faces suggested that they had either cared greatly for the late first lady, or they feared for their continued existence, now that she was gone. This defeatist perspective was especially prominent among those who were part of The Cumberland Group. It was a well-known fact that President Montgomery had tolerated his wife's political folly. Most assumed the group would be liquidated in the not too distant future.

Others in the vast congregation wore looks that proclaimed what could only be their thinly-disguised relief that Mollie O'Brien Montgomery was no more. Their presence, by invitation only, was less about mourning the deceased and more about assuring their doubting minds that the enemy had truly been vanquished. And in such a situation as this, you didn't refuse a presidential invitation. Not even for a funeral. Especially for a funeral. There were days in the future when politics would once again trump gut-wrenching grief, and no one wanted to be caught lacking. Then there were those few whose motives were more voyeuristic in nature. Americans, Patti reminded herself, were bad wreck rubberneckers at their best, and where better, never mind the motivation, to see and be seen?

For Patti, however, who had been almost an appendage to

47

the first lady over the past few years, no location for a memorial service rang more insincere and phony, or more pretentious, than the National Cathedral, only a few miles from the White House. Mollie Montgomery, Patti knew, cared little for organized religion, and the massive edifice run by the Episcopal denomination would have been her very last choice as a location. Whenever she had to declare a spiritual allegiance, the first lady had called herself Baptist. Patti had always found this to be somewhat amusing, given that Mollie's own mother had been put out of the little Baptist church in Sugar Grove, Alabama, because of her openly entrepreneurial sexual actions. Her daughter had even been denied the right to go to Sunday School there.

If there had to be a memorial service at all, Mollie would have been the first to insist on something small and low key. She and the President attended church most Sundays when they were in Washington, at a small church near Blair House across from the White House. Attendance was more for the PR factor and less about true worship. When they managed to escape to Dog Island, to their remote tropical getaway off the Alabama coast, they usually skipped church. Island population numbers were strictly controlled, which meant the closest the press could get to their quarry was dockside in Mobile. On the island, both the President and the first lady felt safe and comfortable to abandon all pretense of religion and just be themselves.

In this case however, if the first lady's death was going to be successfully exploited by the President's re-election campaign committee, then the service needed to be as high profile as possible. And to satisfy the Secret Service's rabid obsession with security, the National Cathedral answered all needs and demands for both objectives.

The melodic strains of *Adaigo from Toccata and Fugue in D minor* began to compete with the background gabble of many different conversations, as the cathedral organist began the preservice music. Patti didn't know who'd selected the funeral music, but she did know that Mollie Montgomery, if she could, would have protested this as well. Pattie realized as she settled herself in the seat she'd been assigned in the section reserved for the press, that she was one of few in the congregation who probably recognized one of Bach's more famous pieces. Classical music had long been an obsession with her, and was yet another way in which she and her fiancé didn't see eye to eye. Lee Stanton loved country music. Worshipped it, especially Patsy Cline, Loretta Lynn and Dolly Parton. It was country music for him, and nothing else. When she was with Lee, Patti was forced to put her own musical preferences aside.

It had been ten days since the TV airways first informed the country's population that the first lady was dead from a massive mid-air explosion. From those first news reports on the missing presidential aircraft, known as Air Force Two, because the president wasn't aboard, to the later confirmation that indeed, all had been lost, it had been a non-stop barrage of information. Not all of it accurate. Much of it was unadulterated fiction. Wreckage of the first lady's aircraft was scattered over several miles on either side of the Colorado-Kansas state line. Patti had seen all of this for herself, and understood why there was no casket, nor even an urn containing the remains of the woman who had literally been larger than life itself.

But just as there was no clear evidence of the deceased first lady's presence in the service, save several large photos of the woman mounted on easels around the chancel area, there also was no clear explanation of exactly what had happened. Rumors, Patti knew, were rampant. Accuracy, on the other hand, left much to be desired. All that Patti Hobgood could say with any assurance was that her gut told her there was more to the story than she and the rest of the country were being told.

There was just something about how information on the travesty was being released that made her journalist mind skeptical. One of her media professors at George Washington University had zeroed in on Patti's ability to read people and situations. She had, he insisted, uncanny accuracy and recognition of detail. It would, he had predicted, stand her in good stead in investigative journalism. There was a fluttering in her stomach, and a little voice behind her left ear, that usually showed themselves whenever she was confronted with deception or even outright lies. Right now, as Mollie Montgomery's service got underway, Patti could feel the many doubts she had converging to stage a coup.

Thanks to her high profile placement among the White House press corps, she was able to secure a second row seat with direct viewing access to where the President would be sitting, and also the pulpit where various speakers would utter the words necessary to hopefully bring about closure to Mollie Montgomery's earthly life. Never mind that some of those words might be totally lacking in accuracy, or even sincerity.

As she reflected on the woman who had made the last few years of her life's work so interesting, the nation's president entered from a side area and made his way to the seat that had been designated for him. He and Mollie had never had children, and he was an only child. James Madison Montgomery, Sr. hadn't lived to see his son in the Oval Office, and Mollie's mother-in-law, she knew, resided in a swanky assisted living facility in Mobile where, according to leaked reports, the old she-wolf had lost most of her memory and along with it her venom. Mollie had always understood that she had several half-siblings, thanks to her mother's line of work, that had been given up for adoption at birth. She had never known for certain who they were, and had never been inclined to search for them, not even after DNA genealogy research became so popular. She had reasoned that having those relations surface might have pushed her mother-in-law over the edge.

At James Montgomery's elbow this morning, when that front pew should have been packed with grieving family to help the widower through the ordeal, was Vice President William J. Reynolds and his wife, Catheryn Yelverton Reynolds. The image of the trio was, for Patti, unsettling at best.

*He's all alone! Totally alone.* She had never seen the president look so absorbed. But it was the sight of the other man, the man whose place on the ticket had assured James Montgomery of his first term win that drove home the point of how big a hole his wife's death had left in the President's life. While the President had never been overly-robust, his custom tailored suit that now literally hung on his frame, and the ever-darkening circles under his eyes offered mute testimony to how much sleep he was losing. But the biggest indication of the depth of his grief, was the sense of isolation so real it could literally be seen. Under any other circumstances, the president would have been working the room, pressing the flesh, and leaving a permanent understanding that he'd been there. But this time, it was as if he didn't even understand that anyone was there.

He had no one to whom he could turn. Unlike Presidents

Kennedy and Johnson and a couple of others who had been better at hiding their downlow proclivities, this chief executive didn't even have a mistress. There was no one with whom he could seek solace. James Madison Montgomery might have been a first class wimp, but from all reports, he had been slavishly faithful to his wife. And if the oft-shared Capitol Hill rumors were even half-believable, Vice President Reynolds was totally grief-stricken that it had been Mollie Montgomery, and not her husband, who was blown out of the mid-American skies.

The sitting VP had higher aspirations than being equal to a bucket of warm piss, as one of FDR's second in command once described the prestige of the vice presidency. In fact, inside the Washington Beltway, even before the first lady's death, odds were already being laid about whether he would or wouldn't challenge the president. And what better way to get a leg up, than to have the sitting president removed from office and replaced with the ever-faithful vice president? Now, with Mollie's death, quietly whispered conversations confirmed, Vice President Reynolds saw his chances of successfully challenging the sitting chief executive rapidly going down the drain.

As the service got underway, Patti had a chance to glance around without being overly obvious. For certain, the mourners made up a who's who of official Washington. What's more, in the room this day, Republicans and Democrats who were miles apart politically, were sitting side by side without benefit of a literal or figurative aisle to separate them. The irony of the moment wouldn't have been lost on Mollie Montgomery, who, Patti knew, would have certainly commented. Wherever the first lady was at that moment, if she was able, there could be little doubt that the woman was rolling on the floor laughing.

One person who wasn't there that day was Lee Stanton.

"I wasn't invited," he'd informed her the previous evening when she'd finally managed to get him on the phone. "You don't truly expect me to crash a funeral, do you?"

While his words had contained a modicum of sincerity, Patti had easily picked up that he was actually happy to get out of attending the service. And she knew for certain that had it been anyone else, he would have been right there, front and center. As part of his job as chief of staff for Texas Senator Albert Rawlings, he was at the senator's left side. Always. Absent was Sharon Rawlings, the senator's ex-wife, who had made a big splash in D.C. society upon her initial arrival, but had wearied of the Beltway tango many years before, and departed the capital and her marriage for greener pastures in Wyoming. The standing joke in Washington was that the senator couldn't even manage to go pee without his chief of staff giving him instructions. But those on the front end of the joke were severely ill-informed.

"So Senator Rawlings isn't coming to the funeral, either?"

*I guess if there's one elected official in town who would have the brass to thumb the president's nose in this situation, it would be Rawlings.*

Patti knew that ideologically the senator and the president were poles apart. They had both come to congress at the same time, and had managed to clash early on. Neither had any use for the other, as Lee would remind her every chance he got. Still…

"Of course he'll be there," Lee replied, and the tone of his words quickly let her know that he considered the question the height of stupidity.

"But you won't?"

"Isn't that what I just told you? You wouldn't believe how we've had to revamp the Senator's schedule to work in the funeral. I'll be going in a different direction so that he can, in effect, be in two places at one time."

*Well, you ought to be good at that, because that pretty much describes our relationship.* Literally two ships that sometimes pass in the night. Patti thought it, but didn't give voice to her deepest feelings. She certainly thought them, however. The reality that Lee hadn't been concerned enough about her when she should have been on board the first lady's plane still wrankled. And since her return from Colorado, except for a hurried dinner one night, from which he left early and suddenly, she hadn't seen him, not even in passing. Neither had he been available by phone. Not for the first time she'd grilled herself, trying to learn what it would take for her to declare, "Enough is enough."

The service wound on for more than an hour and a half, and she found herself becoming more and more uncomfortable. Mollie herself had understood and even embraced that she was far from angelic. She might have been a piece of work at times, but she wasn't two-faced. By the time the final amen was pronounced, however, it appeared that heaven's highest archangel had been displaced in a bloodless coup. Mollie Montgomery had definitely developed wings, if not an oversized halo to go along with them.

Patti found herself feeling uncomfortable for the late first lady, and knew for certain that the woman in question would have protested vehemently and colorfully. Mollie Montgomery had a vocabulary that would cause a hardened sailor to cringe in reaction. Most of the time, she kept that side under wraps, but given all the blarney that had been dispensed that morning, Patti was certain, she wouldn't have been able to govern her words.

She stood with the rest of the congregation, finally, moving slowly, lest her stiff joints protest too loudly. As the president shuffled his way up the aisle, like a terribly old man, to strains of music that Patti couldn't immediately identify, her eyes roved over the crowd that she knew in just moments, would be jockeying for the fastest exit. Official Washington didn't stop the entire beltway world very often, and the vast majority of those there were more than anxious to return to their normal orbits. One of those anxious to escape turned at just the right moment, and his and Patti's eyes locked. Mutual recognition happened, and Patti somehow knew she wanted to revisit that point in her life, when she and Harmon Bostwick had both been students at George Washington University. From the look of delight on his face, even from some fifty feet away, it was obvious that the senior reporter for *Nation's News* magazine was equally glad to see a familiar face.

Her colleague motioned for her to stay where she was, and Patti watched as he began threading his way against the flow of departing mourners, headed her way.

"Patti!" He exclaimed as they finally got close enough to embrace. "You don't know how good it is to see you."

"You, too, Harm." While she was definitely glad to see her former classmate, Patti couldn't quite manufacture the same degree of delight. "How long has it been?"

"Too long, Patti. And when I heard about the first lady's plane exploding in mid-air, you're the first person I thought about." He dropped his eyes, then said more quietly, "I was suddenly afraid that I might never see you again."

"Why, Harm. Thank you for being so concerned." She hugged him again. *This guy could give Lee Stanton some caring lessons!*

"So I guess you've been pretty busy these past ten days. The only reason I take **The Times** is to read your stories. You've had at least a couple of pieces in every issue."

"It's been pretty hectic," Patti conceded. "And I've got to hurry back to my computer. Herb wants a story on this service in time for the late afternoon edition."

"You can do it," her friend said. "You know, you deserve so much more than **The Times**. Maybe this will give you a ticket to something better."

"Something better. Like what? Not all of us are *Nation's News* caliber, you know."

"You're so right," he said, as he socked her lightly on the shoulder. "But you aren't one of those losers. No ma'am, you're one writer who could go big, and the sooner the better, I say."

Patti pointed toward the nearest exit. "We better take this chance to make our escape, or we may be standing here two hours from now." Her friend turned, surveyed the landscape, took hold of her elbow, and they began to move slowly toward the main entrance, following in the wake of the many mourners still in the cathedral.

"Maybe someday I will be looking for something else, but

right now, I've got all I can do to keep up with this story that only seems to get bigger instead of smaller." *Lee has already decreed that once we're married, I won't be working anywhere.*

She patted her friend's arm. "Hey, it's great to see you again, Harm. But I really do have to get back to my computer."

"Well, what about dinner tonight? We've both got to eat. Let's grab something and really catch up."

*Lee may not like me making plans apart from him, but that's how he does me almost every day. He can just get over it.*

"I'd enjoy that," she told him, as she spotted an opening in the crowd and speeded up to take advantage. She fumbled in her purse, then withdrew a square of cardboard. "Here's my cell number. Text me the details."

Harm took the offered card and tucked it in his shirt pocket. "Will do. But before you go, I've got a question."

"Shoot." Patti assumed he was about to inquire about her preference for dinner, and her honest answer would be, "It doesn't matter."

"Do you buy the "official" explanation… he used both hands to pantomime quotation marks… that the explosion was caused by mechanical failure, or do you think there's more here than what they're telling?"

"Uh… uh… I… I really can't say." In truth, she had spent many moments since first learning of the first lady's death playing around with her gut feelings, and what were some very obvious discrepancies. But she'd confided her doubts in no one except her fiancé, who had promptly dismissed her concerns. What's more, he'd actually lectured her about making waves. After that, she'd kept her thoughts to herself. Never mind that it all didn't add up. Many of Washington's legitimate happenings were math deficient anyway.

"It's just too neat, somehow. It's like something's not kosher," Harm said, as they started to go separate ways. "I guess we can talk about it tonight, because it just doesn't smell right."

*I'm not the only one who thinks something's bad wrong. Could she actually have been murdered?* The concept was as frightening as it was beyond reason. Or was it?

Yes, they would definitely talk about it over dinner. "Text me," she said. "Right now I've got a story to write."

# ALIVE BY DEFAULT

(

# CHAPTER FIVE

Thanks to many years of covering major events at a frantic run, and with little time to waste when it came to generating a story on deadline, Patti knew she could finish her work in short order. Already, the opening paragraphs of her account of the morning's funeral service was rattling around in her head. By the time she slid under the keyboard, the story was practically writing itself. In less than forty-five minutes she'd banged out the first draft, then edited and polished, until she was totally satisfied with the finished thirty-six inch story Herb had assigned. She wasted little time hitting SEND and marking one more task off her ever-present to-do list.

In the middle, just as she was getting into the groove where the words were literally gushing into life, her phone rang. A quick glance at the screen led her to believe that the call was from Harm. But she couldn't break the flow. He would understand, and she would return the call as soon as she finished her assignment.

When she did call back, Harm's phone rang and rang, and she was about to give up. Perhaps he would call her back, especially when he saw he'd missed a call from her.

"Don't hang up," a man's disjointed voice suddenly ordered, and she felt somewhat intimidated by his presumed authority. "Be right with you, Patti."

*At least he knows it's me.* She was pretty sure the voice had been Harm's, but she had numerous questions about what had his attention. As she waited for him to return, she remembered again his question before they departed the cathedral. "Do you buy the administration's explanation that the explosion was caused by mechanical failure, or do you think there's something more here than they're telling?"

The words echoed throughout her head. Was there something more than what the president himself and various other officials had revealed? She'd been around politics long enough to understand that there were various shades of truth. Often that truth could be found more in the unsaid, than in what passed as verbal fact. Did Harm know something she didn't know? Her mind began to skim back through all the research she'd done since that fateful day.

*President Montgomery doesn't really have a backbone. He's proven that time and again. But surely he wouldn't lie about the catastrophic happening that robbed him of his very anchor and counselor, and the woman he loved more than all the Montgomery money and prestige. Unless… unless…*

Patti could accept that perhaps there were aspects of the destruction of Air Force Two and the tragic loss of seventy-one lives that the politicos would rather not share. After all, if some mechanic at Vandenberg had gotten sloppy, the system was going to protect the truth. She didn't agree, but she did understand how politics worked.

Then her thought processes went deep, too troubling to even give voice to. If, on the other hand, terrorists had somehow breached the highest levels of Vandenberg's security, that definitely wasn't something that would make the administration look good. But she couldn't wrap her mind around the possibility that President

James Montgomery was deliberately lying. Surely, if the cause was anything more than mechanical failure, he would want to be up front and totally transparent. After all, this was his wife who was dead. Then the flip side of the truth presented itself, and Patti was right back where she had been minutes after that first unbelievable news blast changed everything.

*Unless… what if his handlers are lying to him, and they've used Mollie and him both to further their own private agendas? Is it possible that the president himself doesn't even know the truth?*

Because the truth was, without Mollie by his side, without Mollie protecting his back, the president would be rudderless, totally lacking in direction. He'd already exhibited this several times in the days following the explosion. Fortunately, for him, the public had chalked it up to extreme grief. But Patti knew he wouldn't be able to sustain that wave of sympathy for long. If nothing else, his and Mollie's enemies on Capitol Hill would smell the blood. In truth, sharks were probably already circling.

Harm had finally come back on the line and apologized for leaving her hanging. "My maid was about to leave, and I had to pay her," he explained. "So are we still on for dinner?"

When she assured him that her deadline was met and she could now go to dinner with a clear conscience, he'd offered up several different dining options. "And, Patti," he'd said with marked somberness, "we really gotta talk."

It was against this checkered backdrop of doubt and the unknown that she dressed for dinner. They'd agreed to meet at Maurice's, a tiny pub a few blocks south of the Hill, where many of the drones that labored in the august halls of democracy would escape whenever they got the chance. In addition to some of the best hand-crafted libations, the little hole-in-the-wall had a long-standing reputation for their burgers and homemade fries.

Obviously, Harm either knew something, or at best, he'd picked up something that made him question the specifics surrounding the first lady's death. The one thing Patti knew about her friend was that he was meticulous when it came to research and verifying facts. If there was any doubt at all, the old Harm she knew wouldn't even drop hints, never mind publishing the article. If he was questioning exactly how Mollie Montgomery had died, it appeared he had good reason.

*Does he know something I don't?* That possibility alarmed her.

What's more, Patti suddenly realized, she also desperately needed to know the truth, whatever it was. Never mind who it implicated or who it exonerated. After all, it had been more than just the first lady whose life had been snuffed out. And yet, she knew she'd been spared, and took absolutely no comfort from it. Somehow, that seemed to be a mandate to discover the facts. If for no other reason than all those whose lives were extinguished so suddenly, and who would never receive the attention that had come to Mollie Montgomery. Patti realized she owed it to them.

Indeed, the past few days had seen her at one funeral or another every day, as she said goodbye to colleagues who had perished, and as she thought back on those services, not a single one could begin to compare to all the hoopla that had surrounded Mollie Montgomery's send-off. Suddenly, she realized, Mollie for all her brashness and "up yours" attitude, would have been equally horrified. Mollie, she understood, would have gone to all those other funerals and memorial services.

President Montgomery, on the other hand, had kept himself barricaded in the White House, staying for hours on end in the bedroom he'd shared with Mollie. Rumors had quietly run rampant that he was so out of touch with reality, Russia could have bombed the capitol, and he wouldn't have reacted. To say that he was still deeply in shock was an understatement.

*Is he even fit to govern?* As soon as the question formed in her mind, a feeling of shame overridden by doubt flooded over her. The last thing Washington or the country needed was doubts about the president's grip on reality. And one person who certainly would be most interested in the validity of those whispered confidences that were anything but confidential, was none other than Vice President Reynolds himself.

As she left her Georgetown apartment headed to meet Harm, Patti couldn't shut out the rumblings that had been circulating inside the Beltway over the past few months. It was no secret that there was absolutely no love lost between James Montgomery and William Reynolds late of Texas, and a long tenure in the halls of congress. Referencing the famous quip from FDR's vice president John Nance Garner that the vice presidency wasn't worth a bucket of warm piss, Mollie had offered more than once to baptize Vice President Reynolds with a bucket of the golden elixir. There were, she'd viciously maintained, many who would be willing to contribute to the contents of the bucket.

Reynold's selection for the number two spot, Pattie knew,

had been made to ensure that Texas's thirty-eight electoral votes went for James Montgomery. The future first lady had understood the practical necessity, but that didn't mean she had to like it. Or that she had to keep quiet, and she hadn't even attempted to bridle her tongue. Indeed, on more than one occasion, she'd upbraided the vice president in front of witnesses. There was little love lost between those two.

Once poorly kept word of the vice president's possible plans to challenge his boss for the top spot in the upcoming election reached Mollie's ears, the little respect she had for the barrel-gutted giant from the Texas hill country had eroded faster than an Atlantic City beach in the clutches of a cat five hurricane.

"I'd sooner see an orange and purple spotted homosexual orangutan in the Oval Office," Mollie had sputtered within earshot of enough journalists to ensure that her assessment made every broadcast of the news that evening. CNN had actually broadcast it minutes after the words were uttered, and by the next morning, it had been thinly disguised war between the Montgomery and Reynolds' camps.

The vice president, she knew, lusted after the digs at 1600 Pennsylvania Avenue. If he chose not to oppose the current president's chances for re-election this time around, it was a foregone conclusion that he would be on the ticket in four years. Even President Montgomery had halfway endorsed the man who had single-handedly delivered his victory, when caught off guard by a question from one of the media people a few weeks earlier.

"I would love to see Vice President Reynolds throw his hat into the ring for the presidency," he'd said in response to the reporter's question. "But in four years. Right now, he and I have a job to finish. I look forward to having him by my side as we go to victory next November to buy another term."

*I need to research what has to happen for the president to be declared incompetent to remain in power. Because if Reynolds could force that action now, he'd have an automatic toe-hold on the seat of power.* And knowing the vice president as she did, Patti had no doubt if the man could ever grab the reins, he would do everything in his power to resist giving them back.

James Montgomery had been a lackluster chief executive at best. He'd never been raised to work and manage. His parents had seen to it that their son never had to lift a hand, and his slightest whim was their command. They had moved heaven and earth to make certain he understood that he was different from everyone else. Mollie was the first person who'd ever challenged him, and it had been her determination that had propelled him to Washington. It was also her savvy insight into the political processes that evaluated everything and advised her husband what his position and his responses should be.

More than once he'd ignored her commands, and had lived to regret it. Nevertheless, it was a lesson he never totally learned, and now that his wife was dead, Patti wondered how long the man could last. Vice President Reynolds might be a bully and a closeted wife abuser, attested to by high placed individuals who had photographic evidence, but he was also on the inside track, and knew how dysfunctional the president would be. But would he capitalize on this time of upheaval? Patti feared he would.

William Reynolds was the son of Texas oil millionaires, and

if his government salary had dried up, the man's lifestyle would never have noticed the difference. In fact, according to his tax returns, he donated all of his salary to charitable causes. And unlike the president, William Reynolds' parents had demanded that he perform some of the most demeaning work in the oil industry to "earn" the more than healthy allowance he'd drawn since he was in the fifth grade. His fingernails appeared eternally stained from the backbreaking, grungy labors he'd performed. Obviously, he'd never availed himself of the manicurist that handled the president's nails on a weekly basis in a little salon in the sub-basement of the White House. As a vice president, she would have been easily available to him, subject only to the commander and chief's needs.

Mollie Montgomery had subscribed to the theory that you keep your friends close and your enemies even closer. Toward that end, she'd insisted that her husband keep his vice president in the loop. There were many photo ops when the Montgomery-Reynolds team appeared on the evening news as a unified front and a cohesive team. Behind the scenes, however, it was a slightly different story. The vice president was only given the most basic of information before the fact, and when it came to sharing information after the fact, the number two guy often got his details just like the rest of America -- from the six o'clock news. The first lady understood the Texan's political aspirations, and was determined that he would not achieve those goals on her husband's coattails.

The vice president had been less than happy with how he was treated, and while she didn't want to assume facts not in evidence, Patti couldn't help but speculate on how his revenge would look. In her mind, it wasn't a question of would the man capitalize on the first lady's death, but exactly how and when would he even the

ALIVE BY DEFAULT

score? It did cross her mind that the vice president might have had a hand in Mollie Montgomery's death, but as soon as she considered the possibility, Patti chided herself that the man might be a wife-beater, but she couldn't see him as a cold-blooded murderer. And for certain, if it was determined that human hands had deliberately caused the explosion, those hands would be those of a murderer many times over. William Reynolds was, by all accounts, a slimy piece of humanity. But would he actually sacrifice an entire plane load of people in order to gain the presidency? Patti couldn't see it.

Harm was waiting when she finally arrived at Maurice's fifteen minutes after their appointed rendezvous, thanks to a greater traffic jam than usual around Dupont Circle. Patti hurried ahead of the hostess who was trying to seat her, suddenly desperate to feel the connection with her friend. Obviously, she still hadn't totally gotten beyond the gnawing guilt trip that knowing she should be dead had heaped upon her.

Harm stood and motioned the employee away. "I'll take care of her," he said, as he reached to embrace Patti. "I was getting concerned," he murmured. Patti wasn't certain about the basis of his concern, but didn't bother to ask. As if he didn't really expect a response, Harm pulled out her chair, and seated her.

"Traffic was hell," she said, and when there was no response, Patti knew that her friend understood. Nobody who worked inside D.C. would question the insanity that seemed to infect even the shortest commute on an almost daily basis.

"Glad you didn't let it discourage you," Harm said. "I really wanted us to have a chance to compare notes." His voice not only got softer as he spoke, but Patti picked up on a more somber tone.

69

Only thing was, she didn't quite know how to interpret either his words or his body language that practically screamed discomfort. Or was it desperation?

Before she could broach the question, a server appeared, introduced herself, and took their drink order. Because they each already knew what food they wanted, the server took that as well. In only a matter of minutes, a Sam Adams draft was set in front of Harm. Patti had struggled between beer and a glass of wine. When the server set a glass of her favorite merlot at her place setting, Patti immediately regretted her decision. But there were more pressing issues on the agenda. Red wine it would have to be.

As soon as the server's back was to them, Patti wasted no time. "What's so urgent? You know something." She zeroed in on his eyes, and refused to back down. "Don't deny it." She tapped his hand with her finger. "Don't keep me in suspense, Harm."

For the longest time he said nothing, and Patti had to wonder if, after all the build-up, her friend was going to clam up. "That's the problem," he said, finally. "It's nothing concrete that I know. But there's way too much scuttlebutt going around. There's something that's not right about this whole deal."

"Such as?"

Harm fiddled with the bowl of sugar packets on the table, then finally he said, "All the aeronautical people I've spoken with, and I'm talking people really in the know, don't buy that a mechanical failure brought that bird down."

Patti chewed on the inside of her jaw as she contemplated all the unsaid in his explanation. "If it wasn't mechanical, that means it had to be human related."

"Exactly." While his one-word answer definitely confirmed her belief, it also created several more questions. Patti wasn't certain she could give voice to those questions, because the can of worms that would be opened was downright frightening.

"So, was it simple human error or deliberate human sabotage?" Harm had identified the crux of the issue. Patti well knew that human error wasn't anything to covet. At the same time, when compared to the possibility that someone had intentionally destroyed the presidential aircraft killing almost six dozen innocent people in the process, Patti found herself craving to know that it had been a mechanic who made a critical mistake. If it turned out that unknown forces had managed to penetrate the security that normally surrounded all presidential aircraft, this created even more frightening possibilities.

But the question that haunted her revolved around how a single human error could have triggered such a massive explosion.

"My sources say it's unlikely that a mechanic was simply having a bad day," Harm said. Patti didn't want to hear his words, because to hear them meant they had to be owned. It meant she had to believe that sinister forces and means had brought down Air Force Two. Either way, those who were killed were still just as dead. But if it turned out to be a deliberate attack, that meant a mass murderer was on the loose. Identifying and ultimately capturing that murderer was another matter entirely.

"Tell me everything you know," she said at last. "I don't know if I can handle all of this, but I don't like being in the dark, either."

Harm glanced over his shoulder, then surveyed the restaurant again. Patti knew there was no one close enough to be able to easily overhear. Could their table somehow be bugged? Did they need to take their conversation outside? She couldn't justify feeling so paranoid, but neither could she banish the feeling that something bigger than all of them was at work.

"I'm talking with several people who are convinced beyond a doubt that the plane was sabotaged."

*Sabotaged!*

"Mere mention of the word conjured up all manner of images, each one playing leapfrog over the other.

"But how, Harm? Tell me how." She mentally envisioned the huge aircraft. She'd been on board enough times over the past three years to know the procedures and protocol for getting on board. "That plane was under constant surveillance in a very secured area of a military installation. How could someone have gotten to it to do the job?"

"That's what no one can say for certain," he told her, then quickly went quiet, as their server set plates in front of them. "No, nothing else, we're fine," he said in response to the server's query. "And this is on one check to me," he told her.

"No, Harm, you don't..."

He held up his hand. "No discussion," he said. "We've got more important matters to thrash out."

Patti heeded his words, and dropped her protest. She would repay him some other way.

After the server returned to the kitchen, Harm continued. Over the course of the next few minutes, Patti was amazed at the depth and the thoroughness of her colleague's investigative research. In truth, she was mentally kicking herself. She could have done everything Harm had done. But she hadn't. If Herb Martin discovered how lax she'd been, he was apt to yank her plum White House assignment.

*It would serve me right if he did. Which is why I'm not about to confess. But I will take Harm's information and run with it.*

Instead, she paid close attention to everything her friend had to share, and doodled notes on a napkin she'd yanked from the caddy.

"Air Force Two was given its customary thorough check once the plane touched down at Vandenberg. There were four mechanics that had flown out from Joint Base Andrews." He stopped, took a bite of his burger and chased it with several of the restaurant's fresh, hand-cut French fries.

Patti understood the scenario. The American public rarely ever saw all of the background work that accompanied a trip by either of the first couple. Whether it was Air Force One with the president aboard, or simply Air Force Two, the protocol was much the same. On a huge military transport that left ahead of the official plane, was presidential ground transportation, and many of the ground support personnel. Among them, the hand-selected mechanics that would examine every inch of the aircraft to ensure that a safe return flight was guaranteed.

*Only this time, something didn't work like it should have.*

"But who? What, Harm?"

Her friend swallowed another bite of his burger. "Believe you me, the brass has grilled those four guys for hours and hours. I understand it's been brutal. But it's also been a hard matter to find any blame on their part."

"Meaning they didn't let some mechanical issue slide by, or that none of them deliberately crippled the plane?"

"Both." He slugged down the last of his beer, and held his empty mug aloft as a signal to their server that he needed a refill. "You need your wine refreshed?" He eyed her half-filled glass, then glanced at the burger that was getting cold with only one bite missing. "You better eat that burger. Didn't your mom ever teach you it's a sin to waste food?"

"Come to think of it, she did mention that once or twice. But then I've never been famous for doing everything she told me. Besides, the possibility of the first lady's death being something more than an accident has kind of robbed me of my appetite." But to show that her heart was in the right place, never mind her desire for nutrition, she took a healthy bite of her burger. "But don't keep me in suspense. What about those mechanics?"

Harm waved his hand, as their server approached with a fresh mug of beer with foam still running down the side, and a new glass of wine for Patti. "Thank you," he said. "We're ready for the check when you are."

As the young woman made her departure, he said, "Basically, those four guys came out smelling like roses. The one with the shortest tenure has ten years working on that bird to his credit. And

74

you know how stringent the qualification process is. Nope..." he took another bite of burger. "Those guys didn't miss anything, and for certain, none of them deliberately did anything that would have caused that plane to fall out of the sky."

"Harm. What, exactly, are you saying?"

"According to witnesses on the ground, several of whom actually saw pieces of the plane raining down, it was one more massive explosion. It would have to have been a major mechanical problem that blew that bird to pieces. Even then, if it had been a mechanical failure, the plane more than likely would have failed in flight, and crashed to the ground. But this was a explosion that ran from one end of the bird to the other. That plane and all the people on it were already in little pieces long before anything ever hit the ground."

As much as Patti wanted to know the truth, the visual image Harm's description created in her mind's eye was not just troubling; it was terrifying.

"You're saying..."

"It almost had to be a deliberately set explosive of some description, and a complex one at that. It could even have been remotely detonated. There's no other explanation that can withstand the sniff test. This wasn't an accident. It was deliberate, and so far there's no indication that any of the plane's maintenance crew is responsible."

"They're sure?"

"As sure as it's possible to be, in the absence of any witnesses or other definitive explanation."

"Then I'll ask it again. How? HOW, Harm? Fort Knox is totally unguarded compared to this plane. How did someone do it? And who was it?"

Harm swallowed another mouthful of his beer, almost as if he was looking for courage to continue, Patti thought. Whatever her friend had on his mind, it was freaking him out. And that was nothing like the level-headed Harm she knew.

While she was expecting further explanation, what she got instead was a question that immediately put her on her guard. "Have you heard anything on the grapevine about shady happenings going on in The Cumberland Group?"

"The Cumberland Group?" Patti asked, as if she hadn't heard correctly. "Sure. We all have. Remember. Depending on who you're talking to, and which side of the aisle they normally sit on, The Group is either lily white or terrorist infiltrated.

"No," Harm said, as he glanced around. His hesitancy was beginning to freak Patti, but she was hesitant to let him know it. "That's business as usual over at The Group. This is something else. Something much darker, much more explosive than even the bomb they built."

"As explosive as the blast that blew that plane and seventy-one people to hell and back?"

"Exactly."

Pattie chewed on her response, before finally she said, "Then, no I've not heard anything, but obviously you have. Spill it!"

Harm checked yet again before he spoke, and even then, his voice dropped several decibels. "Blackmail."

76

Patti didn't know what kind of explanation she was expecting, but that hadn't been anything close. "Blackmail? Did I hear you right? Who was blackmailing who?"

"Look, Hobgood. I'm gonna level with you. But if you're smart, you won't take this any farther until we know more. Anybody who would blow seventy-one innocent people out of the sky wouldn't even hesitate to retaliate against either one of us if we threaten them." He regarded her with eyes so black and serious, Patti's entire body was consumed in an involuntary shudder.

"You've got my word. But don't keep me in suspense."

"It appears that Mollie Montgomery has been blackmailing somebody important. And that somebody may have gotten fed up."

Patti was broadsided. If someone had been blackmailing Mollie Montgomery, Patti would have had no problem considering it a viable possibility. Lord knows the first lady had been guilty of a number of unreported shortcomings. Patti could have named several of them herself. Some enterprising enemy wouldn't have hesitated to capitalize on the first lady's vulnerability, and she would have paid the ransom. But for her to be blackmailing someone else? That was a different matter entirely.

"Harm? Are you sure?"

Her friend studied her for a couple of seconds before he answered. "Oh, for sure, the rumors are out there. They're buried really deep, and most of my sources won't even talk about it. Never mind denying or refuting it. But it does appear that the first lady had a most involved pay to play deal going on."

"So you're saying you think the person she was extorting

money from got tired of paying and decided to play ugly?"

"It makes sense, doesn't it?"

"Well, yeah. I mean, I guess. But who could that person be?" Then she connected the dots. "And how would this person manage to sabotage presidential aircraft?"

"Perhaps, somehow, he did. Or maybe he hired somebody to do it. Those are answers I don't have. Or at least, if I have them, I don't recognize them as such?"

"So how, exactly, how does a first lady blackmail somebody? The Secret Service keeps her totally under wraps whenever she's out in public. Even then, all of her guests to the White House are screened."

"There again, Patti, I don't have the answers. But I do have to question if there's a mole buried deep inside The Cumberland Group. It's the only thing that begins to make sense."

Patti considered his premise, and allowed her mind to wander over the inhabitants of Mollie Montgomery's political action committee. For certain, there were a couple of guys on staff that she didn't totally trust: McCallum Kennedy, Mollie's VP of communications, was one. Anybody who garnished perfectly good vanilla ice cream with salsa definitely couldn't be trusted. And she had always questioned if Hal Warren, Mollie's right arm and CEO, was as trustworthy as Mollie believed him to be.

She reviewed everything she knew about both gentleman, and then the image of P.A. Mayhew, the gulf coast shrimper's daughter who coordinated the first lady's agenda between the East Wing of the White House and The Cumberland Group came to mind. In truth, Pascagoula Annie Mayhew would have had the most opportunity and the most information on what the first lady was up to, and when and where.

*If it's true, could it have been P.A.?*

Patti's head began to throb. The half a hamburger she'd finally put into her stomach began to revolt. Not since that day on the cool tile of the bathroom floor in her apartment, when this nightmare first began, had she felt so sick. But she'd had good justification that day to be sick. Now, to think that some of those whom Mollie Montgomery trusted most had somehow had a hand in the conspiracy to kill her, along with many others, caused a complete gastronomical revolt in her gut. Without even begging his pardon, she left an open-mouthed Harmon Bostwick in her wake, as she made a mad dash for the ladies' room on the far side of the restaurant.

Of the many questions plaguing her brain right at that moment, the one most prominent was would she make it on time, or would the undigested remains of her evening meal christen innocent, unsuspecting diners along the way instead?

\* \* \* \* \*

As dawn seeped through the blinds of her eastern facing bedroom the next morning, Patti pulled herself from bed with both reluctance and dread. Her return home the previous evening had been fraught with humiliation and awkwardness. Harm had insisted on following her back from the restaurant, and about half way, as downtown D.C. traffic had slowed her passage, Patti had wished her friend was driving. Somehow, she managed to make it into her designated parking space.

"Are you okay?" Harmon had asked, as he escorted her to her front door. "Am I being too nosy? What happened back there?"

As nauseated as she still was, Patti couldn't send her friend away without an explanation. It just wasn't right. "Come on in, and let me sit down, and I'll explain."

"You sure you're up to guests?"

"I'm up to you coming in. For a few minutes," she said. "But I'm not hosting open house tonight."

"Gotcha!"

When they were seated in her small living room, and Harm had gotten her a ginger ale from the refrigerator, Patti quickly filled him in on both how she'd learned of the first lady's death, and equally troubling, how she'd literally cheated death.

"Wow, friend. That's heavy."

"It was," Patti assured him. "It still is, when I let myself think about it. And now, to have to consider that someone close to Mollie Montgomery deliberately engineered her death, it just made me sick to my stomach. Literally."

The two chatted for a few more minutes, and when Harm left, Patti was amazed to realize that she was reluctant to see him go. Suddenly, the prospect of being alone in her apartment wasn't a comfortable feeling. She had lived there for almost four years, and never had there been a time that she was frightened. But that was then and this was now.

As he left, Harm Bostwick had pulled her to him in a half-hug. "I'm sorry I made you sick. But call me if you need somebody."

Patti giggled in spite of the nausea that was still chasing around her gut. "You didn't make me sick. It was the news you shared that got the best of me."

"Either way, I'm sorry to be the bearer of bad tidings, but from the rumors I'm hearing, there was definitely more to the first lady's death than meets the eye. Certainly much more than we're being told."

Patti watched until he'd gotten back into his car, before she engaged all the locks on her door, and headed for her bedroom. The turmoil in her gut had subsided somewhat by the time she had brushed her teeth and gotten into her pajamas. Bed was looking very attractive, and she was almost asleep, when her phone chimed the theme song from "Beauty and the Beast."

*Lee Stanton.*

It had been several days since she'd even heard from her fiancé, and given how rough she was feeling, Patti juggled the question of whether to answer or let it go to voicemail. Lee didn't like for his calls to go unanswered, but she didn't particularly care about being held hostage to his schedule and his needs, either. Despite the temptation to ignore him, in the end, Patti answered.

"Where are you?" She wanted to keep their conversation civil, but the anger in her system, teamed with the discontent in her gut, caused her to demand, "And where have you been? Do you realize how long it's been since we even had a phone conversation?"

"I'm at a meeting between the senator and a large industrial firm that's looking to relocate its headquarters to Texas." There was no mistaking the irritation in his voice. "Here I take a minute away from work to touch base with you, and what do I get for my concern? An interrogation with an attitude to boot."

His voice trailed off, and Patti realized that he was obviously waiting for her to apologize and beg forgiveness. There was a time, once, when she would have been quick to do just that. Perhaps it was the queasiness in her belly. Or maybe it was just that she was very tired? Or perhaps escaping the grim reaper changed the way one looked at everything?

"Thanks for calling, Lee. You'll have to excuse me, but I'm a little under the weather, and I just really don't feel like talking tonight." The gasp of breath from the other end was painfully obvious, and spurred her to say what she might otherwise have left unsaid. "I'm sure the senator is adrift without a rudder, so why don't you get back to work. I'll reach out to you tomorrow. If I can find the time."

Then, for the first time in their relationship, she unceremoniously mashed the disconnect key with probably more force than was required, and separated herself from her future husband. There would be, she understood, as she laid her phone back on the bedside table, a penalty to pay for her actions. Nobody stood up to Lee Stanton. But for the moment, she realized she really didn't care. She had bigger fish to fry.

As she fought through the fog of sleep that still dogged her, despite the sun shining brightly, Patti fought the urge to turn over and scoot back under the covers. It was the queasy feeling in her stomach that reminded her of the events of the previous evening, and like a flip chart, the memories that began with Harmon Bostwick's suspicions, revisited her.

*Oh, my, gosh. I hung up on Lee! What was I thinking?*

The realization of how angry her fiancé probably was at that moment was the momentum that got her out of bed. That, and the realization that she had a staff meeting, propelled her on to the shower. Forget discovering exactly how the first lady had died. If she missed the meeting, Herb would not be happy. The truth about Mollie Montgomery's last few moments would have to take a back seat. For the present, anyway.

It took cutting every corner she could, literally, and a hefty dose of luck for her to make it to the office in time for the hastily-called staff meeting. Still weak from the digestive revolt of the previous evening, by the time she slid into her customary chair around the large oval table, her legs were trembling, and she was weak as water. So fearful that she would hold up the meeting and be the target of Herb's famous wrath, she hadn't even taken time to scoot by her cubicle and deposit her tote bag and purse. Patti had learned early on that her boss was a stickler for punctuality. Thankfully, however, it was Herb himself who was running late. Not that she nor any other of her colleagues would dare call attention to his tardiness. And she understood he would never apologize for keeping them waiting. One thing she knew about her boss was that it was all about him. No apologies were ever offered. At least, as she told herself, it gave her a chance to catch her breath, and to calm down. Don't look a gift delay in the mouth, she kept saying silently to herself, almost as if it were her new mantra.

She felt her boss's presence before she heard his gruff greeting. "Glad to see everyone could give up some of their precious time to join us this morning." He slammed the door to the conference room with such force, Patti marveled it hadn't jumped out of its hinges.

"Time's wasting," he informed them. "Let's get down to business, because I've got things to do, even if you don't." Then he looked at each of them, going around the room, his already ugly face further disfigured, as if he'd eaten something exceptionally sour, before he said, "And anybody who doesn't have something else to do needs to clear out their desk and be gone by the time this meeting is over."

Patti felt more than heard the harsh intake of breath that the group collectively drew. No one challenged him.

*He's always in a foul mood, but today's is especially bitter.* One of her father's favorite sayings came to mind, and she couldn't help but ask herself who had pissed in his Cheerios® this morning.

Unfortunately, as it turned out, she didn't have long to wait to find out what had set her boss on the warpath.

*He shouldn't be so difficult this morning. This whole scenario is a dyed-in-the-wool true newsperson's dream. There's no end to the story possibilities out there.* She could remember her time in the weekly newspaper business back in Kansas, before she made the big time, when the biggest story was the winning dahlia at the county fair being won by the same woman for the tenth year in a row. Nope, there was plenty of story material here to go around.

Then the situation went south.

"Okay, you deadbeats. Channel 16 News questioned if there's a move afoot to put Reynolds in charge, while Montgomery takes time off to grieve. They sounded like they were pretty sure. How come we didn't know about it? How come you didn't know it, Hobgood?

*Oh, my gosh. That's the worst thing that could happen. None of my sources inside the Oval Office have contacted me. But I'll have to check it out.*

"Hobgood!"

The suddenness and the amount of venom in his voice jerked Patti back to the matter at hand, and she realized with horror that her boss was evidently targeting her.

*But why?*

"Yessir?" She wondered if she should have called in sick.

"How come you haven't already turned in a story on this? What are you working on for today? Deadline's in six hours, and we need something new. Something that no one else has." He hesitated, then banged his clinched fist on the table top, before he said, "Don't let me down."

Patti struggled to know how to answer him. What Harm had shared with her the previous evening would indeed be a dynamite story. It was also a story that had to have a lot of research and confirmation. To go public with what she'd learned without further investigation was simply asking for trouble. The last thing she needed was to share this information with Herb Martin. Not now. Not yet. And for certain, she couldn't write anything about the VP stepping into the president's shoes until she could get with her confidential sources. She didn't put it past the Reynolds' camp to deliberately plant that story. They could have done it to gauge the nation's level of acceptance for such a transition, temporary though it was supposed to be. Such informal "polls" were status quo in political circles.

*If that snake in the grass ever gets his hands on the presidency, it will take World War III for Montgomery to get it back. So what am I going to tell Herb? He's expecting something that I don't have to give him.*

In truth, she'd been so shocked by Harm's revelations last night, and then being sick all night, she hadn't given the first thought to what she would contribute to today's mix of stories about one of the most horrific incidents in modern American history.

"Well, Hobgood? Don't tell me you've gone dry on me."

"Er, no sir," she said finally, grasping painfully for words that would satisfy this news tyrant, while not committing herself to something she couldn't, or shouldn't, deliver. "It's true that President Montgomery is barely functioning. In fact, a couple of my well-placed sources say he would have to look at his driver's license right now to know his own name."

"Hell, Hobgood. He was almost that bad before his wife got blown to smithereens. Tell me something I don't know." He favored her with a look that spoke much louder than any words he might have uttered. "Better still, tell our readers something they don't already know."

"Any of the rest of you got anything worth contributing? If so, make it good." He glowered at her again. "There's a chance we may be in the market for a new Chief White House Correspondent, so knock my socks off."

"Hobgood, I'll see you in my office ASAP." With that, the burly, bear-shaped editor steamrolled out of the room.

"Oh, boy!"

# ALIVE BY DEFAULT

# CHAPTER SIX

"Stanton," the querulous voice demanded. "Stanton!"

Lee Stanton ran his fingers through the curly red locks that crowned his head. In his other hand, he held a land-line telephone, on which he was in the midst of explaining to the governor of Texas why the state's senior senator wouldn't be present at a big pork barrel reception the next afternoon.

As he tried to make the chief executive understand that the senator had bigger fish to fry, but without coming right out and saying so, that same senator's voice was suddenly demanding attention via the inter-office communication system.

"Stanton, damnit, answer me. NOW!"

Lee finally held the phone away from his ear, although distance did nothing to soften the language coming all the way from Texas. With his other hand, he punched the TALK button on the console in front of him.

"I'm here, senator."

"Boy, when I call you, I expect you to answer immediately. No one is more important than I am." Lee heard what literally sounded like a dog's growl. "You got that?"

"Yes, sir. I understand. What do you need?"

"Boy, I don't like your tone of voice."

"Yes, sir. I'm sorry. I'm just trying to find out why you called me."

*Jackass, calling me boy. If I didn't need this job to help me get a better one when he finally retires after this term, I'd tell him where he could go and what he could do when he got there.*

"I'm expecting two very important visitors later this evening, and they are not to be kept waiting. No one must see them arriving at my office, and under no circumstances are their names to be entered in the daily visitors' log."

*Great. More secret visitors, and more exclusions from the log. If I ever get caught, the good senator won't hesitate to deny all knowledge and throw me under the bus.*

Since the Capitol riots in early 2021, security at all the legislative office buildings had been over the top. Twice before, Lee had been tasked with bringing anonymous individuals, who definitely weren't constituents, to the senator's private office. All strictly against clearly-defined policy, but whatever Senator Rawlings ordered, Senator Rawlings got. Never mind what it cost anyone else.

Evidently Lee didn't respond as quickly as the senator expected. "Boy, did you hear me?"

"Yes, sir. I'm just making a note. What time, and how are they arriving?"

"I'll call you on your cell phone when they alert me they're here. Sometime before four o'clock this afternoon. Then you'll meet them at the usual place."

*The usual place.* The freight area in the bowels of the Richard B. Russell Senate Office Building. An area regularly patrolled by armed capitol security. Making the task of breaching that security even more precarious.

"Yes, sir," he said, resignation heavy in his voice. It would do no good to contest the senator's orders, and they both knew it. In some ways, it made Lee's life much simpler.

"Mr. Stanton. Mr. Stanton!" The sound of an irate voice nearby made him remember the land line phone he still held in his other hand. "Mr. Stanton, I demand that you talk with me."

*Crap!*

Lee gazed at the innocuous looking phone with alarm. The Texas governor was still on the other end. He hadn't even put the call on hold. How much had the governor heard? Lee frantically searched his mind, trying to remember all that the senator had said, most of it not for outside ears.

"Yes, sir. I'm here. I'm sorry, Governor."

"Yes, I'll just bet you are. Well, you tell the almighty senator that it's a good thing he's already announced his retirement. Otherwise, he might well have found his sorry ass voted out of office next time around."

"Yes, sir, Governor Perry. I'll be sure to relay the message."

*When pigs fly. I'm not about to get in the middle of that mess.*

Lee knew that the rift between his boss and the sitting Texas governor had gone on for more than twenty years, ever since the brash and sadistic Rawlings had beaten Albert Perry for the state's second U.S. senate seat. It had been a very close race, and word on the street was that Senator Rawlings paid several hefty bribes to secure what had ultimately been one very close and heavily-contested victory.

But Albert Rawlings had survived the election itself, and gone on to establish a full-time, high profile home inside the District. While many members of Congress had to content themselves with small apartments, sometimes sharing with other colleagues as roommates, Senator Rawlings had bought a home in the same exclusive, high-profile neighborhood where Donald Trump's daughter and son-in-law had lived during his four years as president. The Rawlings home, Lee knew, had been featured in prominent architectural magazines following his wife's extensive renovation. He had, from all appearances, come to Washington to stay a while.

*I'm not the first person to question how Rawlings can afford to live like he does. And I guess the answer is that he does what he damn well pleases. Like making me a doormat whenever it suits him.*

If he was honest, the senator had been a bastard to work for since day one. Lee had been warned by former staff members, of whom there had been legions over the more than twenty years the old man had dominated Washington. If you were successful in the job, it would be because the senator literally owned you. But the chance to work for the dean of the senate had been a heady one. Plus, the opportunity it laid in his lap for a climb up the ladder toward a full-fledged political career for himself in a few years, had caused him to throw caution to the winds. There were days, however, when he would gladly have walked away even if it meant he had to check groceries at Walmart.

As Lee returned to the reports he was compiling about the national opinion on a piece of pending legislation, he was still smarting considerably. Not only had his boss been in a particularly cruel and sadistic mood of late, but his demands had been dogmatic and actually unreasonable. Some of them were in clear violation of established congressional policies, violations that could have earned Lee jail time if his actions ever came to the attention of the authorities.

Lee couldn't help the way he was reacting to the senator's abusive behavior. That was nothing new. If truth were known, he was still off-kilter from his telephone conversation the evening before. His fiancée had not only been very snide and abrupt with him, she'd actually ended the conversation by hanging up. Totally out of character, and even more unacceptable. After all, she was but a mere newspaper writer. There's no way she would have had entrance to so many in the government had it not been for the perks his job had afforded for both of them.

He would definitely speak to her about it, but as he pondered how to set the situation straight, something told him that now, while the entire city was in turmoil following the death of the polarizing first lady, might not be the most opportune time. But he would have his say. In the meantime, he still had to somehow satisfy the senator who demanded nothing but one hundred and ten percent loyalty, along with no questions asked. Ever. He must slavishly follow orders, be blind to all particulars, and tell no tales out of school.

He hadn't realized until it was too late, that the freedom to simply throw up his hands, tell the senator to stuff it, and walk away simply wasn't an option. That job scanning items at a discount store would have to wait until the senator had tired of him, and kicked him to the curb. That, too, he'd been warned, would also happen. Almost three years of being a twenty-four-seven appendage to the senator had left him with no doubts. The warnings were accurate.

The promised call came just before four o'clock that afternoon. He'd been so busy all day with paperwork that seemed never to end, he'd forgotten about the senator's special visitors.

"They're here," was all the senator said, when Lee answered. And with a particularly offensive click, the man was gone.

Lee made his way down in the elevator toward the freight area in the very far end of the building's sub-basement. Whether it was printed matter, office supplies, new furniture, or even gourmet kibbles for another senator's Alaskan Husky who went everywhere he went, it arrived in this area. There, security personnel would scan everything, including even the dog food, for hidden explosives or other contraband that might harm people or real estate.

Human deliveries weren't accepted in this area. In fact, humans were strictly verboten. They were supposed to enter via any of several security stations on the main level, where they would undergo similar inspections. The rules were very clear. Penalties for violating those rules were equally clear.

And Lee was about to violate those rules. Again.

It was against this background, and already guilty of violating so many policies, that Lee Stanton approached two men who stood just inside the walk-through door adjacent to the dock. Just as he'd feared, a security guard was already interrogating the intruders, and Lee could tell by the man's body language that the visitors were about to be unceremoniously ejected. He had to act quickly. There would be no pacifying Senator Rawlings if these special guests were turned away. Even if he didn't know who they were or why they were there.

One of the men, bearing all the markings of a middle-eastern heritage, short and stocky, had visited with the senator on previous occasions, although Lee had never known his name. It was never offered, and he'd been under orders not to ask. The second man was familiar, but Lee couldn't place him. One of the advantages to his job was the sheer number of people that he crossed paths with daily. But at the same time, putting a name with each and every face was sometimes difficult. This man's face was so familiar, but the bigger question was why two men from such obviously diverse backgrounds should be coming together to visit the senator? It gnawed at his curiosity, but he had an assignment that would earn him a harsh reprimand if he failed. Better to get on with it.

"Good evening, gentlemen," Lee said, as he waded between the men and the security guard. "Senator Rawlings is waiting for you. Let's get you upstairs now, and not keep him waiting."

Believing that it was preferable to ask forgiveness rather than permission, he was attempting to intimidate the guard, whom Lee had never seen before, by invoking the name of the building's most prominent tenant. But then, guards came and went as they were transferred from location to location, depending on what was happening where.

This guard was obviously caught in a hard place, if the expression on his face was any indication. He peered at Lee's security badge, and saw his high level status. "Visitors are strictly prohibited here." His eyes swept over the two men. "Why would they even come all the way back here? They're supposed to enter on the main level."

"What they're supposed to do," Lee told the man, his words clipped and abrupt, "and what they've done are two different things." He spread his hands in a gesture of resigned acceptance. "Obviously, they got confused. Tourists do it all the time. But if you don't want Senator Rawlings calling the head of security, I need to get these gentlemen upstairs." He punctuated his declaration with a hard gaze not unlike the one the guard was giving him. The senator is waiting, and that's not something he does well."

Lee saw the color slowly drain from the guard's face. "Get 'em out of here." He turned to the visitors, shook his finger in their faces, and said, "Don't come back here again. You enter on the main level the next time, or even a senator won't be able to get you out of trouble."

Struggling to keep from laughing, Lee motioned for the men to accompany him, and the three of them left the dock area. The guard, he knew, was speaking his mind so he could assure himself that he'd dealt with the intruders. His words carried no weight, and all four of them knew it.

No words were spoken until Lee escorted the visitors into the private foyer that opened directly into the senator's inner sanctum, where no one trespassed unless invited. He rapped lightly on the closed door.

"Who's there?" came the response from the other side.

"Your visitors, sir."

"Send them in."

Lee heard a lock being released, he opened the door, and stood aside, as the two men entered. Then the door slammed in his face, and the lock re-engaged.

Having been summarily dismissed, he returned to his desk, where despite several hours of work still awaiting him, he found himself unable to concentrate. For one thing, he knew he would be tasked with escorting the men from the building via a totally different route. But more than that, the question of who those two men were, and why they were afforded such close interaction with the senator, plagued him. What could their business be?

* * * * *

Ensconced in his high-backed executive desk chair, a symbol of his power closely akin to the throne of a royal kingdom, Senator Albert Rawlings regarded his visitors. His face displayed no sign of welcome, or of patience. His voice, laced with hardness and total disregard, further validated that these men were not entirely welcome guests.

"I thought I made myself very clear. I want no further interaction with any of you, and for certain, I expected never to see you in this building again. You think you can just disregard instructions?" He glowered at the two men who huddled in front of him. "So why are you here?"

"Forgive us," the man of foreign descent said in heavily accented English. "But there are others who are having second thoughts. They fear they will be caught up with, and what may be uncovered."

"And this is a problem why?" The senator sat back in his

chair, his hands forming a temple, with his chin resting on the upraised tips.

"Because, people talk. When they're afraid, they talk."

"Then you know what has to be done." At the senator's declaration, the somewhat swarthy face of the speaker paled considerably. "You mean…" and his voice trailed off.

"Do it!" the senator barked, "and don't ever bother me again." He rose from his chair, and pointed toward the door through which the men had entered. "I never saw either of you before. Understood? And if you ever come back to this building, I'll have you arrested. Do I make myself clear?" Then, almost as an afterthought, he added, "And don't call me, either!"

Both men were clearly frightened by the senator's response, and could only nod their heads.

The senator pushed a button on his desk, and said, "They're leaving."

In mere seconds, Lee was escorting them through the building, down to the main level, and to a duly marked exit where, under the disinterested scrutiny of more of the security staff, the men departed. But as they were leaving, the foreigner muttered, "Even people who think they're high and mighty can die." As he spoke, his gaze skewered Lee. The man had meant to be heard, and Lee pondered these ominous words as he returned to his office.

Were they spoken as a threat that he was supposed to take back to the senator? Or was the man merely venting his frustration? There was no doubt that the visit had been contentious. It had also been painfully brief. Obviously, the senator hadn't sought them. So why had they even been able to get the man to see them? During his tenure with the senator, he'd witnessed or known firsthand of several underhanded, even illegal actions the man had committed. Senator Rawlings had had absolutely no concern that he might be held accountable. But whatever he was embroiled in now had a much stronger odor of decomposition. Lee just had to hope that none of that stench ended up on him. There wasn't enough money to pay him to share the message with the most powerful man on Capitol Hill, or to protect him should Senator Rawlings decide to kill the messenger.

* * * * *

Patti Hobgood followed her boss back to his cubbyhole of an office. She was not looking forward to the tongue-lashing she was certain would happen. As for his implied threat that her job was up for grabs, this was an all new low, even for Herb Martin.

*He can't be serious! After all the sweat and devotion I've given this job.*

She couldn't decide whether to go in on the offensive, or whether she'd be better served to be apologetic and even slightly submissive. Herb's opening volley made the decision for her.

"You wanna keep your high-profile job, you better start delivering. You hear me?"

"And if you want to keep the best Chief White House reporter you've ever had, you better climb down off my back, because I'm not a horse. Don't ride me, Herb." Her self-esteem buoyed by the stance she'd taken, she said, "I do have other options." She prayed he wouldn't demand details, because it had been almost a year since another job offer had come looking for her. Even then, it paled by comparison to the job she already had.

"You talk mighty high given that you managed to miss this scoop all together. What have you been doing with your time?"

"I've been busting my butt is what I've been doing. And just how do you know I missed it?" she charged. She shook her finger in his face, and was amazed to see him shrink back. "Show me your proof."

"Check out Channel 16's web site. They're hinting it's a done deal, and if it is, they've got it, and we don't."

Patti made the mental effort to get her emotions under control. Herb didn't allow anybody to one-up him, and at the rate they were going, he would still be ranting that afternoon.

*I don't know about him, but I've got better stuff to do. Like verifying this story!*

She gripped the front edge of his desk and leaned across to confront him. "Look, Herb. None of my sources, absolutely none of them, have so much as whispered anything about this."

The editor's head snapped up, and she knew she had his attention.

"Nobody's talking?"

While she still had the upper hand, Patti struck. "Nobody, Herb. And believe me, as badly as the vice president is despised by the inner Oval Office crew, this would have been  devastating for them. Somebody would have let me know."

"Yeah," he said finally. "Looks like they would have. You

suppose Channel 16's gone rogue?"

"Oh, I intend to check this out. You can bank on it. And I'm gonna ask some really pointed questions when I do. But I'll be very surprised if any such move is afoot." She chewed her lip for a second, and decided she might as well go for broke. "The president knows that his handpicked VP would love nothing more than to get a toehold on the top job. Even if Montgomery doesn't have enough sense right now to resist it, his staff does."

As she pled her case, she could almost hear the president's deputy chief-of-staff, Bobby Junkins. If there had been any action initiated by the president's people to allow the fox to invade the hen house, Junkins would have been screaming bloody murder. It would have been the president's top people who would have been forced to work with the Reynolds' camp. Oh, yeah, he would have been livid.

That having been said, her earlier theory resurfaced, and the more she thought about it, the more plausible that theory appeared. But that was all it was. Just a theory. She had to say something to at least temporarily appease her boss. "You know as well as I do, more than once, Channel 16 has had to retract a story with egg on its face."

"You've got a point."

"Look, Herb. I'm going to jump on this in the next five minutes, that is if you're ready to stop chewing my butt and let me get some work done."

"Yeah, I guess," her boss said, all the bravado and venom missing from his attitude. "But be quick about it."

Part of her wanted to confide in her boss what she strongly suspected had happened. But if it didn't pan out, if she was wrong, and there was every chance she was, then she'd just as soon Herb didn't see the egg on her face. Instead, she began backing out of the office. "I'll get you a story, Herb. You can count on me."

*I just didn't say what the story would be, but if I can prove my hunch, it's gonna blow up half of Washington, and we'll have it all over the front page.*

Patti walked past her desk without even stopping. She had neither the time nor the inclination to engage in chit-chat with her fellow reporters, and after the blow-up in the staff meeting, one and all would want details. As quickly as she could spring her car from the parking deck, she headed for Pennsylvania Avenue, where she nosed up to the gate where media were admitted to the White House grounds. She parked in her designated spot – there were some perks to her job – and sprinted toward the press room, where reporters and TV personalities gathered daily to do their jobs.

As she entered the massive room, she'd hoped to spot Cindy Lewis, the assistant press secretary, with whom she'd built a solid relationship. Cindy would talk to her. Mart Harris, the top guy in communications harbored a deep hatred for her, although Patti was at a total loss to understand why. There was no sign of the number two press secretary, but two of her broadcast colleagues were setting up to do a media bite.

"What's up? You're here early."

"You know how it is," she said, addressing the petite blond woman wearing a striking red dress, whose face was well known to every household in the District. She was a fixture on the evening news, and few people tried to best her. While her name was Honey, Patti knew for certain that the woman's private demeanor was anything but sweet. Her on-screen persona and her behind the scenes actions were poles apart.

*That red dress is gorgeous, but I'll bet it cost a paycheck or two. I'm glad I'm writing for print. I can do that in my jeans and a sweat shirt if I have to.*

"Just hoping for a scoop. Surely there's something here we haven't reported on," she joked. "You know, like what brand of toothpaste did the prez brush with today?" Patti knew if she asked for Cindy specifically, suspicion would be raised and red flags would begin to wave. "No," she said, "the boss man was on a tear this morning, and I decided to vacate the building." It was common for the various media to gripe about those they answered to, and it was more or less an unwritten policy that what was said in conversation among the media in the White House press room stayed in the press room. What the president or any of his minions said was another matter entirely.

"As far as you know," she said "nothing's happening before the regular briefing?" She glanced around, and realized for the first time that the room was primarily empty. "Man, this place is really dead. Are you sure the administration hasn't pulled up stakes and moved to Pittsburg or something?"

"That's a good one," Honey said, as she peered into a mirror one of the gophers that always trailed behind her held. "Nope. They're all here. But with the Commander-and-Chief holed up in the private quarters, nothing's happening."

Patti took momentary satisfaction that nothing had been

released from the president's staff about any plans to temporarily relinquish power.

"Then I'll make a couple of other stops and be back before noon." It was a long-established tradition that the daily press briefing happened at twelve o'clock, which allowed time for stories to be written and ready for mid-to-late afternoon deadlines.

There was no reply, as the TV anchor stepped in front of the camera, and began to deliver her spiel. On that note, Patti trotted out to her car. She knew where Cindy Lewis's office was, but to show up there could place the woman in an awkward position, and possibly jeopardize her job. But there was no reason she couldn't call. Once safely in her car, with the doors locked for good measure, Patti fingered her phone keys and was quickly rewarded with the desired ringing sound.

"White House Press Office," an unfamiliar voice announced. "How may I direct your call?"

"Cindy Lewis, please."

"Certainly, may I tell her who's calling?"

"Patti Hobgood, **The Washington Times**."

In a matter of seconds, she heard the familiar voice. "Patti. You not coming to the briefing today?"

Patti knew that all calls within the sprawling executive mansion, with the exception of those that connected with the private living quarters on the second floor of the mansion, were recorded. It had nothing to do with quality assurance, she knew for certain.

"Yeah, I'll be there. Just wondered if you'd be free for lunch afterwards? If I'm not mistaken, you've got a birthday in a couple of days. My treat."

In truth, Patti had no clue when the press secretary's birthday was. In fact, this was their code phrase when one needed to speak to the other, and always outside the White House and off the grounds. It was how reliable and sympathetic sources were cultivated.

"I can't believe you remembered," Cindy said, practically gushing. "I'd love to go to lunch."

Had she been unable to meet Patti, for whatever reason, the other woman's response would have been, "No, it's a long time yet until my birthday. Somebody's been giving you the wrong information."

"Great," Patti replied, "we'll figure out where after you've finished today's briefing."

She ended the call, and was trying to decide how to kill the hour and a half before she would need to be back in the press briefing room. Not really enough time to return to the office and accomplish anything worthwhile. Besides, she would likely encounter Herb, who would demand an update she wasn't prepared to give. Better she steered clear of her desk until after lunch. Hopefully, then, she'd have more answers than questions. But the prospect of sitting in her car, twiddling her thumbs for the next ninety minutes appealed even less than the dreaded prospect of an inquisition a'la Martin.

Unfortunately, as beautiful as the grounds were at 1600 Pennsylvania Avenue, it wasn't the kind of place where one simply strolled about, taking in the manicured lawns and profusion of blooming plants. Not unless one was a member of the first family, and Patti knew she didn't qualify.

Before she could further debate the limited options available, her phone chimed.

*Herb Martin, I'll bet. Why won't he let me do my job?* But when she checked Caller ID, to both her surprise and relief, she saw Harm Bostwick's number. She punched the talk button, feeling like she'd been given a presidential pardon.

"Harm. Wasn't expecting to hear from you again so soon. What's up?"

"I was worried about you after I left last night, so I wanted to see how you are."

"I'm better. Thanks for checking." That's when it hit her. She'd told Lee that she was ill, and he hadn't once checked on her. But Harm was calling, because he was concerned.

"So if you're better, why doesn't your voice sound like it?"

Patti was so tempted to share with her friend the premise for the rumor she was chasing down. And it wasn't that she didn't trust him, but until she could be certain, the fewer who knew, the better.

"Herb Martin, my editor, he's on a tear. Suddenly he's convinced that I'm coasting when there's plenty of material out there to write about." As she thought back over their earlier caustic encounter, a sob rose unbidden in her throat, and she had to struggle to tamp it down. "He even threatened to give my White House assignment to one of the other writers."

"He didn't!"

"'fraid, so. Told the group that anyone interested in the job

106

should write a story that would knock his socks off."

"He's bluffing. He'd be a fool to replace you."

"You think that, and I think that, but something's put a burr under his saddle. I just wish I knew what it was."

"So where are you now?"

"Had to get out of the office where I could think. So I came on to the White House, even though I'm having to kill some time before today's briefing."

"What? Are you on the trail of something? And have you thought any more about what we talked about last night?"

*Gosh, after my run-in with Herb this morning, I hadn't given any more thought to Harm's bombshell theory.* Which made her feel doubly guilty about not sharing the possibility that the vice president was trying to make a move on the Oval Office, while the president was not at the top of his game. But until she could feel that she was on solid ground, it was best that she kept everything to herself. *If I didn't tell Herb, I shouldn't tell Harm either.* She vowed, however, that as soon as she could, she would bring her friend and colleague into the loop.

"I'm not doubting you, Harm. But how sure are you of your sources? If this is even partially true, talk about blowing the Washington establishment out of the water."

"That's why I'm digging even deeper this morning. I've got feelers out in several different..." He hesitated, then said, "Patti, gotta go. One of my sources is calling."

Patti sat listening to a dead conversation, and finally decided to go on back to the press room. Sometimes thumb twiddling wasn't all bad. And who knew what she might stumble on while she was killing time?

The media that day was especially contentious, determined, it seemed, to flog already long-dead horses. The magnitude of the first lady's violent death, and the number of rumors surrounding it circulating in a town that already thrived on the implied as much as the factual, had every reporter on edge. Competition for exclusive information was intense, and colleagues who had once willingly shared with others were suddenly close mouthed and viciously territorial.

Finally, however, Press Secretary Harris announced that he would take no additional questions, and advised that if, or when, there were any further developments, the press would be so informed. Until then, no news, he said, was good news.

The entire press crew groaned in unison.

As the crowded room dispersed, Patti saw Cindy heading her way, and she waited.

"I thought that ordeal would never be over," the assistant press secretary said by way of greeting. "Sheesh, what gives with you folks?"

"We are what we are," Patti confessed, "and every one of us is on a short leash held by those unreasonable slave drivers who write our paychecks."

"But enough shop talk," the press secretary said. "Where do we want to eat?"

"How about Napalonian's? It's close and they're pretty good with the service."

Cindy agreed and since the restaurant that specialized in French cuisine with a distinctly American complexion was only a couple of blocks away, the women elected to walk. Patti had called as they were leaving the White House to put their name on a table. The wait was minimal.

Because Patti knew that Cindy's absence from the White House would be well documented, and eyebrows might be raised if she was gone too long, she wasted little time in getting down to business. Their server was at the table almost as soon as they opened the menus, and they quickly gave an order for tea to drink, and each ordered a chef's salad and the restaurant's famous rum buns. As soon as the young lady left to enter their orders, Patti spoke.

"I'm hearing rumors that the president is planning to step aside for a little while and that the VP will be filling his shoes." She favored her friend with a steady gaze. "Off the record, any truth to any of that?"

"Absolutely not," the staffer replied, in words that were delivered with high speed velocity and laced with venom.

"There's no talk at all about the president needing some time to grieve?"

"On the record," the assistant press secretary asserted, "there are absolutely no plans for him to take any time off. If for no other reason than it would give that Texas rattlesnake an opportunity that he doesn't need to have." She grimaced, and said, "But that was off the record."

"That was my hunch," Patti said. "Channel 16 is hinting rather broadly that such is about to happen, and my boss crawled my butt seventeen ways to Sunday this morning, because I had nothing on it."

"You do know, don't you," Cindy Lewis explained, "that Reynolds's chief of staff, Gloria Brownstone, is married to one of the high muckety-mucks at Channel 16."

Patti didn't know it, and immediately began running down the leadership at that TV station, but wasn't coming up with a match. Her confusion must have shown on her face. "How did I possibly miss that?"

"Gloria doesn't use his last name," Cindy clarified. She hesitated as a server approached with their food. Once the young woman had gone, and they'd both dressed their salads and begun to eat, she continued, "We all figure this was a deliberate plant to try and force the president to step aside. But I can assure you, it ain't happening."

"What is the administration's official stance going to be on the information Channel 16 is putting out? You can't just ignore it?"

"We'll simply say that while the president is heartbroken over the loss of his beloved Mollie, the love and support he's received from across this great land has given him the strength to continue to do the job the American people elected him to do, while he continues to grieve this horrific act, and that he appreciates the Vice President's willingness to help."

"Wow," Patti said, and couldn't halt the giggle that escaped her lips. "You've got that line down pat." She giggled again, and said, "I'm sorry. I don't mean to be sarcastic."

"I know it, because I wrote it," Cindy said as she blotted salad dressing off her lips. "You should have seen the crap those bozos in the Oval Office put together. Mart was away from the office, and I told them that they needed to leave the writing to the professionals."

"How'd that go over?"

"How do you think? They slunk away with their tails between their legs and in five minutes I had the official wording in place."

"How come it wasn't released at the briefing today? I would have thought you would want to get that on out there before Reynolds shows up on the front doorstep, luggage in hand."

"Simple," Cindy said. "The administration's position is that such an arrangement doesn't even exist. However, if some reporter asks the question, we have the answer ready."

The light bulb came on. "And nobody asked."

"Bingo!"

"You want me to ask at the next briefing?"

"Why, Patti. You know I can't collude with you like that."

Patti understood the unsaid. If no other reporter asked it in the meantime, and she felt so inclined, Patti knew she would be bringing the issue to a head.

"So let me ask you something else." She halted, looked around to gauge if anyone was close enough to be able to overhear and still dropped her voice even lower. "Off the record, again, is the president convinced that this whole nightmare was truly a mechanical accident gone horribly wrong? Or is there something deeper, more sinister at work here?"

If her query startled her luncheon companion, Cindy gave no outward indication. However, neither did she respond immediately. Finally, she said, her voice low and its tone very matter-of-fact, "The president is confident that the plane was mechanically sound." Again, Patti thought, her response sounded more like a crafted media response. And she noticed that Cindy didn't address the more serious option that Patti had offered up. It would be necessary to read between the lines and especially from the unsaid.

*She's actually saying there's suspicion that this was a deliberate killing. But by whom? And, why? Had it really been necessary to kill seventy other innocent people just to get the first lady?* The prospect of such was chilling to consider.

"I've really got to get back," her luncheon companion informed her. "Mart is adamant that at least one of us has to be in the White House 'round the clock." She rose from her chair, grabbed the strap of her purse off the back of the chair, and said, "Mart's actually sleeping on the premises right now."

Patti couldn't contain her thoughts. "Are things that dire?"

"Let's just say the president is really in a bad way. And I'm going to leave it at that."

Patti elected to probe no further, and the two were soon walking briskly back to the White House. They parted company in the area where Patti's car was parked, and Cindy continued on inside, headed, Patti knew, toward her office.

"See you at tomorrow's briefing," the press secretary called back over her shoulder. Patti remembered her responsibility to question the rumor about the vice president stepping into power. "See you," she called back.

Once in her car, she debated what to do next. But whatever she did, it had to translate into a story that would satisfy Herb Martin, at least for the moment. Knowing that her story wouldn't write itself, she pointed her car toward her apartment. She might have to write something, but it was going to happen from home. It was going to require some phone calls and questions she didn't want anyone else in the office to overhear.

*Herb won't be happy that I didn't return to the office, but if he wants a story, this is how he's going to get it.*

# CHAPTER SEVEN

The digital clock over her computer read three minutes to deadline when Patti finally finished polishing the story to her own rigid standards and hit the SEND key.

*For a few minutes there, I wondered if I could make it happen.*

It wasn't that Patti doubted her ability to churn out a story while racing the clock. She'd discovered over the years that the adrenalin rush that accompanied making it happen just under the wire was actually a wonderful feeling. This time, however, because she was writing a story to satisfy her boss, instead of writing the story her gut told her would be a huge bombshell, the writing process felt like she was slogging through waist-deep thick mud.

She rose from her chair and headed to the kitchen to grab a ginger ale, all the while plotting what her next step should be. She was sitting on a much bigger story than any she had ever thought possible. And the crux of that story was that someone with a dastardly mission had taken down the wife of the president of the United States, along with seventy other totally innocent people. Which meant that he, or perhaps even she, wouldn't hesitate to take out anyone else who got too close to the truth.

Without further debating the issue, she grabbed her phone and called Harm Bostwick. Even though she knew Herb Martin would never approve her partnering with someone outside the newspaper's staff, what Herb didn't know wouldn't hurt him. Or her.

"What's up, Patti?"

Before she lost her determination, Patti said, "We need to put our heads together again. Can you come over here tonight?"

"Was planning on crashing on the couch tonight, but I can change my plans."

"I think it's important that we compare notes," Patti said. "Come on over and I'll order a pizza. I've got beer."

"I can be there in about forty-five minutes, but are you sure you don't want to just meet at a pizza place? You pick where."

Patti wondered if her response was going to come across as totally paranoid, but she trudged ahead. "Right now, I'm not comfortable having the conversation we need to have anywhere but in my apartment." The possibility that her place was bugged suddenly flashed into her mind. "And I'm not totally SURE that I'm even comfortable here." As she looked around, waiting for his response, Patti wondered if she should search for a listening device? Or should she bring in a pro to sweep the place?

*You're out of your mind, girl. It's ridiculous to think someone would want to bug you.*

But as she quickly told herself, it was no more ridiculous than the idea that someone would blow presidential aircraft out of the sky just to take out the first lady, never mind all those other innocent people.

"You've got information," Harm charged.

"That's the problem," she replied. "I'm not sure if I do or not, but I'm not going to explore all of this anywhere that we can be

116

overheard." She was fingering a menu from her favorite pizzeria, debating what to order, when Harm said, "I'll be there ASAP. Leaving now."

She called up the text function on her phone, and placed an order for pizza, breadsticks and salad, and asked that her order be delivered, knowing that her guest was going to expect to leave full of information and confirmed fact, as well as a belly full of pizza and beer, she grabbed a legal pad and began to list everything she knew. Then she began a second listing of what she suspected. And when she finished, she was shocked and even somewhat frightened to see how closely some items on the two lists dovetailed.

Yep, she was definitely on to something. Now if only she knew what it was.

* * * * *

Hal Warren sat in his darkened office at The Cumberland Group. It had all seemed so simple in the beginning. Clear cut, but vital that a powder keg be defused for the ultimate good of The Group. And while he hadn't been anxious to be involved, he'd justified his decision, and the actions that followed, as being critical to national security, as well.

But it had gone farther than that. So very much farther. And like the small pebble tossed into the lake waters, the resulting ripples that were already widening, promised to affect so many more people. Innocent, uninformed people, who never had the first clue they were even involved. He held his head in his hands, uncertain of what his next move should be.

*This isn't what I signed on for.*

117

However, there was no chance now for regrets or resignation. He was too deeply involved to be able to pull back, and powerless to dictate going forward.

There was much work on his desk that demanded his attention. The first lady might be dead, but the many-faceted activities of The Group hadn't stopped. And even if The Group was to be closed down, it wouldn't happen overnight. There were many arrangements to make, and projects that had to be brought to some conclusion. As CEO, it was his responsibility to orchestrate the logical conclusion to it all.

He reached over and fingered the switch on the lamp on the corner of his desk. He couldn't do what he had to do in the dark, as comfortable as the shadows were, given his present state of mind. But he knew what he had to do. He'd always known that much of the daily work at The Group was on his shoulders. There had been a time when the job had been challenging, cutting edge, even. But as time passed, almost without his realizing it, what had once been exciting and rewarding had become more of a thankless burden.

Take tonight, for example. His daughter was performing in a musical recital, and once again, he was missing her performance. The image of her disappointed face when she looked out into the audience and realized that he wasn't there was prominent in his mind. In truth, he wasn't interested in tackling any of the tasks that awaited his attention. Never mind that others on staff couldn't do their jobs the next day if he ducked out. Nevertheless, he half rose from his chair, very close to making the great escape.

The office was lonely, and while he'd worked there alone more nights than he could count since Mollie Montgomery hired him, suddenly, he felt very uneasy. It was a sensation that wouldn't go away, and almost without thinking, he reached into the top desk drawer on the right. As he felt inside, his fingers brushed over the textured butt of the handgun kept there. Mollie Montgomery had mandated that every staff member would be armed with a registered handgun and taught to use it. The gun had stayed shoved in the back of the drawer and had never been fired again after his last practice session. Hal couldn't remember the last time he'd even held it.

*The office is locked, and the security system is armed. I know, because I armed it myself.*

Yet he couldn't shake the troubling feeling that something wasn't right. He made his decision, shoved the drawer closed but not before he removed the gun, turned off the light, and proceeded to the office door. The staff would be angry come morning, when he didn't have everything ready for them, but just this once, he was going to play it safe. Suddenly, he needed to hear his daughter's performance at the keyboard. He would probably be out of a job very soon, but Alma would always be his daughter. He found that he was excited to know that he could make it in time to hear her play.

* * * * *

Lee Stanton was putting down his computer, more than ready to call it a day, when he felt more than heard the presence of someone else in his office. He glanced back over his shoulder, expecting it to be one of the secretaries that routinely worked until they'd finished their tasks, never mind the time. Only it wasn't a secretary. And while he didn't know what was about to happen, he had no doubt that it would create total havoc with his carefully

119

crafted plans. This was one of those rare evenings when there were no social functions that demanded his attendance. Knowing that he had the evening free, he'd worked all day planning to go home early, order in food and put his feet up. Then he'd call Patti. Oh, yes, he'd call her, alright!

*I still haven't forgotten that she hung up on me. If she thinks I'm going to overlook it, she's got another think coming.* But something told him that he might not get to deal with Patti's insubordination. It was painfully obvious that his plans were about to change.

"Stanton!"

There was no mistaking the bark, nor the vicious dog attached to the voice that brooked no resistance.

"Yes, Senator?"

"You're not leaving already?" He glanced at his watch. "It's nowhere near time to knock off."

"Well," Lee said, unable to look the senator in the face. "I've finished what I had to do, and thought I would call it a day a few minutes early." He felt the man's heated gaze on him. "That is, if you don't have any objections."

Senator Rawlings' silence told Lee that yes, his boss did have objections. What's more, he'd worked for the man long enough to be able to read his moods and his actions. It was a good thing he hadn't already ordered his take-out.

"You still engaged to that newspaper reporter, Mattie somebody or another?"

"Patti," Lee said. "It's not Mattie. Her name's Patti.   Patti

Hobgood."

"Yeah, she's the one."

"The one what?" Lee couldn't grasp where the senator was going.

"You see her article in this afternoon's paper?" He pulled a folded copy of a newspaper from his side and waved it in the air. "She's something of a loose cannon you know? It might not look good for you to be associated with her."

*Is he making a threat?*

Lee had no use for **The Washington Times**, as he had made abundantly clear to Patti on numerous occasions. He not only hadn't seen that day's edition, he deliberately never read the paper, unless he was forced to. And he'd gone so far as to order that when they were married, she would resign her position with the paper. *And I mean to see that she does just that!*

Now it appeared that she might be putting his job in jeopardy. "No sir, I haven't seen today's issue."

"Well, you might want to check it out, and you need to spend a couple of hours tonight at your desk. We work around here, you know." Without another word, he tossed the paper on Lee's desk. "And while you're at it, you need to spend some time dealing with your fiancée's destructive journalism." He turned on his heel and strode from his assistant's office, and over his shoulder, Lee heard him mutter, "Show her who's boss and show her the error of her ways."

That the senator had come to his office wasn't lost on Lee.

Senator Rawlings rarely mixed with his staff members, always entering and leaving by the private doorway. Only a select two or three employees were ever granted entrance to his private office. Lee was one of those. The senator had come to Lee's office to make a point. And as badly as Lee was smarting both from Patti's actions and the senator's reaction, he had to concede that the man's point had been well-made.

Lee dropped back into his chair, flipped open the paper to the front page, where a large photo of the president leaving his wife's service dominated the page. Next to it a large headline proclaimed, **Grief-stricken president unable to function.**

There was nothing in the headline that Lee could see that the senator might take exception with. True, the message it delivered wasn't at all complimentary, but at the same time, he knew for a fact that Senator Rawlings had absolutely no use for the sitting president. And it went much deeper than their political differences. More than once he'd heard his boss comment that President Montgomery's death would do the country a gigantic favor. There was definitely no love lost, because for all that he could see, both the president and the late first lady had viewed Rawlings as a massive, puss-infected boil on the butt of the nation.

So what was the senator angry about? It had to be something in the story itself, and he forced himself to begin wading through Patti's words. He got to the bottom of the story, no better informed than when he started. In truth, there was nothing in the story which dealt with previous occasions when the president hadn't been mentally or emotionally up to the task at hand, beginning from his earliest days in Washington. At least nothing that wasn't already common knowledge. So he began to read again, and was nearing the end, when two sentences jumped out at him.

*Unconfirmed reports from the highest echelons of Capitol Hill hierarchy indicate that not only is there a move afoot to replace the president while he's most vulnerable, but other rumors hint that the first lady's death was orchestrated from within the Beltway. Authorities are actively investigating these new revelations.*

The very breath caught in Lee's throat. He'd heard none of this, so how had Patti come by this information? If there was even a modicum of truth to either of those thinly veiled hints, it would be a bombshell scoring a direct hit on Capitol Hill. But why would Senator Rawlings take exception. There was no connection with him that Lee knew about. Nevertheless, it appeared that he had still more matters to discuss with his fiancée. And discuss them, they would. He would not allow her to cause strife between him and the senator. That is, more strife than already existed.

Lee wasted little time escaping the office before the senator could detain him further. While he had looked forward to an evening of quiet, uninterrupted down time in the privacy of his apartment, it evidently was not to be. He left the Hill and headed toward Patti's apartment. Despite badly congested traffic, even at that hour of the night, he was there in less than twenty minutes, and quickly made his way to her door. He rang the bell, and when it wasn't immediately answered, he punched the button again, this time more viciously, repeatedly. He could hear the frantic sound of bells pealing, until finally the door swung open.

"What's the meaning..." The shock on Patti's face revealed that he'd taken her totally by surprise, and Lee found that he took great pleasure in that. "Lee, you've got your nerve showing up like this and abusing my door bell! Why didn't you let me know you were coming?"

"We have to talk," he said, totally ignoring her question, as he shoved his way into her foyer. "And we have to talk now!" He'd counseled himself on the trip over to keep a close rein on his temper, but now that he was in her presence, and she'd dared to question his motives, Lee found it impossible to temper his words. After all, her actions were making him look weak and powerless before his boss, which could clearly place his job in jeopardy. The last thing he needed was to give the senator additional grounds on which to kick him to the curb.

"We're not talking about anything until you calm down and stop acting like a jerk," Patti informed him, and as if to underscore her feelings, she placed her hands on her hips. "In fact, you can leave now, until you can show me some respect." The glare she flashed him should have forewarned that he was on shaky ground. "And call next time before you come by."

Her words flew over him, and he pushed his way farther into the apartment. "Hell, no, I'm not going to call before I come back by," he informed her with a sneer on his lips, "because I'm not leaving until I'm good and ready to leave." He turned so quickly Patti had to jump back. "You've got several things to answer for, so this may take a while."

"Look," she charged, "you may be real impressed with yourself right now, but I'm not. And I don't tolerate fools or jerks easily, so why don't you go on home and we'll talk later." She extended her index finger and poked him in the chest. "I'm not in the mood to talk tonight."

"Don't you dare…" He was positively trembling."How dare you…."

"Patti," a man's voice interrupted Lee's tirade. "Is everything alright?" Harm Bostwick's head appeared around the corner.

"Who is this?" Lee demanded. "And why is he here?"

Without waiting for Patti to answer, Harm strode across the hallway with his hand outstretched. "I'm Harmon Bostwick," he said, by way of introduction. "And you are?"

"I'm wondering why you're here with my fiancée is who I am," Lee responded.

Patti, who'd been doing a slow burn, finally found her tongue. "Harm is a long-time friend, and we're simply catching up on old times." For reasons she couldn't totally explain, Patti wasn't comfortable telling Lee that she and Harm were comparing notes on the first lady's death. "I don't owe you any kind of explanation and he sure doesn't." She moved in Lee's direction. "In fact, I wish you'd leave. Now." She directed what she hoped was a murderous gaze his way. "If it's so important that we talk, then we can do that when you decide to stop acting like a jerk and not before."

Lee felt himself so overcome with anger, he was actually seeing red spots before his eyes. Almost as if he was functioning in a fog, he groped his way toward his fiancée. If he could just get his hands on her, he'd jerk her until she understood her place.

As he reached for her, and she backed out of his way, he said, "I'll show you who's giving the orders around here. You need to understand…" But that was as far as he got, before two strong arms encircled him.

"And you need to understand that not only are you not going to put your hands on this lady, but she has asked you, very politely, I might add, to leave." Harm gave Lee a shove in the direction of the door. "But I'm not as nice as she is. You need to get the hell out, and don't come back until you're invited back." With that, he shoved the angry man through the still open front door, until Lee was standing on the outside stoop.

As Harm released his hold, Lee shook himself as if he was ridding himself of unwanted debris, as he screamed, "Just who the hell do you think you are? This 'lady' happens to be my fiancée, and I'll come here any time I get ready."

"So this is how you treat the woman you love and plan to marry? I'd hate to see how you treated one you intended to abuse." Harm stood totally barring the doorway, preventing Lee from re-entering. "Now you get on home, before I call the cops and report you for domestic abuse."

"You SOB! Just call the cops. I dare you!" At the same time, the small amount of reason still left to him cautioned that getting arrested for anything would probably buy him an immediate one-way ticket out of Senator Rawlings' office.

Harm said nothing, but pulled his cell phone from his pocket and began to finger the keypad.

What occurred next happened so quickly, Patti wasn't totally sure she saw it. With one vicious swipe of his hand, Lee knocked Harm's phone out of his hand, and it landed in the shrubbery right outside the door.

"Oops, my bad," Lee announced, with absolutely no trace of

contrition in his voice. "I'm gone." He peered over Harm's shoulder in Patti's direction, as he said, "But you can't keep this guy around to protect you twenty-four/seven, and we will find time to talk. In fact, you can count on it."

He turned on his heel and strode down the short walk to where his car was parked. Patti recognized the rigid set of his spine, and the way his head appeared to be in danger of snapping off his shoulders. Oh, yes, she told herself, he's furious. There would definitely be a future price to pay.

*First you hung up on his call, and now you've kicked him out of your home. Lee Stanton will not take this quietly.*

"You okay?"

The query came from her rescuer. It was a jolt to return to the present reality and to understand that she and her guest for the evening were still standing in the foyer, where that guest had just shown her fiancé the door.

"What? Huh?"

Harm moved closer to her, but didn't reach out. "I asked if you're okay. That jerk was threatening you with physical abuse, and for certain it was verbal abuse."

"I'm sorry, Harm. He's always at work, or at various receptions and cocktail parties. I didn't expect him to come by tonight."

"So do you have to have his consent to entertain people in your own home?"

His question jarred Patti. When had it reached the point that she was expected to kowtow to Lee's many whims and dictates?

She couldn't answer Harm's query, but she knew for certain that he was on solid ground. *Lee acts like he owns me, and can order me around whenever and however he pleases. What's more, I've let it happen.*

"No," she said at last, "Lee may think he controls me, but he's got another think coming." She linked her hand through Harm's elbow. Come on back. Our pizza's good and cold by now, but more importantly, we're not through with the work we're doing."

Lee's actions weren't discussed further, and the two turned their attention and their comments back to what they now both knew in their guts was the deliberate murder of Mollie Montgomery. The fact that seventy others had lost their lives along with her made the crime that much more horrific.

"I'm not sure how we proceed further with this investigation, but let me have overnight to give everything some thought," Harm said, after he'd helped clean up their dinner remains, and was preparing to leave. "After all, I don't imagine anything else could happen overnight that would make a major difference one way or another."

Patti bade him goodnight, and closed and locked her door with his admonition echoing in her mind. *He's right. Nothing's going to change overnight.*

\* \* \* \* \*

Hal Warren's body was found the next morning by two secretaries at The Cumberland Group who arrived a few minutes before clock-in. The fact that the main door was unlocked and the security system was disarmed gave them no cause to suspect anything was wrong. That is, until they almost stumbled over the bled-out body of their boss lying crumpled in the floor just outside his office door.

One of the women had been totally overcome with hysterics when she looked into the still open but sightless eyes of the man she'd assisted for more than ten years. But it was the bullet hole squarely in the middle of Hal Warren's forehead that totally freaked her out. The other employee had retained enough sanity to place a call to the police. And before she totally gave way to the trauma she was witnessing, she'd also called McCallum Kennedy, The Group's VP of Communications.

"I'm on my way," Mac had said, after he'd recovered from the initial shock of the news. "Let the police in, but don't say anything more than you have to, until I can get there to deal with them."

Patti learned of the death thanks to the periodic news segments of the early morning shows. She'd just stepped out of the shower and was grabbing her towel, when through the open door, she heard the voice on the bedroom TV saying, "Reports just in that Hal Warren, the CEO of The Cumberland Group, the left-wing think tank established by the late first lady Mollie Montgomery, was found dead inside the group's office suite earlier this morning. Preliminary reports hint strongly of suicide. We have a reporter and camera crew on the way, and we'll bring you more details as they become available."

Patti dropped her towel to the floor and sat down on the end of her bed. It was hard to know which of her emotions to indulge first. To believe that this man, whom the first lady trusted with her very life, was dead, was beyond comprehension. As for the premise that he'd committed suicide, she found that possibility to be even more unlikely. *He just wasn't the type!* But one thing was for certain, The Cumberland Group was her beat. She had work to do.

Before she pulled out of her parking space precious few minutes later, she'd texted Herb Martin that she was on her way across town to the high rise commercial building where The Group had been housed for a number of years. While it had been established when James Montgomery was still a senator, when he won the presidency and it was obvious that Mollie's time would be more divided and controlled, she'd relocated the office from just outside the D.C. boundaries to an address very near the White House. As she had explained, the rent was significantly more, "...but the Secret Service is happy, and that's all that matters!"

Chaos reigned supreme outside the building as she pulled to a stop in a restricted parking space. Hoping to keep her car from being towed, she placed one of several special signs she always carried in her trunk under the windshield wiper, and sprinted up the sidewalk. With any luck, the message that her car belonged to a special consultant to the White House would keep any overzealous cop from running her license plate or having the car towed. Most of the time, it worked. She crossed her fingers and prayed for success.

After flashing her press card several times, Patti finally gained entry to the lobby of the building where The Group occupied space on the fifth floor. The first thing she saw was the crude signs posted on all the elevator doors declaring that the entire fifth floor was off limits.

"My boss is going to fire me," a woman standing nearby in the crowd said, "if I don't have those reports ready for his ten o'clock meeting." She moaned, and clutched her purse close to her, "When he let me leave early yesterday, I assured him everything would be ready when the clients arrive."

"Hey," her companion said, "if we can't get to the fifth floor, chances are neither he nor the client can, either."

Patti saw the light bulb flash on, as the first woman said, "Hey, you're right. He can't fire me over this." She surveyed the crowded lobby. "Maybe I could even get the day off with pay since I can't get to my desk."

She definitely couldn't get the day off, Patti knew, and whether others could access the fifth floor or not, she had no choice. Somehow, she had to find a way to get to the murder scene.

As she was contemplating how she might accomplish that goal, she spotted a crew from the coroner's office pushing a cart of their equipment, parting the crowd in the lobby in much the same way that Moses had parted the Red Sea. Without stopping to debate the merits of her actions, Patti pushed in with the group, and was successful in gaining entry to the elevator. Now if only no one on the crew noticed her and blew her cover.

The ride to the fifth floor was swift, and thanks to the cumbersome cart, those involved were occupied with jockeying it out of the lift and into the lobby hallway. Patti took advantage of the distraction to slip away, and actually walked in the opposite direction from the crime scene, until she could get her bearings and formulate a plan. As she rounded the corner, which bought her a momentary bit of safety, her phone pinged. An incoming text; probably from Herb.

There were times she hated being right. Update? UPDATE!! It read. She dived into the doorway of a darkened office, and quickly composed a reply. On TCG floor. Don't bother me. Back to you ASAP. Herb wouldn't be happy, she knew. But at least she wasn't at the office to have to absorb his wrath firsthand, although she pitied the others who were. There were simply times when that man got on your last nerve.

A quick tour of the rest of that end of the building revealed many more darkened doors. Meaning that those employees not already on the floor before the cops arrived were probably still being held hostage in the lobby. She wondered if the two women she'd overheard were employed in one of the deserted offices. She could only see one way to get what she needed.

Throwing caution to the wind, she hid anything that might give away her true status, fixed a perplexed expression on her face, and started down the hall, back in the direction of The Group's office suite. When she was challenged, she already had her cover story in mind.

She actually made it into the outer lobby of The Group's office before a uniformed officer stopped her. "Don't know who you are, lady, but you need to get out of here." He moved to physically bar her from going farther, and from the congestion of people in the hall some twenty feet behind him. She had found the crime scene. Indeed, the crowd was gathered very near the doorway to Hal Warren's office. She knew this, because she'd met with the first lady more than once in her own office next door. This would, she knew, lend credence to the early report that the deceased was indeed The Group's CEO.

"But I'm here for a job interview."

"No job interviews happening here today," the officer informed her, as he slapped his thigh with the night stick he held in his right hand, and his face betrayed the suspicions that Patti saw were starting to flood his mind. "In fact, how did you even get up here? You need to move along."

"But, you don't understand," she protested. "The employment agency said to be here at nine o'clock, or don't bother to show up. Said these folks were real particular, and I really need the job."

The officer was losing his patience, and Patti knew she was skating on thin ice. "I'll go if you say I have to, but I don't understand what's happening here." She drew herself up a little straighter, before she said, "Is there anyone who works here that I can talk to, to make sure they know I was here?"

It was obvious that the officer was analyzing the situation, and she held her breath. Finally he pointed across the room, opposite the body, to two doors that Patti knew were administrative assistant offices. "There's a couple of ladies in there who might help you."

"Oh, thank you," she said, and fled in the direction he'd indicated. The first office was empty, although the lights were on. In the second office, two women huddled together, and as luck would have it, one of them was Janice Burnstein, Hal Warren's right hand. Patti knew both of them by name, and she noted that the woman's pale, tear-stained face indicated that the woman was taking things hard. Marian Whitfield, the other woman, was speaking to her in hushed tones, and delivering a lot of consolation.

It was Marian who first realized they had company. "Patti!

What are you doing here? How'd you get in? They won't let any of the rest of the crew, not even Mac Kennedy, up here."

"Never mind how I got here. Just tell me what's going on. Quick. Was Hal the victim?"

Both ladies' heads nodded in the affirmative. "It was him," Marian confirmed. "We literally stumbled over him."

With no warning, Janice looked at Patti and said, "I don't care what they say. Hal didn't commit suicide. He didn't have it in him." Her words were spit out on wings of sheer venom. Her eyes drilled into Patti's own eyes. "Do you hear me? He was murdered. Just like the first lady." Then she burst into tears.

Patti knew her time was short, and as if her thoughts were a self-fulfilling prophecy, the office door opened, and the policeman stuck his head in. "You need to finish up your business, you hear, and clear out. This is an active crime scene." He gestured with his thumb over his shoulder.

"Sure," she said, desperate for another minute with the two women. Knowing that Janice was too emotional, she targeted her comment on Marian instead. "Let me write my name and phone number down for you, so you can let me know when I can come back to interview." She grabbed a notepad from the desk next to her, and began to write. But instead of her contact information, she wrote, "HAVE to talk with you ASAP. PULEEZE call me ASAP." She added her phone number.

"I really need this job," she said, and winked slightly at Marian, hoping that the woman understood. She tore the sheet off the pad and handed it to her. "You can call me at this number. It's my cell phone, and it's always with me."

Marian took it, looked at it, and folded it in half. "Thank you," she said. "We'll be in contact."

The cop, who still stood in the door, made it clear that she'd worn out her welcome, and he escorted her all the way to the elevator. The last thing she saw as the doors closed was his rigid stance that sent a definite message that she had been trespassing. But she'd gotten as good as she could get. Now it was time to go in a different direction.

Once she reached the lobby, she went in search of the public information officer for the Metropolitan D.C. Police, for the official information. And she kept her eyes open for Mac Kennedy. Mac was single, she knew, reportedly married to his work. She had no doubt that wherever he was, he was spinning the details for release to the public.

Two hours later, she was back at her apartment, about to settle down to write the story. She still had about three hours until absolute deadline, so she indulged her boss and called him.

"Where are you?" he demanded, when he recognized her voice.

"Relax, Herb. I've just gotten back from The Cumberland Group."

"So what's...?"

"Pipe down, Herb, and listen. Officially, Hal Warren put a bullet in his head. Unofficially, it looks a little more complex than that, and I'm working on that angle now. You'll have a story by deadline. And I know you have a photo of the deceased in the file. Dig it out."

Then before he could further muddy the waters, she ended the call.

*I'm getting rather good at cutting other people off at the knees.*

# CHAPTER EIGHT

When the story was finally complete to her exacting satisfaction, Patti hit SEND and collapsed into her desk chair. She'd had no breakfast and no lunch; it was now two o'clock, and she was tired in every way that one could be exhausted. As she was trying to determine the least labor-intensive way to get some food, something that didn't require that she get up from her chair, her phone that she'd laid on the edge of her desk rang.

*I'll just bet that's Lee, ready to put me in my place. Only he's picked the wrong day to pick on me. I'm too tired to deal with his crap. It can go to voicemail. Serves him right.*

As the phone continued to ring, curiosity forced her to pick it up and check the display.

*Oh, my gosh. It's Harm!*

She punched the TALK key probably a little more viciously than was required. "Hello!"

"Patti? It's Harm. Didn't know if I would catch you or not. Have you filed your story? I figured you were all over Hal Warren's death."

"It's in," she told him. And I'm wiped out. Been a hard and frantic morning."

"It wasn't suicide, you know."

"That's what they're telling."

"Logistically, it doesn't work."

"What do you mean? I didn't see the body, although I was only about twenty feet from it. But one of the women who found his body was insisting that it wasn't suicide."

"Cause of death was a gunshot to the head, but if you're going to put a bullet in your brain, you put it in the side of the temple, or beneath the chin. Hal was killed by a single bullet through the very center of his forehead."

Patti attempted to picture the scenario without being overcome by the gruesomeness. "You've lost me."

Pretend you're holding a gun. Point it right in the middle of your forehead. It's awkward. You're going to slant it to one side or the other. They said the one bullet that killed Hal went in the front and exited out the back. Almost a straight shot."

Patti pantomimed what he was saying. "You think because it would be difficult to hold the pistol steady and straight, that it would veer off to the right or left."

"Exactly."

His theory was as troubling as it was on target, she decided. But if Hal Warren didn't kill himself, who did? She voiced that question, and when Harm's response so closely mirrored her own thoughts, she felt a chill consume her.

"Whoever fired that gun had to have been fairly close to Hal, probably somebody that he knew. Otherwise, how could they get so close to him?"

"Sounds right. So do you think his death is connected with the first lady's death? I mean, what are the chances that the top two people at The Cumberland Group are both murdered? And within a few short days of each other, at that?"

*Murdered. Just the word sounds so very sinister and ominous. But as my daddy used to say, if it looks like a duck, walks like a duck and quacks like a duck, there's a pretty good chance it's a duck!*

"I don't believe in coincidences," Harm said by way of answer. "And we both know that Mollie Montgomery and, by extension, Hal Warren, have stepped on a lot of toes and made a lot of people mad."

She agreed. "So how do we narrow down the suspects? Who knows how many crackpots out there would have loved to take their lives?"

"Oh," Harm said, "I'm sure there are more than enough to fill the Houston Astrodome. But we have to keep this in mind. If we adopt the premise that both deaths are related, remember," he paused for a second, and Patti wondered if he was having second thoughts about talking with her. "Sorry," he said, "if both deaths are related, the person involved also had to have the ability to somehow breach security at Vandenberg in order to sabotage that plane."

Patti understood. "And just any average joe with a grudge to avenge wouldn't have the means to infiltrate a major U.S. military facility."

"You got it."

"Oh, boy," Patti said. "Talk about things getting more and more complex."

"Say," Harm said, "have you had lunch? I'm about to starve."

Her exhaustion was just as pronounced as it had been, but the growling in her gut reminded her that she was equally famished.

"Me, too." She said.

"Then meet me at the sandwich shop down the street from your house. We can't work on an empty stomach."

"You mean Rudolph's?"

"Yeah, that's the one. See you in about twenty."

The sandwich shop was only three blocks from her apartment, and knowing how congested parking was in the area, she elected to walk. Harm would have to have a space. If he was lucky.

She strolled down the crowded sidewalk, dodging those walking in the opposite direction. Congested pedestrians was one of the negatives about living in Georgetown. It also occurred to her that it was now approaching mid-afternoon; she'd heard nothing from Lee.

*Knowing him as I do, I didn't really expect an outright apology. But the fact that he hasn't reached out in any form is so telling.* She fingered the impressive looking diamond on her left ring finger, and was shocked to realize that she was thinking about taking it off. What she would do after removing it remained to be seen, but the idea, the temptation, was definitely there.

It had been so beautiful the night Lee placed it on her hand. Almost as beautiful as the setting and the event, where he got down on one knee to pose the immortal question that prospective grooms have uttered for centuries. And she'd been thrilled to respond as brides down through the years have done. But, suddenly, not only had the diamond somehow lost much of its luster, so had the prospect of being joined with Lee Stanton until death parted them.

*Have I just been blatantly blind, or has Lee changed, somehow or another?*

In the end, because she couldn't answer that question, or the many others that sowed doubt in her mind, she elected to leave the ring in its rightful place. For the moment. But she had to question if it could ever again be as special and beautiful as it was in the beginning.

As she walked, taking in all the little things that made Washington such a special city, her phone rang. Thinking it was Harm saying he was delayed, she answered without checking the display.

"Patti. Cindy Lewis. You missed the daily briefing."

O.M.G. In all the excitement and confusion of the morning, she'd totally forgotten her intent to pose a certain question at the news conference. Knowing that she was otherwise engaged, Herb would have sent someone else in her place. But they wouldn't have asked about plans for the VP to step in for the president.

"I'm sorry, Cindy. I was tied up with Hal Warren's death; then I had the story to write."

"Not to worry," her caller assured her. "Carole Lincoln from Channel 11 about threw her shoulder out of the socket to get to ask the question."

"So I can run with it? Do you have any more information

than what we knew yesterday?"

"Check your email. I just sent you the official statement, but I can tell you, strictly off the record, of course, that a leak out of the VP's office tells us that Reynolds is furious that his carefully placed innuendo isn't generating the groundswell of public encouragement he anticipated."

"I wouldn't wonder."

"To say the least. Not that I need to tell you how to do your job, but posing a couple of very pointed questions toward Reynolds's staff might get you some very interesting responses."

"You better believe it," Patti said. She hurried on toward the sandwich shop, and had managed to snag the last available booth, just minutes before Harm arrived.

"Took me forever," he said, as he slid into the other seat. "Thanks for meeting me."

"You've got new information." There was no question mark at the end of her question.

"I do," he said, as he glanced over the menu board over the counter. "I don't have much time, so let's order, then we can talk."

"I've got news, too," she said, as a server approached.

They quickly gave their selections, and as soon as the young woman was out of earshot, Harm said, "While the official word so far is that Hal's death was a suicide, there's a lot of doubt on the part of the investigators. But there's also a lot of pressure from somewhere up top, trying to convince them to stick to their original cause of death."

"I spoke with two of the secretaries at The Group this morning, and they were supposed to call me when they could talk. But I've heard nothing."

"From what I hear, the police still have the fifth floor cordoned off. They may not have had a chance. So what's your news?"

"It's come pretty straight that the vice president has deliberately leaked information that the president is going to step aside, only temporarily, of course, and that Reynolds will take over. The VP assumed that the American people would get behind the plan, out of sympathy for the president, and it would give him the leverage he needed to seize control of the Oval Office."

"I assume the trial balloon didn't get very far off the ground."

"Not yet. And I'm about to start asking some questions that will further impede his efforts."

"Interesting."

Patti hesitated, then decided she had to give voice to her deepest suspicions. "Harm, there's too much coincidence here. The first lady is killed. Hal Warren is murdered. And Vice President Reynolds has his eyes on a bigger prize." She ceased speaking, before finally saying, "As crazy as it sounds, is it possible that the VP orchestrated Mollie Montgomery's death? Could he have set up a domino effect so that he could shove a grief-stricken president aside and become the new president, even if only in a caretaker role?"

"That's a heavy premise," Harm said, after considering the matter for a few moments. "But at the same time, it all makes perfect sense."

"Perfect sense," Patti said. "Especially, when you know the real Vice President Reynolds. He's a crook, no doubt about it. But is he the kind of monster that could be so power-hungry he would sacrifice the lives of dozens of innocent people, just to satisfy his own despicable, sick needs?"

They looked at each other, and in unison, said, "Vice President William J. Reynolds." And while their answers had been somewhat flip, the gravity of their accusation wasn't lost on either of them. The idea that any human could be so twisted was almost impossible to conceive.

"If he did this, and it sure seems possible that he did, given the man's determination to be president, somehow, some way, then he and Hitler are right up there together."

A logical accusation, however, was miles removed from adequate evidence for a conviction.

\* \* \* \* \*

After she and Harm parted company, Patti made her way back home, where she emailed Herb Martin to give him a heads-up on the articles she had coming for the next day. Almost immediately, her phone rang.

"How certain are you on all of this? I don't relish the furor these stories will ignite if we can't substantiate them."

"We'll be able to substantiate them," she assured him. *Sheesh! One minute he's crawling my butt because he thinks I'm not doing the job, and the next minute he's afraid I've gone too far. Maybe Harm's right. Maybe it is time I looked for something else.*

"I'm doing my homework on this, Herb. And I'm naming names and citing quotes."

"Go with it, then," he said finally. "Give me some projected story lengths ASAP, so we can plan."

"Will do, Herb." She ended that call and began to place the next call on the list she and Harm had compiled. And in the middle of all her outgoing calls, while she was making a few additional notes before her recall of the conversation got cold, a call incoming from a number she didn't recognize sent her on a new tangent.

"Patti?" the quiet, definitely hesitant voice of a woman inquired.

"This is she." Patti was frantically trying to decide if she recognized the voice. While she wasn't always comfortable answering calls from unknown numbers, when she was on a big story, it was professional suicide to ignore any call.

"This is Janice Burnstein," the voice said. "Hal Warren's secretary..." her voice faltered. "At least I used to be." Patti heard the tone of defeat that was front and center in her demeanor, and felt for the woman.

"I know this has come as an awful shock to you," she assured her caller. "Is there anything I can do?"

It was as if her words had suddenly ignited a white hot fire under the woman. "You can fight the theory that Hal killed himself. I worked for that man for more than ten years, and from an emotional standpoint, I knew him much better than Marjorie ever did."

"Marjorie is... was his wife, right?"

"That's right. Sweet, sweet woman. I think the world of her, and I know if I'm hurting, she had to be absolutely devastated." Patti thought she detected a sob, and prayed the woman wasn't about to lose it again. "And poor Alma. Her daddy loved her more than life itself."

Hoping to get the conversation steered toward something concrete that she could use in a story, Patti asked, "I agree. I don't think he killed himself, but I didn't really know the man." Her voice dropped, as she positioned her fingers over the keyboard, and triggered the voice recording device. "I'm interested in your thoughts, and I'm going to record our talk so that I can refresh my thoughts while I'm writing."

"Well," Janice said, hesitancy clear in her voice. "I guess I don't mind. Not if it will help you prove that Hal was murdered." A ragged breath followed, after which she said, "Because he was murdered."

"Okay. Tell me everything you know."

"First of all, Hal was a devout, practicing Catholic. Suicide went against everything he believed. Second, he loved Marjorie, and Alma was the brightest light in his life. He always felt so guilty about missing so many of her soccer games and her musical performances. There's no way he would have put this kind of hurt on her."

Patti had to admit that Janice's premise, so far, at least, made reasonable sense. "Do you know more beyond that?"

"Hear me carefully, when you live with a person ten, twelve, sometimes even fourteen hours a day, you come to know them. I mean, really know them. You can zero in when something is bothering them. They don't have to tell you."

"I would agree," Patti said, as her fingers worked over the keys.

"Marjorie slept with him every night, and he was never, ever unfaithful to her. But I was with him much more than she was. Awake anyway. I was his office wife, and there was absolutely nothing physical between us. But there definitely was an emotional connection, and I know that the first lady's death troubled him greatly. But more than that, for the last five or six weeks before she was killed, Hal Warren was a very troubled man."

By the time Patti ended the call some thirty minutes later, she had several pages of notes that painted a pretty clear and convincing picture that Hal Warren had been a man in turmoil. Something, his administrative assistant insisted, had been haunting his soul and dogging his every footstep.

"I don't know what it was," Janice had insisted as the call drew to a close. "But he did let a few things slip that made absolutely no sense, raised no red flags at the time. But in looking back now, I can see things."

*Now, maybe, I'm about to get something that I can use.*

"What kind of things?"

"Things at The Group were always hectic, and often tense. But Hal had the ability to ride above it all, until about two months ago. He always put in long, full days, but suddenly he was there before seven every morning, and would often be there as late as midnight."

"And you were working those same hours?"

"Not really," she said. "I often did work until six or seven in the evening, and would sometimes come in before eight. And I offered to stay later than that, after I realized he was putting in so many hours."

"You offered."

"That's right, but he insisted that I go on home. Always said he wouldn't be much longer, but that was a lie. At least it was one night for certain."

Patti wanted to prod Janice to speed up her story, but she feared she'd spook the woman, and cause her to clam up entirely.

"And you know this how?"

"A friend and I had gone to a movie. It let out at 10:30. It was her birthday, and in my haste to get away from work that day, I'd left her present, a gift card to her favorite boutique, in my desk. So on our way back from the movie, we detoured by the office."

Patti knew what was coming next. "And you discovered your boss still hard at work."

"More than that," she said, "he had two visitors in his office, and from the sound of the raised voices, they were having one more heck of a disagreement."

"Was it unusual to have after-hours visitors?" She thought of The Group's function, and common sense told her that there could often have been visitors following the close of the traditional business day.

"It wasn't the time they were there, although after eleven o'clock is rather late." She hesitated, almost as if she knew once the words were spoken, they couldn't be taken back. "It was Hal's reaction to me knowing they were there."

"I don't understand."

"I could hear them yelling from the moment I unlocked the office door, plus I was surprised to see the lights still on. I didn't intend to call attention to myself, so I slipped into my office, grabbed the gift out of my desk drawer, and was about to leave when he caught me."

"He caught you?"

"I guess I made more noise than I realized, because suddenly there Hal was. And the fury that was all over him... well, it frightened me. I mean, I've never, ever seen Hal so angry."

"What happened?"

"I explained why I was there," she said, "but the entire time I was talking, he was literally pulling me toward the outside office door. He didn't want me to know those men were there. In fact, he practically threatened me... threatened... ME... with my job if I ever breathed a word of what I knew."

"Wow!"

"And you're the first person I've ever told. I didn't tell my friend who was waiting in the car. I didn't even tell Marian."

"How was he the next day?"

"Obviously, we didn't talk about it. But from that day forward, it was like there was an invisible wall between us, and I could never decide if he didn't trust me, or if it was himself he didn't trust."

"That must have been difficult." She glanced at the clock and knew if she was going to get her other remaining calls made, she had to wind up this conversation.

"It was. And then after the first lady was killed, his entire demeanor changed. For the worse."

"Well, as closely as he and Mollie worked together, it's natural that he would feel an extreme sense of loss."

"Agreed. Except, if you ask me, it wasn't loss he was feeling, as much as it was guilt. That poor man was absolutely dogged with guilt. It was written all over his body."

"Guilt? Like over something he'd done?" Her mind began to run on high, as she allowed her brain to consider all possibilities. There was absolutely no way Hal could have killed his boss. Was there?

"No, more like something he hadn't done, or hadn't done well enough."

Janice had given her some interesting information, but at the same time, all that additional information had mainly created more unanswered questions.

"Okay, Janice," she said, preparing to bring the conversation to a close. "Thanks for everything you've shared. If anything else comes to you, you've got my number."

"I'll sure call you," Janice promised. Then, as they were about to end the call, she said, "Oh, one other thing. The two men that were with him that night. One of them spoke English very poorly, and the other one had a very distinctive accent."

"An accent? Like a deep south accent, or the nasal sound of someone from New Jersey?"

"No, a foreign accent. Maybe middle eastern European."

*A foreign accent. At almost midnight. And Hal was very defensive.*

The stories that appeared in **The Washington Times** the next day under Patti Hobgood's byline created quite the firestorm of supposition and accusation within the Washington establishment. Depending on who you were, and what you had to hide, or what you yearned to see exposed, there were different aspects of her story that created within each individual who saw themselves within her tersely-woven words, a sense of uncomfortable vulnerability.

**Rumors: VP connives to "crowd" grief-stricken president out**

A subhead elsewhere in the same story read: **Did D.C. power player orchestrate first lady's death?**

Elsewhere in the same issue: **Hal Warren and first lady: Are their deaths connected?**

\* \* \* \* \*

"Mac! MAC!" The voice of P.A. Mayhew thundered through the intercom on the desk of The Group's communications director MacCallum Kennedy. After several unsuccessful attempts, Pascagoula Annapolis Mayhew left her desk in search of the only person who could understand the ramifications of all that was happening. "I need to see you. Now."

Receiving no response, she left her office, newspaper in hand, in search of the missing staffer. She found him in the break room, full, black cup of coffee at his side, and his head cradled in his hands.

Totally ignoring the standard niceties, she bellowed, "I'm assuming you've seen this." She definitely wasn't asking a question.

Mac raised his head, his eyes bleary and his entire body burdened, and said, "Yeah. I've read it."

"Well, what are you going to do about it?" P.A. flung the folded paper onto the table, jostling the press officer's cup of coffee, which splashed out onto the table and soaked into the offending newspaper. Mac took no notice and did nothing to rescue the paper. *Just like I can't do anything to rescue The Group.*

"There's little I can do," he informed her. "Unfortunately, much of what this young woman says is true. Or at least there's a nugget of truth in everything she says, and she even cites sources."

He leveled a gaze at the woman who would, following the long-established line of succession created in the early days of The Group's existence, be their new acting CEO. He hadn't particularly cared for P.A. Mayhew in her role as the go-between for Mollie Montgomery, chair of The Cumberland Group board of directors and Mollie Montgomery, first lady. It appeared that now she was prepared to exercise her newly-self-appointed clout.

"Well, you'd better figure out something. Did you see this?" She grabbed the coffee-stained paper from the table and flipped to the front page, and began to read aloud.

*"Since the news of first lady Mollie Montgomery's death on board the ill-fated presidential aircraft that exploded in mid-air and killed all seventy-one passengers on board, rumors surrounding that incident have been rife. There have been several theories, maybe several hundred theories advanced.*

*"But one that keeps rising to the top of the heap like rich cream standing in a pail of new milk, is that no less than a Washington insider was the designer of this travesty. Since such a complex task could never have been successfully accomplished by the efforts of a sole assassin, law enforcement authorities are unanimous in their belief that other, possibly high-placed individuals were a part of this dastardly plot.*

*"Day before yesterday, the body of Hal Warren, fifty-one, and CEO of The Cumberland Group was found dead outside his office door, in the offices of The Group. Warren worked hand in glove with the late first lady, and had been in his job since long before Mollie Montgomery began moonlighting as first lady.*

*"Are the deaths of Mollie Montgomery and Hal Warren sadly connected? Authorities have called his death a suicide. No one has been blamed in the first lady's death, but authorities from the highest echelons of federal law enforcement, who have been investigating, are becoming more convinced that mechanical failure isn't responsible for the massive plane explosion that resulted in the first lady's death. That leaves only some degree of sabotage, although authorities remain tight-lipped as to the particulars.*

*"With Warren, the first lady's first-in-command at The Group, now dead as well, the question must be asked: Are their two deaths related? According to Janice Burnstein, Warren's private secretary*

and right hand for more than ten years, the verdict of suicide is wrong for many different reasons. She cites his devout Catholic faith, and his absolute, unswerving devotion to his family.

"First of all, she maintains, 'Hal was a devout, practicing Catholic. Suicide went against everything he believed. Second, he loved Marjorie, and Alma was the brightest light in his life. He always felt so guilty about missing so many of her soccer games and her musical performances. There's no way he would have put this kind of hurt on her.'

"Ms. Burnstein went on to further explain, 'Hear me carefully, when you live with a person ten, twelve, sometimes even fourteen hours a day, you come to know them. I mean, really know them. You can zero in when something is bothering them. They don't have to tell you. "Marjorie slept with him every night, and he was never, ever unfaithful to her. But I was with him much more than she was. Awake anyway. I was his office wife, and there was absolutely nothing physical between us. But there definitely was an emotional connection, and I know that the first lady's death troubled him greatly. But more than that, for the last five or six weeks before she was killed, Hal Warren was a very troubled man.'"

"Yes, P.A., I read all of that already. Three times already. And like I tell you, there's not much I can do, outside of issuing a nebulously worded official statement that acknowledges that we're all grieving Hal, that we're there for Marjorie and Alma, and that we categorically deny that Hal's death is anything other than what it appears to be, a tragic, senseless suicide. And that there is absolutely no connection between Hal's death and the first lady's."

"Well, I know what I can do," P.A. informed him. "I can give

Janice Burnstein her walking papers. She had no right talking on the record to Patti Hobgood, much less allowing herself to be quoted."

"P.A., P.A., I wouldn't do that if I were you. It'll come back to bite you on the butt much more severely than anything contained in this article." He leveled a gaze on her that indicated he meant business. "I promise you, you do not want to go there."

"But listen to the rest of this. What she's saying is absolute dynamite. It's insane, and practically screams that Hal was murdered."

Mac leveled another gaze at her. "How do we know he wasn't?"

"You're not buying this garbage? Are you?"

"I'm doing neither, P.A. But I will tell you this much. Whether Mollie's death and Hal's death are related or not, Hal was a changed man, a different man, those last few weeks before that plane blew up. And since Mollie's death, he was like a man carrying a very heavy load."

"You don't think he killed himself?"

"I'm not saying that. What I am saying is that Hal Warren was a very troubled man, and my gut tells me that his troubles were somehow connected with the first lady's death. He may well have committed suicide. But it was over something that he had absolutely no means to control. And Hal knew how to control everything." He got up from the table, tossed his empty coffee cup toward the trash can and missed. As he stooped to pick it up, he said, "Mark my words, if this is ever solved, you'll see that I'm right." He left the room, and left P.A. Mayhew staring at his retreating back.

"Well…"

* * * * *

"I damn well thought you were handling this, Gloria. You assured me it was under control. Why the hell do you think you're my chief of staff?" As the vice president strode around his office in the executive office building across from the White House, but many light years removed from the inner sanctum of the Oval Office a few hundred yards away, the target of his ire was inching backwards toward the door. The VP, in the meantime, was building up a full head of steam.

"Don't you dare try to dodge this," he screamed, as he waved a newspaper in the air. "It was one thing to plant the idea that the president might want to step aside to grieve. It's another thing entirely to paint it as a deliberate attempt on my part to hijack the presidency. And that's exactly how this damn story reads. Furthermore, it quotes, several times I might add, 'Chief of Staff Gloria Brownstone.'" He swung the paper and hit the corner of the office wall with it. "Quotes you no less than three times!"

He pointed his finger at the young woman whose perky store-bought boobs and trim, petite figure had first caught his attention. And her people skills hadn't been bad either. Up until now, her physical attributes had more than compensated for all her professional shortcomings.

"Just listen to this," he ordered. "Just sit and listen." He pointed to a chair nearby and feeling that she had no say so in the matter, the young woman with the excessively blonde hair took a seat. On the very edge of that seat, poised to make a fast get-away.

Vice President Reynolds planted his feet wide apart, opened and folded down the issue of **The Washington Times**, and began to read to his audience of one.

*"Earlier this week, local TV station Channel 16 broadcast what it basically said was an unsubstantiated rumor that President James Montgomery planned to take some time away from the rigors and responsibilities of the office, in order to grieve his late wife, Mollie. He would be returning in a few weeks a stronger, more committed than ever Commander-and-Chief, the report continued.*

*"'No such plan is underway or even being considered,' Mart Harris, President Montgomery's press secretary has assured* **The Washington Times***, as well as other news outlets who have inquired. Their official statement reads like this: 'While the president is heartbroken over the loss of his beloved Mollie, the love and support he's received from across this great land has given him the strength to continue to do the job the American people elected him to do. He continues to grieve this horrific act, and he appreciates the Vice President's willingness to help.'"*

*"When this newspaper contacted the vice president's office, Gloria Brownstone, Chief of Staff, responded. 'The Vice President is terribly worried about the President. Working closely with him on a daily basis, he sees firsthand the deep grief that has his close friend and colleague in its grip. He wants to do anything he can to help, up to and including giving him some time away from the office. That's why he made the offer to his friend.'"*

"But, sir," she protested. "I was only trying to..."

"Quiet, Ms. Brownstone. There's more." He continued to read, all the while striding about the office.

*"President Montgomery's Chief-of-Staff Buddy Junkins denies having received any such overture from the vice president's office, and echoes Press Secretary Mart Harris's assertion that no such action has even been considered.*

*"Under the provisions of the Twenty-fifth Amendment to the U.S. Constitution, should the president take "bereavement leave," Vice President William J. Reynolds would become president until such time as President Montgomery elected to return. This temporary transition of power has happened several times since the amendment was passed by Congress on July 6, 1965, and ratified on February 10, 1967. Indeed, Section 1 of the amendment, reads, "In case of the removal of the President from office or of his death or resignation, the Vice President shall become president."*

*"This provision has been used six times since it was enacted. When President Lyndon B. Johnson was under anesthesia for gall bladder removal, Vice President Hubert Humphrey was president for the few hours that his boss was incapacitated When President Ronald Reagan was shot and nearly killed by a would-be assassin and underwent life-saving surgery, VP George H.W. Bush assumed all the duties and responsibilities on a temporary basis.*

*"And thereby lies the crux of this matter. Section 4 of this same amendment provides a method by which the vice president and members of congress may deem that, despite the president's assertions to the contrary, he or she isn't fit to return to the responsibilities of the office. By taking certain legislative actions, the president can be forever barred from returning to those responsibilities, and the vice president becomes president until the next federal election.*

*"Given that there is documented hostility between the two*

offices, and the sitting Vice President's thinly-veiled threats that he will oppose President Montgomery at the Democratic Convention for the number one spot on the ticket in the next election, such a transition at this time could be closely akin to a coup. George Washington University political law professor Dr. Franklin Potts says such an action '...would be like ushering the fox into the proverbial hen house, were the Vice President to step in now in a supposedly caretaker capacity.' He urged extreme caution on the part of the Montgomery administration.

"Apparently the "man on the street" concurs with Dr. Potts's analysis. An informal poll taken by stopping people out and about in the city to ask if they thought the President should step away and allow the Vice President to step into the job was overwhelmingly against the prospect. Out of twelve people polled, only two were even willing to consider the possibility."

"Do you see how they're painting me? The President isn't fit to continue in office. Lord knows, without his wife to tell him when to breathe, he's going to be totally over his head." He shook the paper in the air angrily. "Up until this, I could have saved the country from a major internal catastrophe. But not now. Hear what she's written next."

"When asked about this, Chief of Staff Brownstone declared that the Montgomery camp was simply running scared and seeing boogers where there were none. The Vice President has no interest whatsoever in the Oval Office. You may quote me on that'."

"Have you lost your mind?" The Vice President asked, although the scream that propelled his question into the open indicated the degree of anger that consumed him. "Of course I'm going to be president. And if Montgomery keeps playing the poor, bereaved spouse much longer, I could have had a good chance to get there. Sooner, rather than later, because I've got the votes on Capitol Hill. Or at least I did."

Gloria attempted to speak, and he held up his hand stop sign fashion. "There's nothing you can say, Gloria, without digging yourself in deeper. Because there's still more." He turned the page and continued to read. *"According to members of his close staff, President Montgomery believes his wife's plane was brought down by a deliberate act of sabotage. Investigations reveal no evidence of mechanical failure or even sloppy mechanical maintenance. Instead, officials are now looking at very high profile individuals within the government on Capitol Hill. It's a given that they're targeting several people, because it's clear this wasn't the action of a single individual.*

*"With the recent death of Hal Warren, CEO of the first lady's The Cumberland Group, that investigation is now expanding to examine whether there's a connection between the two deaths. And if so, what that connection is."*

"Now I ask you," he practically bellowed, "who is more high profile in this town besides the President?"

"Well, it doesn't mean…"

"Yes, it does mean, Ms. Brownstone, they're looking at me. They think I'm desperate enough to be president that I would kill the first lady. God knows, I had no use for that spawn of a whore, but I wouldn't have killed her." He strutted around the office, before he said, "I would have gladly disgraced her and dragged her name through the mud, but I'm no murderer." He held up his hands as evidence. "You'll find no blood on these hands!"

He stopped in front of his chief of staff. "It pains me to do this, Ms. Brownstone, but I think you need to take some time away from your job, with pay, of course, until all of this shakes out and I can decide how best to go forward."

"But, sir…"

"Go. Now," the Vice President ordered, "before I totally lose my temper."

Knowing that she had no choice, the young woman spun on her heel and headed to the door. Under her breath, she mumbled, "The little frog never leaps so high but what he falls back to the ground on his little butt. Quite frankly," she added, her words laced with venom, "I can't wait to watch your butt skid across the Capitol parking lot."

"I'm sorry," the Vice President said, "what did you say?"

"I said, thanks a lot." Then she slammed the door behind her and grabbed her purse and her cell phone. There were calls to make.

* * * * *

Three miles away on Capitol Hill, yet another elected official was livid about the stories Patti Hobgood had written for that day's edition.

"But Senator," Lee Stanton protested, "I have no control over what she does."

"If you're a man, and especially if you intend to marry her, you have total control over her. Or at least you should."

Lee picked up the folded newspaper. "Sir, I've read today's stories, and I don't see what you're upset about. Perhaps…"

That was as far as he got. "You. Don't. See. What. I'm. Upset. About." The Senator's words were clipped, and fairly sported ice crystals. He strode across the room, grabbed Lee by his shirt collar and dragged him out of the chair. "You moron," he screamed, putting his face right into Lee's face. "This woman has practically accused me of orchestrating the first lady's death, and hints that I'm involved in Hal Warren's death, as well." He was so angry Lee saw that the senator was literally trembling. "She says people in high places are responsible and who is more highly placed than me?" He shook Lee by the shoulders, before shoving him away, and Lee fell into a heap against the wall. "Now if you intend to work for me, you best get your woman under control. Slap her around a couple of times, and show her who's boss. That's how I whipped my wife into shape."

*Yeah, and she abandoned Washington, divorced you, cleaned your plow, and went to Wyoming.*

The senator's face gradually took on a hue of blood, and his voice dropped so low, Lee had to strain to hear him. "Now, get your sorry butt out of my office, and when I see you again, I expect to hear that you have dealt with the problem." He smiled broadly, but Lee saw no warmth in it. "That is, if you want to keep your job, because I can ruin you and I won't hesitate to do so."

"Yes sir," Lee said, and picked himself up off the floor. As he made his way to the door, his tail tucked tightly between his legs, he remembered the foreign visitor from only a few evenings before. "Even people who think they're high and mighty can die," the man had said after his meeting with the senator.

164

Suddenly, Lee understood just how frustrated that man must have been. And he also realized that the other man with that visitor had been none other than Hal Warren who was found dead hours later.

Which brought him back to the question he'd asked the night those visitors left. Why were those men, mere peons, having an audience with the high and mighty Senator Rawlings? And why had the senator been so freaked over it?

# CHAPTER NINE

The next few days were a blur, as Patti dealt with the fallout from her articles. Herb Martin, however, was thrilled with the public's reaction. In the next day's paper, thanks in part to an anonymous tip received after the two bombshell articles appeared, a follow-up article delivered still more dynamite.

The envelope was addressed by computer, and bore no return address or even postage. It contained a brief, cryptic note.

*You're on the right track with what you've written about the vice president. But you've only scraped the very top off the iceberg. This deal goes very, very deep, and you're the only one courageous enough to turn over the rocks to expose the maggots.*

Like the envelope, the contents were composed on a computer. There was no signature, nothing to provide even a clue as to the sender's identity, or how Patti might contact this individual for additional information.

She'd known in her gut that Vice President Reynolds believed he'd found a shortcut to the Oval Office. Whether he'd had an active role in bringing down the first lady was still under consideration. But the second sentence in the note stood out in stark relief. *"You've only scraped the very top off the iceberg."* That ominous revelation would, she knew, haunt her until she could scrape the bottom of the entire conspiracy she was now certain existed.

"What do you want me to do?" she queried Herb Martin after

he'd had a chance to read the note. "I don't know where, or how, to pursue this. I can do a story about receiving the note, but we can't back it up."

"I think we have to run with it," Herb said.

That afternoon's edition included a front page article that included an image of the actual memo.

*This memo was received anonymously* at **The Times** *office this morning.* Patti had written. She deliberately made it as low-key as possible, with the hope that someone would be prompted to come forward. *We would like very much to speak with the person who's responsible.*

Then she listed the ways she could be contacted – office phone, office email – and wrapped the article up with an abbreviated version of the previous day's story about the rumor that the vice president would step into the presidency temporarily.

As she held a copy of the day's edition and read back through the story she could have recited from memory, she wondered just what kind of Pandora's Box it might open.

That night, at home, chilling, her phone rang. The number was a D.C. exchange, but it wasn't familiar. She'd listed only her office number in the article, but as she grabbed for the phone, she questioned if their anonymous tipster had somehow gotten her cell number. After all, she knew, anyone who wanted to know badly enough this day and time could get the number, if they were willing to work for it.

"Hello."

"Where are you?"

*Lee! He sounds really pissed.*

"I'm at home, and if you're gonna climb on your high horse tonight, I'm hanging up now."

She could literally hear the steam pouring from his ears. When he finally spoke, he said, "We need to talk. I'm coming over."

"If you're coming with your butt on your shoulders, don't come." She wondered if there was any way to make her position any clearer. "I mean it, Lee. I'm not going to be your whipping girl."

"I'll be there in thirty." The line cleared.

*He didn't even acknowledge what I said.* While she usually steered clear of conflict whenever possible, Patti had to acknowledge that this might be one of those situations where going head to head was the only way. *He's not going to roll over me!*

It was actually more than forty minutes later that she heard her fiancé's trademark knock. She could remember a time when her heartbeat had quickened whenever she heard this announcement of his arrival. Now, the only thing her heart felt was an overwhelming sense of dread.

She slipped the security locks off and opened the door. Immediately, she could see the anger in his body language, and the blood in his eyes.

"I'm glad you could spare me a few of your precious minutes tonight. It seems like I always come in dead damn last with you of late."

Patti blocked the door, although she was suddenly aware of how much bulk the man was packing. When things has been wine and roses, that bulk had been enticingly attractive. Right at this moment, however, all that body mass was totally intimidating.

"I told you, Lee. I'm not going to tolerate your lousy attitude." She put her finger on his chest, and felt him draw back. "Lose the attitude or leave."

She saw the motion of his arm before she felt the impact that put her on the floor. "That's my attitude," he snarled, and made no move to help her up. "Like it or not. I could care less."

Patti knew her chances of physically resisting him were practically non-existent. Perhaps the most sensible action was to allow him to spill his venom and perhaps he would leave.

For the next fifteen minutes that felt several years long, her fiancé ranted and raved. She saw his face redden, morph into sickly shades of plum, then extreme paleness, before starting again. There was little coherency to anything he had to say, and he kept repeating, "You have to stop this vendetta against Senator Rawlings. I can't take his crap any more." Several times he repeated this, interspersed with his disgust because she was always at work, and never available when he wanted to see and talk to her.

*Talk about the pot calling the kettle black.* She knew better than to refute anything he said. And while she'd never seen this degree of arrogance and abuse from him, she suddenly had a vision of what the future held for her. It took everything she had to keep from twisting his ring from her finger and throwing it at him. *That would absolutely push him on over the edge.*

However, she was getting weary, and wondered how much longer it would take him to exhaust his anger and leave? Would he leave? The prospect that he might come on in and spend the night sent horror flooding through her. If he insisted, there was no way she could prevent it.

"Is there some kind of problem here?"

The question was posed by the authoritative voice of a uniformed cop she hadn't seen approaching. From the way all the color drained out of Lee's face, he hadn't glimpsed the officer either. Nevertheless, he managed to get in the first word.

"Nothing's wrong, officer." He assured the man as he turned his back on Patti and favored the man with his brilliant politician's smile that Patti had learned long ago was as bogus as a three dollar bill. "My fiancée and I are just having a small disagreement." He glanced at the officer's left hand. "I see you're married. You understand how unreasonable wives can be sometimes."

Taking advantage of Lee's turned back, she was shaking her head at the officer, and mouthing the words, "Help Me. Help me."

Without giving any indication that he'd gotten her silent message, the officer said to Lee, "Why don't you step down here and talk to me."

"There's no need for that," Lee had responded. "Thank you for checking on us, but you can go on your way now."

Sir," the officer said, his voice suddenly having lost its easy, bantering tone, "I need you to step away from the door and step down here on the sidewalk. Now."

"But you don't understand. You don't know who I am."

"Sir, it doesn't matter who you are. I've given you an order, and so far, you haven't complied." He put his hand on the butt of his gun, and said, "We can do this the easy way or the hard way." He caressed the gun again. "It's totally up to you."

"But I'm Chief of Staff for Senator Albert Rawlings. You have no control over me."

Patti knew Lee well enough to know that he was very close to losing control. She couldn't decide if it would be safer to help nudge him to that edge, or whether she should just divorce herself from all that was happening. Deciding to look after herself while her fiancé was distracted, she began to slowly scoot backward into the foyer. The cop, she could tell, understood what she was doing, and he was keeping Lee occupied. As soon as she could, she kicked the door with her foot. It shut with a bang that sounded like a small explosion, and almost immediately, the sound of a whirling dervish attacking the other side of the door horrified her.

Just as quickly as the assault had begun, it was over. In just a couple of minutes, the doorbell rang and a man's voice said, "This is Officer Barnett. Are you okay? It's safe for you to open the door."

Patti pulled herself up from where she still sat on the floor, surprised at how stiff she was. When she opened the door, she could see past the officer to where two more cops had Lee subdued and in handcuffs.

"You're Patti Hobgood?"

"That's right." She looked past him to where Lee was still resisting. She could hear him swearing and ranting. "Is he going to be okay?"

"We're not worried about him right now. Are you okay? I can call an ambulance for you."

"No. No, I'll be okay. A good long soak with essential oils in a hot tub and I'll be fine." She hesitated, then blurted out, "But I don't want him back here. Not tonight. Not ever."

"Ma'am, we're going to make sure he won't be back tonight. But you may want to seek a restraining order tomorrow. Do you live here together?"

Patti held up her left hand where the engagement ring was still in its customary place. "We're engaged, but we don't live together."

She couldn't contain her curiosity. "How did you come to be here?"

"Your neighbor, Mrs. Tennant heard him yelling and called nine-one-one."

*When I think of how often I've fussed about that old woman being so nosey, I'd love to go over and hug her neck. But not tonight.*

"We're going to take Mr. Stanton to the jail tonight. Whether he stays there depends on whether you file charges against him. You have grounds for a family violence warrant."

Patti knew if she did press charges, Lee's high profile job was probably toast. At the same time, she reasoned, if he couldn't do the time, he shouldn't have done the crime.

"Yes," she said, and took a deep breath before she raised her voice and said, "I will press charges."

As she watched, the man she'd once thought she would marry, suddenly broke loose from the two officers and ran awkwardly in her direction, screaming. He'd evidently heard what she said, and the flow of profanity that spilled from his mouth shocked even Patti. She heard language she'd never known Lee to use. The three officers tackled him and brought him to the ground. They got up, jerked him from where he was sprawled, and Officer Barnett barked, "Get him out of here."

As the two officers forced him down the walk toward the cruiser that had pulled up at the curb, inspiration hit. Patti twisted the diamond ring from her finger, extended it to Officer Barnett, and said, "Give him this, please. He'll know what it means."

The cop saluted and said, "Yes, ma'am. I imagine he will. But I don't think he's gonna like it."

* * * * *

"Serves him right," Gloria Brownstone muttered, as she listened to the news broadcast from her husband's TV station. The anchor had just reported that the vice president's office appeared to be in a state of chaos, with much turmoil ongoing. "Conspicuously absent from all the confusion is Chief of Staff Gloria Brownstone. According to other staff members not authorized to speak on the matter, Brownstone left the office yesterday following a contentious confrontation with Vice President Reynolds, and hasn't returned."

*And won't be returning, either. So don't look to me to pull your bacon out of the fire, you crooked, pompous SOB.*

One distinct advantage to being married to a TV station

manager was the easy ability to get information out there without begging, and was a reliable source of inside information.

"When asked this afternoon by a reporter about Ms. Brownstone's absence, the Vice President responded, 'Oh, is she absent? I hadn't noticed.'"

"But you're gonna notice before I'm finished with you, because I know where the bodies are buried," Gloria vowed, as she began to pace her living room. "And so will the rest of the world. You don't screw around with Gloria Brownstone."

She slapped the back of a wingback chair, visualized it as the vice president's face, and said, "You ain't seen nothing, yet, Mr. Vice President. I know too much."

\* \* \* \* \*

Had it not been for Lee Stanton's notoriety with Senator Rawlings' office, his arrest on domestic abuse charges would probably never have made the newspaper. After all, if the press covered every case of family violence in the District, there would be no newsprint space left for the crooked politicians and the lobbyists who played both ends against the middle. As it was, Lee's case garnered only about an inch and a half total.

*Lee Stanton, age 30, originally from Abilene, Texas, was arrested last night on charges of abuse against his fiancée, Patti Hobgood, a writer for **The Washington Times** and the newspaper's Chief White House Reporter. Stanton, Chief of Staff for Senator Albert J. Rawlings (R) Texas, is also charged with resisting arrest. Ms. Hobgood, according to reports, is bringing charges.*

Patti had read the snippet so many times, she had it

memorized. Herb had written the blurb himself, after she had alerted him to what had gone down the evening before. And later that day, she had indeed followed through on her vow to bring charges against Lee. It would, she knew, be the bitter end to their relationship. But instead of sadness, she realized that relief edging onto euphoria most accurately described her emotions.

*I guess I really should thank Lee for pushing me to do what I didn't have the courage to do on my own.*

But her appreciation didn't extend to turning a blind eye and allowing the man to escape responsibility for his actions.

"I'm sorry, Lee, to have to feed you out of the same spoon you fed me with."

\* \* \* \* \*

It was the third day after publication of Patti's bombshell stories, before things began to heat up. In the meantime, there had been more than enough conflict and confusion to make her wish that she was back in sleepy Council Grove, Kansas, writing about Sadie McCoy winning the flower show grand prize. Again.

Harm had called her as soon as he saw the article about Lee. "Why didn't you call me?" he'd demanded. "This is the same guy who came by the night I was there." Patti had assured him it was, and they had talked about Lee's position with the senator. "You know," Harm had shared, "there's long been talk on the Hill about an unholy alliance between Rawlings and the Vice President."

"How have I not heard that?" she asked. "Is there anything to it?"

"Depends on who you talk to," he said. "Depends on who you choose to believe."

"Have you heard any more on either the first lady or Hal's death?"

"My sources have gone strangely silent. But I'm still convinced there's a connection."

Patti had told him she agreed, and they ended the call by promising to keep the other in the loop.

In the meantime, the scope of the conflict between the Vice President and his Chief of Staff was garnering more and more press, and Patti had been obliged to post a story on it. She'd reached out to Gloria Brownstone, but her voicemails hadn't been acknowledged.

It appeared, she told herself, as if suddenly everyone who knew anything had dropped off the radar. Because they had nothing else to reveal, or because they were afraid to reveal the rest of what they knew, Patti couldn't be sure. Even direct contact wasn't eliciting anything new. It was as if all of Washington had battened down the hatches and gone underground. And, maybe, she thought, maybe she should do likewise.

Just when she thought things couldn't get any more disruptive, a call from Janice Burnstein had given her investigation a badly needed injection of information and inspiration.

"We need to talk, somewhere private, somewhere that we can't be seen together," Janice had informed her.

Patti was immediately intrigued, although she quickly recognized the tone of sheer panic in her caller's voice. *She is totally freaked.*

"Okay, tell me where, and I'll meet you."

"Union Station, one o'clock today, the east entrance. Pull up to the curb, and I'll jump in."

Accordingly, Patti was in the prescribed place at the prescribed time. She'd barely pulled to the curb into a space intended for a taxi, when the passenger door was jerked open, and a woman slid into the seat. "Drive," she ordered. "We can't take a chance that either of us has a tail."

The woman's words and actions were so reminiscent of an old, bad detective movie that Patti had to stifle the desire to laugh. *This woman is truly afraid.*

It was a few minutes into the journey before Janice spoke, and Patti had begun to wonder if the woman was ever going to break her silence. Almost as if she was reading Patti's mind, Janice said, "I know you think I'm being too cautious, but when I show you what I have, I think you'll understand. With that, she whipped a small, wire-bound nondescript notebook from her purse. It was, Patti realized, just like many other similar notebooks available for about a dollar or so at any discount store.

"Marian found this in the contents of Hal's desk."

Patti moved her gaze from the congested traffic. Janice's face was pale, and she could see perspiration on the woman's forehead. "Marian has been going through Hal's desk?" She had known Mollie Montgomery well enough to know that the first lady would never have allowed mere clerical people to sort through all that Hal had left behind.

"Not going through his desk, but through the leftover contents."

"I still don't understand."

"P.A. Mayhew allowed Hal's widow and daughter to go through the desk and remove anything of a personal nature. Mac Kennedy fought her on it, and just between us," Janice looked around, as if she thought it possible that someone could actually overhear, "Marian and I didn't agree, either." She shook her head, "P.A. has decided that Mollie would expect her to step in and really take over." There was no missing the snort of disgust the woman made. "Honestly, if Mollie could speak, she would be horrified. Heck, she'd be pissed as hell."

"How so?"

"You knew the first lady well enough to know that she was all about security and secrecy and confidentiality. Hal handled a lot of hot issues, dangerous, confidential issues. There's no telling what was in his desk. At the very least, Mollie would have gone through the entire office herself, before turning it over to his family."

Patti agreed, and said so, as she navigated a tight traffic obstacle.

"P.A. told Hal's wife to take whatever she wanted, and gave her boxes to hold anything she didn't want. Then Marian and I got handed the job of going through those discard boxes." She waved the notebook. "That's how we got this."

"So what have you found that has you so spooked?" Patti decided she would have to take control of the conversation before she burned a whole tank of gas driving all over the city.

"There's nothing in here that's out of place or that can't be explained. Names. Phone numbers. Addresses. Notes about meetings. But this was tucked into the pages near the back." She withdrew a small slip of paper, unfolded it, and said, "It's in Hal's handwriting, as is everything in this book. But this reads,'If anything happens to me, somebody needs to investigate. I've gotten myself into something I can't talk about, because it will cost me my life. It may, anyway!'"

Patti felt the impact of the words.

"Hal didn't kill himself," Janice said, "He did NOT kill himself." Her words jerked Patti back from the many questions that were flooding her mind. "He feared for his life, Patti. He as much as predicted his own death." She held up the slip of paper, then slipped it back into place in the notebook. "Don't tell me this isn't important."

Patti couldn't tell her that, because she knew in her gut that someone had killed Hal Warren. Which, in her mind anyway, increased the possibility that Mollie Montgomery had been deliberately killed as well. But gut instincts and proof were two totally different matters.

"Does anybody know about this book?"

"Just Marian, and she's more frightened than I am, if that's possible."

"And you didn't find anything else in those boxes?"

"Nothing that we couldn't explain; nothing that didn't make sense."

Patti pulled into a parking space behind a large van, and turned off the car. "May I keep the notebook? And the note, too?"

Almost as if the little book was too hot to touch, Janice shoved it into Patti's hands. "Be my guest. But you may be signing your own execution order."

She was only too aware of the danger she was taking on, but Patti understood, even if she couldn't explain it, that this was a critical piece of the puzzle. However, as yet, there was no picture on the box top to show her where this puzzle piece belonged.

"Marian and I are afraid," Janice said. "Something smells so bad, but we don't have a clue what it is."

An angle she hadn't considered before suddenly flitted through, and Patti voiced it before she lost her chance. "What about The Cumberland Group?"

"What about it?"

"Is it going to continue? What kind of contingency or transition plans are there?"

Janice appeared to be weighing her words. "Mollie was a brilliant woman, and she was very savvy when it came to understanding how to navigate politics. But she also had her Achilles' heel."

Patti had her answer. "She didn't plan for a future beyond her lifetime, did she?"

"She did not," Janice said. "And that's the other thing that frightens us. We don't know from day to day if The Group is going to survive. After all, we've lost the top two people within just days of each other, and there's absolutely no plan already in place to save us." The audible sigh she offered bore mute testimony to her discouragement. "Just drive me down to the next transit stop, and I'll catch a bus back."

"So what are you going to do?" Patti asked, as she started the car again. She just would make it to the White House in time for the daily briefing.

"We're already looking for new jobs. There's just too many unknowns right now, and we have to look out for ourselves."

*Don't we all?*

# CHAPTER TEN

"But... but, sir. Sir..." Lee's words were drowned out by the shouting that came through his phone. Lee held the instrument away from his ear, knowing that the only hope he had of getting to have his say was to allow the senator to talk first. If you could classify the profanity-laced tirade issuing from the phone as talking. Finally, that tirade came to a merciful halt. Before it did, however, Lee had heard how his actions had reflected badly on his boss, and had been threatened with the loss of his job at least five times.

Lee had finally gotten home, after spending what seemed like an eternity in a holding cell in the downtown jail complex. In addition to a prominent, ragged growth of beard, and a bodily stench that simply begged to be addressed, he'd made bail and made it home. But not before he'd had to tolerate the inept actions of a public defender and the rage of a female judge, who made her bias against men who abused women very clear. And then he'd been confronted with the restraining order Patti had taken out.

"Bail is granted," the judge had decreed. "But part of your release is predicated on your respect for this restraining order. Ms. Hobgood doesn't want to see you, hear from you, or receive any kind of communication from you." She had leaned across the bench to shake her finger in his face. "Violate this order, and it will give me great pleasure to slap you back behind bars where, as far as I'm concerned, is where you belong. If it were solely up to me, you wouldn't be getting out." She had smiled at him, but he'd seen no warmth in her expression. "And when you go back to jail, it will be without any hope of bail."

While he normally would have discounted her words as mere garbage from a female mouth, his recollection of the time in jail, of the strip searches including body cavities that even his doctor hadn't visited, and the total lack of privacy for even the most personal of tasks, weighed heavily on his mind. It was not an experience he would want to revisit. Not that he believed he'd done anything to deserve the treatment he'd endured.

Before he could actually leave and taste the sweet air of freedom, which was a long way from the co-mingled odors that permeated the entire jail complex, he'd had to deal with a jerk of a bail bondsman.

"How much? You expect me to come up with how much money?" The amount the burly man with the cigarette dangling from the corner of his mouth demanded had been astronomical. Lee had heard the judge set the bail at one hundred thousand, but he'd assumed the bonding company would handle everything.

"Your bond is a hundred thousand," the man informed him with a bored, take-it-or-leave-it attitude." The smirk that punctuated his words did nothing to reassure the man who had assumed that freedom was just steps away. "You have to put up ten thousand, plus my fee."

"Ten thousand dollars. You expect me to come up with ten thousand dollars?"

"If you wanna get out of jail, that's how the game's played.

Or you can stay here at the D.C. Resort. Don't matter to me."

In the end, Lee'd had to call his grandmother to beg for an immediate loan without explaining why he needed the money. Then when he asked her to wire it immediately, rather than sticking a check in the mail, he'd had to lie in order to get her to agree, again without an explanation.

It was several hours later before the bondsman claimed the wired funds, completed all the required paperwork, and Lee had finally walked out the door a free man.

*I gotta get home, get a shower, and then get something to eat.* He'd found the jail food to be both meager in quantity and greatly lacking in quality. *I'm starving, and then I'm gonna take care of Patti Hobgood.* He fingered the diamond ring in his pocket, still smarting from the attitude of the cop who'd passed it along with a message. "She said you'd understand."

Oh, yes, he understood alright. And by the time he was through with her, she was going to understand, too.

He'd stopped on his way home to grab some quickly-prepared take-out. Once he'd finished his food, he stood in the shower repeatedly soaping and scrubbing and rinsing, in an effort to forever wash away the stench of his hours of imprisonment. His phone rang, and he jumped out from under the cascade of hot water, grabbed a towel, wiped his eyes and checked the Caller ID. *Senator Rawlings' private number.* He'd sent word from the jail that he needed to take the day off. Probably the senator was pissed, because he didn't believe in days off.

Lee had answered the call, expecting to be chastised for his absence. Instead, the senator's wrath was directed at his arrest, and the charges that resulted.

"Don't you understand," the senator was saying. "You're an idiot, and I can't have someone working for me who's been charged with domestic abuse."

*How did he find out? I didn't say anything about it when I called in this morning.*

He realized that it was up to him to defend himself. "But that's what you told me to do."

The explosion his words triggered could have been heard all the way back in Texas, Lee decided, as he tried to withstand the onslaught of venom and curses that spewed without mercy from the phone.

"Th' hell you were doing what I told you." The senator sounded like a menacing, angry bull snorting and pawing the ground. "You ain't gonna lay this one on me."

"But, sir..." Lee could feel the proverbial ground literally eroding from beneath his feet. "You told me to deal with my fiancée's involvement in all those newspaper stories. That's all I was doing." As he struggled to find some way to level the playing field, the senator's much earlier words came back to him. "You said you had to do the same thing with Mrs. Rawlings."

"Of course, I did. But I didn't do it on the front steps where the entire world could see me. And, unlike you, I came out on top, and nobody was the wiser." Lee could hear the man's ragged breathing, but wasn't certain if it was from exhaustion, or if his boss was dangerously close to going over the edge. "Believe me, by the time I slapped her around a few times, gave her a few beauty marks and showed her who was boss, there was no fight left in her. And I dared her with much worse than that if she so much as whispered to anyone about what had happened. She and I came to..." he hesitated, and Lee couldn't decide why. "You might say we came to an understanding."

*Yeah, you had an understanding alright. She took you for a bunch of money and moved to Wyoming. That was one strong woman. In fact, right now, if I could join her, I would.*

"So you understand," the senator said, totally unaware of the thoughts crowding into his aide's mind, "that we're going to have to part company."

*What did he say?* "Excuse me? Part company?" The light bulb began to glow, and with it, the sense of dread in his gut multiplied like black mold. "You're... you're not firing me?" As if on cue, all the advice he'd gotten from previous staffers who'd tried to warn him began to flood his mind. *And now it's happening to me. All I did was exactly what he would have done, and he's throwing me under the bus.*

"I've already had your office and your desk cleaned out," the senator informed him in a very matter of fact manner. "Everything will be delivered to your apartment by private messenger in about an hour." His dictates were issued with a total lack of emotion. "Your security clearance and office credentials have already been canceled."

*I'm washed up. I'm a nobody with nowhere to go.*

"And Mr. Stanton."

189

"Sir?" Lee wondered if his boss was about to make the parting a little easier.

"Forget you ever even heard of me." The hardness of his voice told Lee there was no wiggle room in this scenario. "Because I'm sure as hell going to forget that I ever knew you." The sound of the handset being slammed down was the concluding point of the conversation.

Lee plunged his hands into his pockets to try and calm anger so intense he even feared himself. When his fingers connected with the diamond ring, he jerked it out, looked at it, and with a scream of agony and vengeance, flung it against a nearby wall.

*Damn you, high and mighty "Senator" Rawlings. And damn you, too, Patti Hobgood.*

\* \* \* \* \*

"It looks like all of Washington is imploding," Patti said to Harm when they met shortly after lunch to compare notes. In part because of their two different schedules, and partly because they had become paranoid about talking anywhere that someone could overhear, they were speaking in the media parking lot following that day's press briefing that had been a whole lot of rerun information. Patti had managed to make eye contact with Cindy Lewis, whose facial expression conveyed her own negative thoughts.

"It would appear that you're right," he'd agreed with her assessment. "And is it just me, or is everything that's going down right now somehow tied to Mollie Montgomery's murder?"

While there was scant proof to prove murder, and even less evidence to identify those behind the killing, both Patti and Harm had begun to refer to the first lady's death as a murder.

Patti alluded to as much when she said, "And does it appear that no one is really investigating? Looks like they're just going through the motions."

"Meanwhile," Harm said, "the people responsible are sitting out there feeling pretty sure of themselves, and laughing up their sleeves."

"But to tell you the truth," Patti confessed, "there's so much turmoil and confusion in so many different arenas, I'm not sure what I know and what I don't."

"You're right there, so I think what we have to do before we go any farther is to make a list. No..., wait. We need to make two lists."

"Two? I don't follow you."

Harm held up one finger. "On the first list, we put down everything we know that's happened. The second list will be of those things, those people we suspect, and pieces of evidence we need but don't yet have."

"And may never have," Patti offered. "My gut tells me there's so much more to this story than even we realize."

"All the more reason why, before we set off looking, we need to be sure what it is we're looking for."

The two agreed that overnight, each would create the two lists. "Let's meet for breakfast in the morning and compare what we have." They settled on a time and location, and parted company. Patti returned to her apartment, slid under her keyboard, and put together a story that was as boring as it was lacking in anything new, any real update on anything old.

*Herb's probably going to chew my butt again, but I can't manufacture news. For sure the daily briefing was dull as well. With the president still hiding in the private living quarters, nothing's happening.*

She reviewed her story one additional time, threw caution to the wind, and hit SEND, all the while vowing to do better tomorrow. *Although what better will be I have absolutely no idea.*

Later that evening, after she'd ordered food delivered, and had cleaned up after her meal of Chinese vegetables and rice, she curled up on her sofa with a legal pad and began her first list, which was fairly easy. The second list was much harder, and when she finished almost two hours later, she knew there were still aspects she'd forgotten. The entire scenario beginning with that plane explosion was a convoluted, multi-layered set of events and people. There was no way she'd thought of everything, and she could only hope that what she'd forgotten, Harm had included on his list.

Bedtime was next, but the entire experience was far from peaceful, forget restful. Instead, it was a night of tossing and turning, waking up, and dreams that further muddied the already murky waters of the whole situation. Including Mollie Montgomery's reaction when she realized she'd been killed. That dream had caused Patti to sit straight up in bed, with perspiration breaking out all over.

Finally, just as a new day in D.C. was dawning, she abandoned the effort to rest, and got up. Following her shower, she dressed, grabbed her tote bag that went everywhere with her, and struck out on foot to her breakfast meeting with Harm.

They'd agreed to meet at Willie's, a long-time Washington hole in the wall that made a greasy spoon look like fine dining. No self-respecting tourist would be caught dead in the place, and the younger crop of politicians turned its collective noses up as well. Which suited the longtime D.C. locals, and those who'd come to Washington long before posh and trendy congress members had sullied the dining scene.

*But you're not going to get a better breakfast.* Patti was looking around the long, narrow room that would seat maybe forty people in a pinch. Another reporter, now retired from **The Times'** staff, had introduced her to Willie's. That was the first time she'd ever had pancakes made with beer, and it had ruined her forever for them prepared any other way.

"You beat me," Harm said, as he slid into the other side of the booth. He glanced around the room that was quickly filling up. "Glad you got here and got us a table."

"We could've eaten at the counter, but I felt like we needed a little more privacy." She couldn't help the sorrowful expression that crossed her face. "Besides, I didn't sleep well last night, and when I got up, I figured I might as well come on down."

A waitress with a cigarette in the corner of her mouth, holding a green-lined order pad approached. "What'd ya' have, hon?" Patti was used to the rough exterior of much of the wait staff who'd been there forever, and took no offense. "Grandma's pancake breakfast, sausage, and scrambled eggs. Coffee, cream and sugar."

Harm duplicated her order, and quickly their server was

gone.

"I didn't tell anyone we were meeting here," he said, as he fished papers out of his tote. Patti pulled out her own batch of papers. "Neither did I, so we should be safe."

Over the next few minutes they compared their respective lists. Just as she'd hoped, Harm's list contained several items she'd forgotten. Likewise, she had a couple he'd overlooked. And there was much duplication.

"Now what?" Patti asked. "We know what we know, and we know what we don't know. But where do we go from here?"

"For starters," Harm said, "I think..." he stopped talking. "I think here comes our food. Let's eat while it's hot. I can think better on a stomach that isn't grumbling."

As they enjoyed their breakfast, Harm asked about Lee, and about his and Patti's status. "I'm not trying to be nosy, even though I am." He grinned wide and warm. "But I'm also concerned."

Patti told him what little he didn't already know. "If I'm honest with myself, I've been dissatisfied for quite some time, but it's come to a head since the first lady died. He had no way of knowing that I wasn't on that plane, and he was making absolutely no effort to find out anything about me."

"That's cold. Especially for somebody you're about to marry."

"Well," she told him, "I'm not about to marry him now. I sent his ring back by the police, just before I got the judge to issue the restraining order."

"You know he's lost his job in Senator Rawlings' office."

That news hit Patti squarely in the gut. She hadn't heard it, but at the same time, she knew the magnitude of his firing. Rumors regarding how Rawlings disposed of staff in much the same fashion that a mother discarded her baby's dirty diapers were rife in Washington. She didn't doubt the truth of what Harm was telling her.

"And I'll get the blame for him getting fired."

The look Harm gave her spoke more loudly than anything he might say. Nevertheless, he said, "You probably will. But that doesn't mean there's any truth in it."

Patti reconciled herself to the fact that there was nothing she could do to put Lee's toothpaste back in the tube. Better to spend the time designing a course of action for uncovering the truth about who was behind the deaths of now seventy-two innocent people.

Harm shared some new information he'd uncovered, and Patti brought him up to date with what she'd learned.

"I'm going to throw something out, and you're welcome to tell me I'm crazy," Harm said. "Unless I'm mistaken, I'm seeing a faint pattern emerging here, and if I'm anywhere close to right, it's frightening as hell."

"Lay it on me," she invited. "You've got my curiosity aroused, if nothing else."

By the time he finished, Patti found herself speechless. Her mouth was hanging open. "You're crazy," she said, and punched the air between them with her finger. "You've lost your mind. And yet," she hesitated, as if looking for the words she wanted, "it all makes perfect sense."

"On the contrary," he said. "Absolutely none of this makes any sense. But looked at as the big picture, it does explain a lot of things that make absolutely no sense otherwise."

"Okay, we have our premise. Now what do we do about it?" She played with the packets of sweeteners in the little caddy on the table. "How do we prove it?"

"On that," Harm said, "we're going to have to brainstorm." He glanced at the large clock over the counter. "And I've got to run if I'm going to make this morning's staff meeting." He slid out of the seat, grabbed the check, and said, "On me this time. Let's talk this evening."

Then he was gone.

Patti sat for a few more minutes, savoring her refreshed cup of coffee. And as the warmth of the stout brew wormed its way into the channels of her still sleep-deprived brain, an idea slowly began to form. It was, she acknowledged, a totally crazy, out in left field plan. It could cost her a job she loved, if Herb Martin would even agree to participate. And the fallout if the plan worked would be as explosive as the blast that brought down the first lady's plane.

In fact, after taking a second look at it, the plan was totally screwball, and only an idiot would even give it a second glance.

Which is why she was determined to carry forth.

* * * * *

*"It's been only three weeks since first lady Mollie Montgomery died in an explosion that brought down one of the presidential fleet of aircraft, killing the first lady and 70 other passengers on board.*

196

*Nothing was left of the bodies to recover, and explosives experts speculate that had the same bomb been detonated on the ground, at least two city blocks would have been leveled into nothing more than rubble.*

*"Almost two weeks later, Hal Warren, the CEO of The Cumberland Group, an extremely left-wing think tank headed by the late first lady, was found dead inside The Group's office. Initially, the first lady's death was thought to have been caused by mechanical malfunction. And Hal Warren's death was first called suicide. It has now been determined, more by the process of elimination than by concrete evidence, that both the first lady and Hal Warren were killed deliberately. In some circles, this is also called murder.*

*"Which begs this question. Who? And why? Is there a connection between the two deaths? Did the same person(s) kill both?*

*"Almost a month into the investigation, many theories have been floated, examined, and ultimately discarded. However, those involved have gotten sloppy, authorities say, people are talking, and slowly, a horrific scenario is developing. To be certain, those investigating these deaths confess that their theories make little sense. But at the same time, they maintain, when looked at from an overview perspective, their sinister theories make a tremendous amount of sense, and paint the only picture possible to explain all that has happened.*

*"The two most prominent elected officials in Washington, after President James Montgomery, are his Vice President William J. Reynolds and Texas Senator Albert A. Rawlings, the dean of the senate. It's a badly-kept secret that Vice President Reynolds covets the presidency. He has hinted rather broadly that he would oppose*

*President Montgomery in the next election, and should he succeed, would deny the incumbent president a second term. What's more, since the first lady's death, the vice president has floated the idea that he should step into the presidency, and allow the president to take some R&R to grieve for his wife. President Montgomery has declined the offer that some say was more assumed on the part of the Vice President than was actually offered.*

*"Senator Rawlings has already announced his intent to retire at the end of this term. Individuals speaking on the matter, who have requested anonymity because they aren't authorized to speak about it, have revealed that Reynolds and Rawlings have quietly formed an unholy alliance. Reynolds would seek to gain the presidency by any means necessary, including killing the first lady, some say, in order to drive the president out of office and seize power under the provisions of the Twenty-fifth Amendment. Then once he was in the presidency, Reynolds would select Rawlings to be his new vice president.*

*"But things haven't gone exactly as planned. President Montgomery, while deeply grieving his wife, has shown that he is committed to serving the people of this country who elected him. He has declined to take 'time away,' thus apparently thwarting Vice President Reynolds's clandestine efforts to seize the Oval Office without benefit of an election.*

*"Reynolds can still seek to oppose the president in the next election, but the American people have seen the price President Montgomery has paid to serve his country, namely the loss of his wife. Political pundits now estimate that Reynolds had almost a fifty-fifty chance at deposing President Montgomery at the upcoming Democratic Convention. Their revised odds for his chance are now*

*calculated at one in five.*

*"And now, carefully calculated plans once nurtured in darkest secrecy and at the highest level of deception appear to have fallen apart. As they've disintegrated, those who assisted in the execution of what can only be called a very bloody but unsuccessful coup, have begun to run scared. And scared people are prone to talk, investigators say. It's just a matter of time, before somebody in the know talks to the wrong person, and this diabolical scheme will blow up in its planners' faces, authorities familiar with the situation believe.*

*"The Washington Times reached out to both the vice president's office and that of Senator Rawlings to ask for comment. Both queries elicited a, 'We have nothing to say,' response."*

Herb's voice faltered, but his eyes said far more than his mouth ever could. "My gawd, Hobgood. Do you know how volatile this story is?"

"If what I've written there is true, it's more explosive than either of us could ever imagine."

"What do you mean, 'if it's true?'"

"Just what I said, Herb. There's no proof I can put my hands on to substantiate the more sinister elements of this story. But those involved, those who would know they needed to fear for their freedom and their very lives, don't know that we don't have the goods on them."

"So you're hoping this story will spook them, and cause them to give themselves away."

"That's about it, Herb. You'll notice that I quote rumors and unnamed authorities. Very little is specific, but again, those who're behind all of this don't know that."

"I don't know," the editor said. "This could get dicy." He fingered his chin. "Definitely for the paper, but also for you."

"I'm in the mood to gamble," she said. "How about you?"

"And you've talked to both the vice president and the senator's offices?"

"I haven't," she confessed. "But I will, if you agree to run the story."

Herb rose from his chair and paced the postage stamp size office. Finally he looked at Patti as if he was trying to see inside her head. "Okay," he said. "It still seems to be too dangerous, but if you're determined, call for those comments, which we both know you won't get, and then run with it."

"Thanks, Herb." She left his office working under a mandate. Calls to the two elected officials elicited not just the expected responses, but much stronger answers. Most of which couldn't be quoted in a family newspaper. She amended the last sentence of the article, added her byline and a proposed headline, and hit the SEND button to transmit it to composing.

The fall-out would be something to behold. She wondered where she could safely ride out the storm that was guaranteed to erupt.

* * * * *

Chaos reigned supreme at the White House press briefing the

next day. Patti's story had hit the streets late the previous afternoon, and even though time was short, the six o'clock TV newscasts were already on the matter, and everyone who was anybody was suddenly speaking up and voicing an opinion. But nothing could compare to the media free-for-all that characterized the daily info session.

"Quiet! Quiet down!" Mart Harris called out, as he pounded on the podium with his fist. "Order. Order."

Finally the modern version of the Tower of Babble began to cease its frantic conversations and the various individuals present took seats. But that was where the civil behavior ended, because as soon as Press Secretary Harris spoke, he was immediately besieged with shouts from all sides of the room. Finally, unable to bring the room to order, Mart Harris announced, "Meeting canceled." Without another word, he turned on his heel, motioned to Cindy Lewis and another aide, and together the trio left the dais.

"Well," Patti said to the older woman seated next to her, one of the writers for the L.A. Times based in Washington, "This was a big waste of time. But at least I've now got something to write for today's edition." She extended her hands into the air. "White House holds Press Conference that wasn't".

"I don't know why you're surprised. That bombshell story you posted yesterday was guaranteed to stir the waters." She grinned at Patti. "And it sure did."

Patti had to agree, although she didn't say that. After she'd gotten home the previous evening, the various TV newscasts began to break with different details all spawned by the story a few hours earlier in **The Times**. Her phone began to ring as well, making her wonder how many people out there had her number. Too many, she

201

decided, for her to feel totally comfortable. She just let all the calls go to voicemail. Until Harm's number showed up in the display.

"Hey, friend. You don't know how good it is to hear from you."

"Been besieged, huh?"

"You wouldn't believe it, but yours is the first call I've answered."

"Want me to come over? Have you eaten?"

"I haven't eaten, but too many people in this town know what I look like, so I'll starve before I go out to eat."

"Starve not, m'lady. Give me an hour and I'll be there to assuage your hunger."

True to his word, it was just about an hour later when Patti's doorbell rang. "It's me," she heard Harm's voice say. She hurried to the door and released the locks, admitted her visitor and his carry-out bags of food, and locked the door behind him.

The fragrance from the food announced the arrival of the evening meal. "Yum-yum," she said, as she relieved Harm of his delivery. "What do we have here?"

"Cuban sandwiches."

"Oh, I love those." She set the sacks on the end of the kitchen counter and motioned for Harm to take a seat on the couch. As he moved into the living room, she removed the takeout containers and brought them to the coffee table. "Beer?" she asked as she set the food out.

"Yup."

She grabbed two bottles from the refrigerator, set one in front of Harm and opened the other for herself. After settling on the other end of the sofa, she opened her plate of food and took a hefty bite of her sandwich. "Ohhh, this is soooo good. I don't think I realized how hungry I was."

While they ate, Patti brought him up to date on all that had happened since they'd met for breakfast the day before. In turn, Harm shared all the scuttlebutt he was hearing on the street.

"And believe you me," he told her, as he wiped a dollop of dressing from his chin. "There's a lot out there to hear."

"But what are you hearing from the top? Reynolds or Rawlings?"

"That's the most interesting of all," he shared. "The VP's office isn't saying a lot, either way, but then you know they're in total chaos up there. Since Gloria Brownstone left, they don't know up from down."

"But Rawlings. How about him?"

"He's been very vocal, denying any and all connection with Reynolds, and declaring that, as far as he's concerned, you are a danger to the safety and welfare of this country." He took another generous bite of his sandwich. "In fact, he's vowed to bring you down, and he's given the impression that anything that takes you out is still on the table." He hesitated, as if trying to decide what else to say. "The senator has decreed that Washington would be better off if you were dead. BTW, unlike the vice president's office, Senator Rawlings' office isn't showing any signs of chaos, even though your fiancé has been relieved of his duties."

"Because of me," she said quietly. "And he's no longer my fiancé."

"All the more reason to watch your back."

She couldn't stop the sharp intake of breath that expressed her shock. Cold chills shot up her spine. She knew from things that Lee Stanton had said in passing that Rawlings was totally lacking in either ethics or scruples. Lee had called him ruthless, and as a result, she would put nothing past him. *But death? Would he really go so far as to kill her?* But somebody had killed both the first lady and Hal Warren. If not Senator Rawlings, then who? The blood was as likely to be on his hands as anyone.

"You've as good as put a target on your back, you know."

While she'd known reaction to her stories would be vicious in some corners, it hadn't occurred to her that someone might actually mark her for elimination as a result.

"I guess you're right, but I don't know what I can do about it. Especially now." She suddenly felt particularly vulnerable, and couldn't fight the urge to move around.

*It's hard to hit a moving target.*

"You can take extra precautions, that's what. Don't go anywhere alone, and be careful who you surround yourself with."

"But I have to work. I can't stay holed up here, or even at the office."

"All the more reason to be careful." He joined her where she stood peering out a front window, almost as if she expected to see someone out there waiting to grab her. "We're dealing with ruthless killers. If they would kill a first lady, why would they hesitate about a meddlesome newspaper reporter?"

For the first time since she'd heard the early reports announcing Mollie Montgomery's death, Patti realized that she actually feared for her own life. It wasn't easy to accept.

After Harm was gone, she double-checked doors and windows, and for the first time ever, she wished she lived near the top of a high rise. Somehow, it just felt safer. However, as she told herself, there were no true high rise buildings in the city, because there was a ban on any buildings taller than the Capitol. She went to bed, but as she would confess the next morning, sleep was fitful, if not downright elusive.

If Harm had been concerned the night before, Herb Martin summoned her to his office the minute she stepped into the newsroom, before she had time to even drop her purse and tote bag in her cubicle. Never one to stand on ceremony or etiquette, her boss remained seated while he gestured for her to come in and sit.

"What's up, Herb?" she asked, as she entered his cluttered office, and she wondered yet again how the man could function in the midst of such confusion. There was no sign of order anywhere, and even the chair he indicated she should take had to be divested of the stack of magazines evidently living there.

"I'm worried about you, Hobgood." He fingered his tie, cleared his throat. "I knew we were taking a chance when we ran this story, but now," he shook his head as if to dislodge whatever was dogging him, "I just don't know."

"What's got you so spooked, Herb?" While she'd been concerned after Harm's revelations the previous evening, the fact that Herb was troubled was positively unnerving. "Where's that newsman's stiff upper lip and rigid spine?"

"They're both missing in action, Hobgood. Instead, my brain's saying we screwed up." He rose from behind his desk and came and perched on the arm of the chair next to her.

"You're running scared, Herb. I never thought I'd see this."

"You bet I'm running scared. People in high places are absolutely coming unglued. Why the owners of this paper have been bombarded with every kind of threat you can imagine, and Senator Rawlings is absolutely out for blood."

"Yeah, I heard he was foaming at the mouth."

"Oh, it goes way farther than foaming at the mouth. He's demanding your head on a post out front of this building, and he's threatening to sue."

While Patti still felt uneasy, she knew if she showed it, Herb would capitalize on the hysteria she recognized was lurking just below the surface.

"He can sue, Herb," she assured him. "But winning is another matter. And don't forget," she reminded him, "we gave his office a chance to comment on the allegations. I read them the paragraphs in question, and in return, I got an earful of obscenities and venom."

"Doesn't matter. The good senator doesn't take kindly to being looped in with insinuations that he had a hand in Mollie Montgomery's death. Furthermore, he's throwing the vice president under the bus, and claims that Reynolds is using him to deflect

206

some of the negative press."

"In other words, he's posturing." It was a common trait among politicians, Patti had been shocked to learn when she first began covering politics. But she also knew that Rawlings had almost a professional skill level in the art. Lee had once described his boss's expertise as smoke and mirrors at its finest.

"Posturing for sure, but I don't trust him, Hobgood. "He's not just dangerous. He's diabolical, and he has no conscience."

"I'm watching my back, Herb. I promise you."

"Nevertheless," he said, and his voice was heavy with emotion, "you are to go nowhere without someone with you, until we know more than we know now."

"Someone with me? But who? How?" The thought that she would have a nursemaid wasn't at all enticing. "Herb, I can't do my job with somebody tagging along behind me." She couldn't begin to imagine how cumbersome that arrangement would be.

"Nevertheless," he said, and she heard the steely resolve in his voice, "that's how it's gonna be."

And that's how it was. When she left the office heading to the White House for the daily briefing that day, a newly-hired intern, Julia Robinson, tagged along. At least that was how it felt. For the next few days, Patti couldn't even feel like her normal self, as it was, if every move she made and word she spoke was apt to be passed along to others.

There was one place where she drew the line, dug her heels in the sand, and ultimately prevailed. That concerned having her detached appendage with her when she was working from home during the day. It was nothing against the young lady, whom Patti confessed to Harm on the third evening, she would have really liked, just under different circumstances. Home was the only sanctuary she had, and she refused to allow it to be sullied. Consequently, she stayed away from the office as much as possible, electing to use phone and email and even text messaging to accomplish her tasks.

Harm had brought burgers from one of their favorite haunts, and they were on the floor in the living room, eating off the coffee table, when he said, "Have you heard the latest out of the vice president's office?"

"What do you mean 'the latest'? They're telling a different story every day."

"Oh, they're mired in contradiction alright. But the VP issued a statement this afternoon that there is absolutely no truth in your story about him and Rawlings colluding to seize the presidency, so that he could make Rawlings his VP."

"So what's changed?"

"This time," her friend informed her, "he's getting down and dirty with you personally."

"With me?" She'd known the vice president had few scruples, but what was there in her life, in her background that he could exploit for his own means?"

She asked Harm that same question.

"He's dragging you through the muck, trying to trash you and cast suspicion on what you publish."

"Vice President Reynolds is trashing me? Me? How?"

"You're the daughter of the janitor at the courthouse in Council Grove. You grew up on the wrong side of the tracks, and then you got yourself engaged to a man who was such a failure, Senator Rawlings had to fire him."

"Is that all?"

"No," he said, and the tone of sadness in his voice caused the hair on the back of her head to stand at attention. "He said that the late first lady was the daughter of a whore, and that the reason you and Mrs. Montgomery got on so well was because you both came from very questionable, tawdry backgrounds."

Patti couldn't stop the deep gasp of breath that left her. She had never been ashamed of how she grew up. Her daddy wasn't just a janitor. He was the mechanical superintendent for the courthouse, and sometimes those duties could get menial and dirty. But it had been good, honest work, even if it meant they lived in the old family homeplace outside of town. Her mother had been a stay-at-home mom, who also ran a part-time beauty shop in the enclosed back porch. No, they hadn't been part of the town's elite, but Patti had never been ashamed. Not then, and not now. At the same time, she'd comforted herself in the reality that Mollie O'Brien had overcome her earliest circumstances. If the first lady could succeed, Patti believed she could as well.

"How dare he drag my parents into this! That's a low blow, even for Reynolds."

"Well, he has," Harm said. "And it's much uglier than I've related to you tonight."

Patti's head dropped into her hands, and she could only

imagine the shame that her parents were feeling, if they'd heard the vice president's remarks. And she was sure they had. They'd been so fearful when she announced she was leaving Kansas to work in the capitol. But as she'd successfully climbed the ladder, their fear had slowly morphed into a deep sense of pride. Although there were times when her mother still confided that she worried every night about her single daughter living alone in the big city.

"I should probably call the folks to reassure them," she said at last. Then she realized that she hadn't yet made them aware that she'd broken her engagement with Lee. Which would be another matter of concern for them. Both parents had expressed relief when she'd told them that Lee had proposed, and that there was someone in Washington looking out for their only child.

*They're not going to take this well.* She checked the clock, knew that back in Council Grove the folks were just finishing their evening meal. Mama would be starting to clear the table. Might as well get it over with.

The call was answered on the fourth ring. "Patti, baby girl, are you okay?" It was Mama's voice, and thanks to Caller I.D., her daughter hadn't been able to slip in unannounced. "I'm good, Mama. There's nothing to worry about."

"But we are worried." It was her dad's voice that answered. Patti knew he'd picked up the extension phone. Neither of her parents used cell phones, but there were three landline phones in the house. "We saw Vice President Reynolds on the noon news today, and what he said about you, what he said about us… well, sugar, we can't help but worry."

"What have you got yourself into?" Mama asked. "I've known

all along that you should have stayed here where it's safe. You could have been the editor of the paper by now."

"I'm perfectly safe where I am, Mama. And I've never wanted to be the editor of the paper there, or of any paper."

"Thank goodness you've got Lee," her dad said. "What does he have to say about all of this?"

Patti took a deep breath, then before she could lose her nerve, said, "Lee and I aren't together any more, Dad. I've given his ring back."

Patti both heard and felt the dual intake of breath on the other end of the conversation.

"You gave his ring back?"

"Yes, sir. He showed me his true colors, and I wanted nothing more to do with him."

"Oh, baby. Why don't you come home for a few days? It's been a long time since we've seen you."

"Mama, I know you mean well. But I've got a job to do. What's more, I'm on the trail of a big story, so there's no way I can leave now. As for the vice president's comments, he's running scared, and he's trying to deflect attention off himself. I'm a good target, but I'm sorry he dragged the two of you into this."

"We're not worried about ourselves, but we are very worried about you."

"I'm fine, Mama. When you work in politics, you have to have thick skin. I'm okay."

Patti continued to assure her parents, but by the time they ended the call, she realized that all the starch in her body was gone.

"That was brutal," she told Harm. "When it comes to Lee, Reynolds can say whatever he wants. I was a fool to ever hook up with him, so I'll take my lumps. But my parents… that's another matter entirely."

"But this should give you a good idea of just how frightened Reynolds and his whole camp are. Ditto for Rawlings, although he's hiding his fear much better than the vice president is."

Patti couldn't stop the grin that captured her face. "Translated, Rawlings' handlers are doing a better job of managing him and the situation than the VP's people."

"Translated," Harm said, "the vice president doesn't have Gloria Brownstone any longer, and it's showing."

After he'd left for the night, Patti recalled his last words, and despite her best efforts, she realized her body was trembling. "Don't underestimate these people," he'd said, as she closed the door behind him. "If there's any connection whatsoever between the first lady's death and these two powerful politicians, your parents are right to be very worried." He hesitated, then said, "You're in danger, Patti. You've got to be very careful."

As she settled in for the night, her parent's words of concern and Harm's advice kept echoing in her head. By the time dawn came, and she was up, getting ready for the day, she thought again about her parents' suggestion that she come home for a few days.

*It's been over two years since I've seen the folks. Three different times they were coming here, and I told them I was too busy.*

Yes, it was time to go home. For several different reasons, her need to see the parents who had sacrificed everything for her was overwhelming. And it would put some distance between her and the venom that was spewing so plentifully in Washington. *Perhaps Harm's right. Maybe I am in danger.*

As soon as she knew Herb was in his office, Patti called him. "Herb, I'm taking some leave time. Starting now."

"What are you up to, Hobgood? You're not going rogue on me, are you?"

"I'm going home, Herb. To Council Grove. My parents are really freaked over that load of BS the vice president unloaded on them. I've got to go reassure them."

"Well, if you think so."

"I think so," she said. "I'll be gone at least a week, maybe a few days longer." She'd already done the calculations and knew that she had more than two weeks of leave time banked, and she reminded her boss of that fact.

"Take the time, Hobgood. Go home. But get back here as soon as you can. I'm convinced we're still sitting on a powder keg."

"Thanks, Herb." Over the next couple of hours, she'd booked a plane ticket on line, and pulled clothing enough for at least a week into her luggage. The last thing she did was call for a cab to take her to the airport. It was cheaper than paying for long-range parking at Reagan International.

As she awaited the taxi, she debated whether to alert her

parents that she was on her way. *But if I do, Daddy will insist on taking off work and driving to the airport to meet me. Better I just rent a car, drive the seventy miles, and arrive unannounced.*

The image of the surprise on her parents' faces would be validation enough that she was doing the right thing.

# CHAPTER ELEVEN

I t was past time to be up and at something productive. Instead, Lee Stanton just lay there and stared at the walls of his bedroom, in the apartment he shared with a roommate. The guy was a first class nerd and a know-it-all to boot, but his half of the rent and utilities in D.C.'s pricy rental market allowed Lee to have money left over each month. Lee tolerated him, but he definitely would not miss the jerk. In the days since Senator Rawlings had so unceremoniously dumped him, Lee had barely left his room. Fired, he was, and for what? That little blurb in the paper that no one except the senator himself even noticed. None of the other media outlets had even picked up on it.

"Rawlings over-reacted," he shouted to the ceiling. "SOB fired me for nothing, and after everything I've done for him." Lee couldn't decide which rankled more, that Rawlings didn't recognize his dedication, or that he'd been so callously cast aside, much like yesterday's garbage. Lee cursed the man, then dropped back onto the bed. What was the use in facing the day? His chances of getting another job comparable to the one he'd lost were somewhere between slim and none. And all of it was Patti's fault.

He rolled out of bed, stumbled to the bathroom, took care of the most urgent piece of business, and stared at himself in the mirror. He hadn't shaved since the day he'd returned home with his tail tightly clinched between his legs. His stubble was fast becoming true beard. Maybe he would grow it on out. But in the meantime, he padded to the kitchen where another bottle of beer provided his morning's nourishment. His diet for the past few days had been primarily liquid, most often alcoholic.

As he crept back to bed for another day of doing absolutely nothing, he couldn't contain his hatred of both his former boss and his former fiancée. The blood of the death of his career was on both their hands equally. Only thing was, he couldn't figure how he could get the revenge he knew was rightfully due him.

When his cell phone sounded off, he didn't answer it. In the days since his firing, not one of his former co-workers had even reached out to check on him. It was as if he no longer existed. And if they were calling after all this time, it was too little, too late. He didn't want to talk with them, and he sure as hell didn't want their sympathy.

It was more than an hour later that curiosity overcame his anger. Sure enough, the caller had left a message. But when he listened to it, shock reigned supreme.

"Call me, Stanton," he heard the gravel voice of Senator Rawlings say. Even though the man didn't identify himself, there was no mistaking his voice. "I may have over-reacted, and there's a way you can make amends."

Even though he could think of nothing he needed to make amends for, Lee wasted no time returning the call.

* * * * *

Patti had asked the cab to be there at eleven-thirty, so when the bell rang at just before the appointed time, she violated her own rule and swung open the door without first checking to be sure who

218

was on the other side.

"Hey, babe. I've missed you," the man on the other side of the door said, as he swaggered against the door jam. "Did you miss me?"

It was Lee Stanton rather than the cab driver, and if appearances were any indication, he was no happier than he had been the last time he stood in that same doorway. His next words confirmed that suspicion.

"Thought you were through with me, didn't you? Sent my ring back, didn't you? Got a restraining order against me, didn't you?" The leer on his face convinced Patti that the man was drunk. "And got me fired, too, didn't you?"

Patti knew she was spitting into the wind, but she wasn't about to let Lee get by with his illegal behavior. She would not allow him to further abuse her, and attempted to shove him out the door, so that she could shut it. However, he anticipated her, and before she could do anything, he was suddenly inside her apartment.

He noticed her luggage sitting in the hallway. "Oh, I see you anticipated me. You're already packed and ready to go. Thanks for making this easy, but you won't need that luggage where you're going."

"Where I'm going," she informed him, "is to visit my parents." She poked him in the chest with her finger. "And where you're going is back to jail if you don't get out of here right now and leave me alone." She held up her phone. "Or do I need to call the cops?"

Before she could stop him, he grabbed the hand that held the phone and twisted it, until she dropped the phone. "You SOB," she spit the words at him. "You do not put your hands on me. Do you understand?"

"What I understand is that you don't respect me, and I'm about to do something about that," he whispered, as he grabbed her hand again.

"What are you going to do?" She couldn't keep the tremor out of her voice.

"I'm gonna show you who's boss, and it's gonna be a lesson you ain't never going to forget." He twisted her arm until she screamed. "Now behave, and I won't have to hurt you any more. But I will, if you push me." He put his face right up in her face, and hissed, "It's all up to you, but it looks to me like the high and mighty White House Reporter has met her match."

He began shoving her toward the door.

"My phone," she screamed. "And what about my luggage?"

"You ain't gonna need none of it." With that, he pushed her out the door and pulled it closed. The next thing Patti knew, he was forcing her into an old, black, solid paneled van. As she was disappearing inside the vehicle, she saw out of the corner of her eye that a cab had pulled to the curb in front of her apartment. But she was helpless to signal the driver, and resigned herself to trying to figure how to get away from the lunatic who held her captive.

Lee ordered her to sit on the bench seat behind the driver, and once she'd complied, he tied her feet and hands and tethered her to the legs of the bench. Then he tied a blindfold over her eyes, and Patti felt a momentary sense of panic when she was totally robbed of sight.

"I demand to know where you're taking me!"

"Well, it ain't back to Kansas, Toto." The laugh that punctuated his response was, Patti realized, something you would connect with a mentally unstable person. Unfortunately, she realized, this was the same behavior he'd been exhibiting for quite some time. She'd just refused to see it. Plus, if present behavior was any indication, it had progressed to a new, higher level of insanity.

*There's no way he's ever going to let me go. I'll be lucky if he doesn't kill me.* It would do no good to plead for freedom; such would only further empower him. She remembered an old saying her dad had favored, "Never expect reasonable behavior from unreasonable people."

Instead of engaging him further in conversation, Patti determined to keep her mouth shut and her ears open. Everything she could hear was her only hope of knowing where they were bound.

It seemed that they rode forever, before Lee swung the van still at too high a rate of speed into what was obviously a rutted dirt lane. The motion of the van flung her against her restraints and despite not wanting to appear weak, she cried out from the pain. "Hey, watch it."

"Shut-up!" If anything, it seemed that he picked up speed, deliberately, and was hitting every pothole in the road. All the way out, he had ranted and accused her of everything he could think of. Many of his ramblings made absolutely no sense, and she had elected to simply let him say what he wished. Nothing that she might say could make any difference.

After traveling for another couple of minutes, he brought the van to a screeching stop. Patti speculated, given the direction he'd taken from her apartment and the traffic sounds, Lee had brought her across the Virginia line, somewhere outside the District of Columbia. But beyond that, she had no clue where they were.

Before she was ready, she heard the van door sliding open. Lee entered the van, untied the ropes from the seat itself, and gave her a vicious yank. She stumbled out of the vehicle, missed her footing and fell in the dirt drive. But before she could even try to judge if she was hurt, he jerked off the blindfold and she saw for the first time a small, rustic cabin that had obviously seen better days. Lee pushed her up the two steps onto a small, covered porch. The door wasn't locked, Patti noticed, because Lee opened it without a key. With him behind her, they entered what passed for a living room, but he pushed her on toward a hall in the back side of the cabin, then into a bedroom.

"Where are we, but also, why are we here, Lee?"

"As long as I know where we are," he replied, as he untied one of the ropes that bound her, "that's all that matters. As for why we're here. Well," his grin was downright evil, "just call this place a school, because you've got several lessons you need to learn. And we're going to teach you here."

*He said "we're." Does that mean there are others involved in this?*

Up until this point, she'd assumed that Lee was acting alone, simply trying to vent his anger at being challenged and embarrassed in the process. It hadn't occurred to her that there could be more people involved in this than she realized. That possibility shot icy

222

cold up and down her spine.

"Get over here," he ordered, and even though her ankles were bound, she managed to painfully hobble the six feet to where her kidnapper stood. "Now let me tell you how this is going to work," he said, as he made quick work of restraining her with a fairly heavy chain that was looped around her waist, and secured with a small lock. The other end he fastened to a new hasp mounted on the bedroom wall near the head of the bed. Then he hung the keys to the lock on a hook outside in the hall. Patti could tell without measuring that her tether wasn't going to reach far enough to allow her anywhere near the keys.

"You've got fourteen feet of chain," he told her. "And it's twelve feet to the toilet." He pointed to an open door a few feet away, and Patti caught a glimpse of a dated bathroom. "But that's as far as you're going to go, until we decide what to do with you."

"Do with me? What do you mean?"

"That's for us to know and maybe, one day, you'll find out." He headed for the door, and over his shoulder, he exclaimed, "Now, don't you go anywhere. Hear?"

Determined to have the last word, Patti said, "Lee, won't you please tell me why you're doing this? I need to understand what it is that I've supposedly done."

He halted, turned, and regarded her as if she was a five year old. "You're slick, Patti. But you may have been too slick, when you poked into matters at the highest level of government that were absolutely none of your business."

"All I've done is my job," she protested.

"And doing your job has threatened important people who aren't used to being threatened." He spat on the floor in her direction. "And those people don't take kindly to what you're doing."

"But what do you have to do with them?" she asked, truly perplexed.

Rather than answering, Lee grinned at her in such a way that Patti felt totally vulnerable. He said no more, but headed back through the cabin. She heard the door latch engage as he left.

Patti sat on the side of the bed, and took in her surroundings. The walls were dirty white, and appeared to be badly in need of a good cleaning, if not a coat of paint. The entire room, and where she could see into the hall and the adjoining bath appeared to be locked into a time warp somewhere in 1998. But regardless of the décor, the fact remained that she was a prisoner in this place, and she had no clue where she was or how she was going to get out.

*Am I even going to leave this place alive?*

Patti pulled herself up on the bed, and stretched her legs in front of her. It occurred to her that she would be more comfortable if she could at least loosen the ropes around her ankles. After working for almost an hour, success was at hand.

She knew that she should be frightened. Perhaps terrified would be a more apt response. And, later, she might well be shaking in her boots. But at the moment, she was still shaking inside with rage that she had allowed herself to be taken hostage.

It was obvious that Lee was simply one of a number of people involved in this plot to abduct her. Question was, who were the others? Lee had made mention of people at the highest levels

224

of government. Surely he wasn't referring to the vice president and Senator Rawlings? Was he?

*Both those guys are ruthless, but I can't believe either of them would be a party to kidnapping, and who knows what else?*

Then it came to her. If either of those men were involved in the first lady's death, then it stood to reason they were also connected to Hal Warren's death. A simple kidnapping would be small potatoes, indeed.

She had no way to tell time, and no way to pass the time, but at some point later in the afternoon, if the sun coming through the blinds over the window next to the bed was any indicator, she had company. The sound of a door elsewhere in the house opened, and she sat forward on the bed, expecting to see her former fiancé. *Right now, even Lee would look good.*

Instead, her visitor was a man she'd never seen. She drew back on the bed, then realized that she couldn't get farther away from him. "Who are you?" she demanded, and hoped the fear she felt didn't come through in her voice.

The stranger said nothing. He advanced on her, checked the ropes that still hung around her ankles, and inspected the chain that was her leash. As he moved about her, Patti took notice of everything she could glean from what she could see. He was short, not over five-six at most. And he was stocky. His closely-cropped dark hair had a few streaks of gray beginning at his temples, and his complexion hinted at a middle European heritage. Finally he spoke.

"You know why you're here, don't you?"

His heavily accented English confirmed her suspicions, but

also added to the confusion that swirled in her mind. How could this man be a part of this equation? Patti was sure there must be a sensible explanation, a connection that she simply couldn't see, but struggle as she might, she couldn't find the common denominator.

"No," she said, and deliberately raised her voice. "I don't know why I'm here. What's more, I demand that you release me and take me back to town."

"You're in no position to demand anything," the man informed her, and as she looked into his eyes, the cold, cruel, sadistic gaze that met her eyes caused her to involuntarily flinch. He saw her reaction, and she could also read his body language. He understood that she feared for her life, and there was no mistaking his satisfaction.

After checking the rest of the room, he left for a couple of minutes. When he returned, he carried two takeout bags and a drink carrier from a chain fast food eatery that he deposited on the bedside table.

"I will be back," he said, and headed toward the door. "We still have unfinished business." Then Patti heard the door latch behind him, followed by the sound of a vehicle starting.

*Unfinished business? Whatever could he mean? And who is he?*

The aromas from the food right at her elbow were overwhelming, and suddenly, she was ravenous. Who knew when she'd get another chance to eat. She delved into the bags, pulled out a burger and fries, and put a straw into one of the drink cups. As she ate, she pondered the situation. Was she being held for ransom?

If so, who were they asking to buy her freedom? Or was she being punished? Since they hadn't taken steps to ensure she didn't know who her kidnappers were, Patti had to question if they planned to allow her to gain freedom by any means other than death. The prospect was troubling, yet at that moment, restrained and isolated as she was, she realized there was little she could do.

As darkness took over the room, she switched on the lamp on the bedside table. One of the most aggravating parts of the situation was the lack of a clock. She had no way to accurately tell time, and the night seemed years long. She slept fitfully, and had finally dropped into an exhausted sleep when the sound of a vehicle pulling up outside her window disturbed her. She raised up, rubbed sleep from her eyes, and waited. Would it be Lee or the strange man who'd brought the food? Or would it be someone else? *How many people are a part of this?*

In a few minutes the sound of the front door alerted her that she was about to have company, and very quickly, Lee was in the doorway. He carried more take-out sacks, which he set down on the end of the bed, then turned to leave. "Breakfast."

"Lee. Wait," she said, "we need to talk."

He stopped, turned back to her, and said, "Too late for talking. We're way past that point."

"But, Lee. I don't understand what I've done. And who is this 'we' you keep talking about."

"What you've done, Patti is to jeopardize many different people who aren't accustomed to such. And it's better you don't know who all is involved." Then he was gone.

Patti watched his retreating back, and understood for the first time that she was a threat to somebody. In that moment, she also understood that her life was ebbing out. They would eventually kill her, which meant she had nothing to lose if she got herself killed trying to escape. Having come to terms with reality, she dived into breakfast. She needed nourishment if she hoped to have enough strength to die if it came down to it.

The next four days were a carbon copy of her first twenty-four hours, and between bouts of terror when she tried not to imagine how gruesome death might be, and how it might occur, she plotted how she could escape. Anything was better than twiddling her thumbs, which was the only outlet she had to relieve the boredom that was almost crippling. She'd fiddled with the chain, with the connection, and could find no way to free herself. She must have conceived and then discarded at least a hundred escape plans. At least it helped to pass the time, as did her detailed search of the room looking for something, anything, that would enable her to cut the chain that held her prisoner. After an exhaustive investigation, a mixed bag of loot had been collected. Twenty-seven cents in loose change had been collected from several places, along with a ballpoint pen, a selection of sex supplies and toys, and a lone business card from a home maintenance service.

At one point, when extreme paranoia took over, she'd had reason to question if she would ever leave that house alive. After all, she must be in the middle of something very hush- hush, and her captors were evidently threatened by her. It was a given that the only way her captors could guarantee her silence was to kill her. The problem was, while she had her suspicions, and dastardly suspicions they were, she knew nothing specific and even less that could be proven. Feeling that she had to do something to give someone a clue in case her body was found on the side of the road, she picked up the business card from the pile, took the pen, and wrote her name, along with a message.

*Obviously this is somebody's love nest, but whose?* Somehow, she couldn't see either Senator Rawlings or the vice president using such a rustic, almost rudimentary dwelling for their downlow assignations. They were more the five star hotel caliber. Patti was far from a prude, but for certain, she had no need for any of the x-rated items she'd uncovered. Her biggest find was a full, unopened fifth of quality bourbon that she laid on the bed beside her.

*If I don't soon get out of here, I may need the contents of that bottle myself!*

It wasn't until the fifth day, when her evening meal was delivered, that she saw a chance to get away. For starters, her courier was a face she hadn't seen before. This man was very young, and if appearances were any indication, he was even more scared of her than she was of him. Could she use his discomfort to her advantage?

He advanced into the room cautiously, and placed the sacks of food on the very end of the bed.

"Uh… uh, is there anything else you need?" He was the first of her captives who'd inquired if she was in need, but she figured his query was more from nervousness than real concern. She wondered, too, why they'd sent this guy. Did it mean something was wrong and the others couldn't turn loose? Whatever the reason, she needed to seize on the opportunity. Who knew if she would get another chance?

"I need this chain around my waist loosened. It's so tight, it's rubbing me raw through my clothes."

From the look on the young man's face, she might as well have asked that he set her free and drive her back to her apartment. "Uh... uh..., I don't... I don't know." He wrung his hands in indecision. "I don't think I'm supposed to do anything but bring your food." He motioned to the bags on the bed, as she noticed him slowly edging toward the door. Her one opportunity to escape was about to walk out. Somehow, she had to keep him there until she could wear him down. He was her only hope.

"I promise," she said, and she dropped her voice to where it was very soft, so as not to spook him. "I promise I won't try to escape or anything, if you'll just loosen this chain." She tried to put on a sufficiently suffering expression. "It hurts so bad, but if it were loosened just a couple of links, I could deal with it."

"I don't know..."

"Look," she said, "the key is on that hook on the wall out in the hall. She pointed in that direction. "If you'll get it and give me a little relief, I'll stand here and hold my hands in the air." She extended both arms over her head. "I won't move from this spot. I promise."

The indecision that obviously plagued the young man was torture for Patti to watch. Under any other circumstances, she would have been so ashamed of trying to deceive him. But succeeding might likely make all the difference between living and dying.

She lifted her hands toward the ceiling again, and said, "Please help me. I promise, I'll never tell any of the others what you did." She favored him with a broad smile. "It'll be our little secret.

230

Please?"

She could sense that he was wavering. "Please?"

When he began to move toward the hallway, she had to question if he was indeed about to help her, or if he was just taking the easy way out and was about to leave. It appeared that his thoughts were mirroring her own, because he came to the keys, hesitated, took a couple more steps, hesitated, backed up and snatched the key ring off the hook. Slowly he made his way back to where she stood.

"I don't feel good about this," he mumbled. But even as he voiced his doubts, the man was fitting first one key, then the second key into the lock. The click that followed was the sweetest sound Patti had ever heard. He removed the lock, allowing the chain to fall to the floor. As he bent to pick it up, when she could no longer see his face, Patti uttered a quick and silent prayer for forgiveness, then brought her arms down around his shoulders, knocking him off balance.

As he began to struggle to rise again, she said, "I'm sorry." And she truly was sorry, but she was also desperate. Without further apology, she grabbed the bottle of bourbon by its neck. Using all the strength that remained in her body, she brought the bottle down on the young man's head. The bottle shattered and the pungent amber liquid poured over him. He collapsed onto the floor, and without stopping to check his condition, Patti made her escape.

She didn't know where she was, how she could get back to some place of safety, or which direction she should go. But never mind that she was totally lost, she was also totally alive, and she intended to keep it that way.

231

# CHAPTER TWELVE

"Mr. Martin. This is Harmon Bostwick. I'm a writer for *Nation's News* magazine and a long-time close friend of Patti Hobgood."

It was such a relief that he'd been successful. He'd had to argue with the receptionist who, at first, had refused to put his call through, explaining that Mr. Martin was on deadline. It had taken almost a full-blown assault before he heard the voice of the man he was desperate to reach.

"Yes, Mr. Bostwick? How can I help you? And I should tell you, my time is severely limited, so if this can wait a couple of hours, that would be better."

"It can't wait, because I'm very concerned about Patti. Hopefully you can put my mind at ease."

"Concerned? Why? Patti's out of the office for a few days R&R."

"Yes," Harm said, as he glanced around Patti's small living room, and noted with concern that the apartment smelled as if it hadn't been occupied for quite some time; as if all the life had been sucked out. He studied again the suspicious tidbits he'd collected in his quick search. "I know she supposedly went to Kansas to visit her parents."

"So, why are you concerned?"

"I've been trying to call her all week, and at first, all my calls went to voicemail. I've left numerous messages, but she hasn't called me back. Now for the past two days, it's like her phone battery has died."

"Perhaps she's turned her phone off and simply isn't taking calls."

Harm couldn't contain the snort that escaped his mouth. "Oh, come now Mr. Martin, you and I both know her better than that. You might have had to call her back from her trip early. Patti Hobgood would not have been without her phone at her fingertips."

Silence on the other end told him he'd struck a nerve. "But I know where the phone is. Along with her packed luggage and her plane ticket and boarding pass. And none of it is in Kansas."

"What's going on here, Mr. Bostwick? Are you trying to run some kind of a scam?"

"I'm worried about my friend and colleague, and given the events of the past few weeks, I think you ought to be concerned as well."

"Where is her cell phone?"

"It's in the corner of her living room, damaged. And her luggage is sitting here in the foyer, and her plane ticket and boarding pass are laying on top of the luggage."

"Have you checked in with her parents?"

"No," he said. "I didn't want to alarm them, unless there was a need to do so. That's why I called you first."

"I've not seen her or talked with her since she called to ask for time off," he said. "But Mr. Bostwick, I have a question. I'm assuming you're in her apartment. What I don't know is how you got in, because I know Hobgood. She guards her privacy very carefully."

"I came by to check on her, after I couldn't get an answer to my calls, and found the front door unlocked and ajar."

"Unlocked? You were able to walk right in."

"Yes, sir."

"Hang up, Mr. Bostwick. I'm calling the police, and I'm on my way. But you don't leave until I get there."

"I'd call the Secret Service, as well, Mr. Martin. Patti was Chief White House Reporter, and we both know that threats have been made against her. I think it's obvious that she never made it to Kansas, and I don't feel at all comfortable about any of this."

Harm ended the call, and continued searching the small apartment without touching anything.

*Oh, Patti, where are you?*

\* \* \* \* \*

Outside the cabin, she made note of the license plate on the older model Ford Taurus in the drive. Hopefully, she could remember the number, because she had no way to write it down. And while she freely admitted that she was totally lost, she also knew that time wasn't on her side. It was a given that the young man would soon be coming through that door, because she realized that she'd only stunned him. He must not find any trace of her, which meant she had to make a hasty escape.

*At this point, going in the wrong direction is preferable to standing here where he can see me.*

There was heavy undergrowth all around, and she wasn't dressed for running through the woods. Neither could she take a chance on sticking to the driveway; she might not have time to get off the road if she heard him coming her way. Patti looked around once again, said, "Eeeny, meeny, miney, mo…" and quickly moved into the tree line while she had the chance, trying to get far enough away that she couldn't easily be seen.

Part of her dilemma lay in the not knowing what to expect of the young man who had unwillingly assisted in her escape. She couldn't see him striking out on foot to follow her. He just didn't appear to be the woodsy type. So would he call someone to come and help him, meaning he would have to confess what he'd done? Or would he simply lock up the house, get back in his car, and leave, planning to play dumb when the others discovered that she was gone? She hoped for the latter, but wasn't overly optimistic.

*I only have one chance, and every minute I stand here thinking about him, I'm jeopardizing my own safety.*

The question most plaguing her was how to get somewhere that she could borrow a phone. Any phone. Everything became more complicated when she realized that she had absolutely no idea where she was. The rural nature of her surroundings tended to validate her earlier belief that she was somewhere in Virginia. She looked about her, and realized that the sun was already dipping in the sky. The western sky, which meant Washington should be in the opposite direction. It was a matter that needed no more debate, and she headed farther into the trees on the eastern side of the drive.

It was rough going from the very beginning. The sandals she'd chosen to wear on the plane weren't very suitable for serious hiking, and she kept hanging a heel on exposed roots and vines. Add to this the fact that the sun was dropping lower in the sky, and she knew she would soon be out of daylight. It was a given that she would be spending a night, alone, and exposed to the elements. Not until the sun rose again would she have the opportunity to find help.

*I've got to find a place to bed down for the night.*

Light was almost gone by the time she found a small, tumble down building. *Looks like it might have once been a utility or garden shed.* A good, hard shove caused the door to open enough that she could squeeze inside. However, she wasn't comfortable going very far into the building. At the same time, she had to wonder just how close she was to the cabin. She'd had to go around so many obstacles to get to this point, she had no clue how far from the drive she'd traveled. Had she walked in circles and did her kidnappers know of the building's existence?

*Better to get inside far enough to close the door. Just in case.* Even so, the prospect of spending the night here wasn't an attractive one. Who knew what kinds of creatures she'd rather not encounter already called the building home. She was definitely the trespasser here.

One of the first things she realized was how hungry she was.

*Why didn't I grab those sacks of food? There's no hope of anything to eat until it gets daylight. And maybe not even then.*

Darkness settled in, and Patti tried to do likewise, knowing she had no choice but to make the best of things. But that didn't mean she had to like it. Plus, the floor seemed to be alive with creepy, crawly things of undetermined denomination. And between the night noises going on around her, and unidentifiable sounds from inside the building, she was becoming more freaked by the minute.

She had spent several years during her childhood with the Girl Scouts, and had a number of survival-oriented merit badges to prove her membership. She was certain, if she was to invade the cedar chest in her parents' bedroom in Council Grove, she could find those same fabric badges still sewn to her sash. Her mother, she well knew, threw nothing away. The badges were definitely there. Unfortunately, the knowledge behind them had long since gone AWOL.

*Too many years have passed, and I've had other things going on!*

It didn't help that she had no idea of the time, or how long she'd been there. For that matter, she had no idea how long she would have to stay there. In an effort to calm herself and to feel like she was doing something positive, she began to try to calculate the time. Knowing that good dark had come at 7:47 the night before she was abducted the next day, and since the days got a minute or so shorter as time moved toward the end of the year, she was able to do some rudimentary math calculations.

*That means it should have been about 7:39 when it got good and dark tonight. Now how long has it been since it got good dark?*

She couldn't seem to do the math, and the futility of her

238

efforts came home to her in a sense of defeat. Perhaps she shouldn't have escaped. Had she jumped out of a bad situation into a worse situation? For certain, it was hard to find any way that she'd improved her lot.

The darkness engulfed her, and she sat in the black surrounds of the little building, totally unable to relax. Sleep would be elusive. However, exhaustion claimed her, and when she awoke and realized she'd been dozing, the inability to know the time was absolutely maddening. Had she been out for any period of time, or had it been a case of nodding off, only to awaken only a minute or so later?

As she tried to calm her emotions, she noticed a change. At the beginning of her stay, the little shed had been totally dark. Now there was a large area of light splaying over the floor. So much light that she could actually make out the clutter and abandoned tools that were scattered about the little building she now judged to be about eight by ten feet. Pulling herself to her feet, she hobbled over to the light, and realized it was moonlight.

*It's a full moon. But why didn't I see it earlier?*

After giving it some thought, she realized that earlier in the evening, the skies had been heavily overcast. Now they weren't.

*All those clouds were hiding the moon, but now that they've blown out, I can see every star in the sky, and outside it's almost as bright as day.*

Without even thinking through what she was about to do, she pulled on the door and managed to get it open far enough that she could squeeze through. The accumulation of dirt and dead bugs and who knew what else that was on the edge of the door wreaked havoc on her clothing. The yellow pants outfit had been one of her favorite pieces, but after wearing the outfit for six days without a bath, it was definitely trash can bound.

She stood in the brightness of the moonlight, and realized that she was still faced with the same dilemma. Which way should she go to try and find help? The last thing she wanted to do was end up back at the cabin. Although, she consoled herself, she no longer feared they were searching for her. But they might have left someone guarding the house in case she did return. Nope, somehow she had to find a different direction. Preferably the best direction.

Thanks to the moon, she could actually see better than when she'd first entered the woods. And if her memory of what she'd learned in scouting was still correct, she needed to head in the opposite direction of the moon's position. Praying that she was right, Patti wasted little time doing just that.

*At this point, doing something wrong is better than being held prisoner to my fears and indecision. If I've made a mistake, I'll deal with it.*

She walked, picking her way through vines and undergrowth, over fallen logs and exposed tree roots that tripped her up more than once. But she continued slogging toward an unknown invisible target, stopping when exhaustion dictated. And, again, she had no clue about the time, or how long she'd been walking.

The only consolation, the farther she went, she could see the eastern sky beginning to lighten. It should soon be where she could truly see her surroundings, and hopefully could finally decide where she was. The lighter the eastern sky became, the more optimistic Patti found herself. Surely it couldn't be long now until she stumbled upon some kind of civilization.

Her energies were flagging, and in an effort to keep moving, she picked up her pace. It was the searing pain that tore through her left ankle, followed by the hard thud when the ground rose up to meet her, that put an immediate stop to her progress.

*Oh. My. Gosh. My ankle hurts so badly.*

She twisted to where she could get a better look and noticed immediately that her painful ankle was laying at an awkward angle, and the toe of her sandal was wedged against a brick that protruded out of the ground. Before she could even take stock of the situation, what few contents were still in her stomach came up and out, further soiling her clothing. The nausea all but consumed her.

*Oh. Great. Just great.*

All efforts to move her left foot resulted in white hot pain coursing up her leg. There was little doubt she'd broken her ankle. What she didn't know was how she was going to get to freedom and safety.

*But somehow, I have to keep plugging.*

When she finally realized that the roiling in her gut had passed, she attempted to stand, and after three attempts that piled her back on the ground, she had to concede that she couldn't make any progress without help. Looking around, she spied a broken tree limb about five feet long. She dragged herself across the rough ground, tearing her slacks and the skin beneath them. It seemed that she was moving in mere fractions of an inch each time, and finally, much later than she would have believed, she finally fastened her hand around the piece she prayed would act as a crutch and allow her to continue walking to somewhere. Anywhere.

The act of pulling up on the limb was excruciating, because even the slightest movement sent spasms of pain through her ankle, all the way up to her hip. But she gritted her teeth, kept trying to find her balance, and finally, was able to lean all of her weight against the tree limb, and take one small, quick step. Her ankle felt as if it was encased in concrete, that it weighed more than her entire body. That made her gait very much off balance, and very labor-intensive. In the end, she'd make one short step, rest, another short step, followed by another rest.

*At this rate, I might make it by Christmas. But I'd planned to spend Christmas in Council Grove.*

Thoughts of her parents, and the possibility that she might never see them again, threatened to push her over the emotional cliff she had been teetering on since she'd been abducted. Tears filled her eyes, and she couldn't corral the loud sob that escaped her mouth. How much was one person expected to withstand?

Patti had no idea how long it took, or how far she'd literally hobbled, when she began to see a thinning of the trees ahead. As badly as she wanted to pick up the pace, her body not only denied her that luxury, but threatened to shut down entirely. The prospect of being stopped so close to what she prayed was someone who could help her was as infuriating as it was defeatist.

*I will NOT give in. I will not let these animals win.*

Her pace slowed, but she continued toward the signs of civilization she hoped weren't a mirage. And finally, when she felt she simply couldn't make it another step, she spotted ahead of her,

242

perhaps fifty feet away, a paved road. She still had no idea where she was, or where the road would take her. But a road that would eventually send a car by her was preferable to what her situation had been for the past six days. When she finally reached the roadside, and could see no signs of automobiles or of human life, she came apart at the seams. Her entire body collapsed on the rough ground of the roadside, and for the first time, she gave herself permission to cry.

*Sooner or later, somebody has to come along.*

But nothing came, and the temperature began to rise and her thirst was almost unbearable. She began to wonder if this small rural paved road was actually a private road within one of the many estates that dotted the eastern Virginia countryside. If so, it might not see any traffic for days. There was no telling how long it might be before someone came by. In the meantime, she was famished, almost sick with thirst, her ankle was swollen to obscene proportions, and she wished she were still chained to the bed back at the cabin.

*If I had died with the first lady, it would have been instantaneous. I wouldn't have known anything until it was a done deal. Nothing like the torture it looks like I'll have to endure before death finally takes me this time.* She laid her head down on the ground on the side of the road, and closed her eyes. *Might as well, because I am going to die.*

\* \* \* \* \*

Harmon Bostwick didn't recognize the number displayed on his phone's Caller I.D. Nevertheless, he answered on the second ring. After dealing with the Secret Service and then officers with the

D.C. Metropolitan Police Department, he dared not ignore any call. If it was spam, or a crackpot, he'd simply deal with it.

It had been a long night, and he'd slept very little. The authorities had checked with the airline and confirmed that Patti never boarded her flight. They had also checked with her parents, and were assured that their daughter was not visiting them. Of course, Mr. and Mrs. Hobgood had insisted on knowing why Patti was supposed to be there, and once they learned the whole story, had announced that they would be on the next flight to D.C.

To his surprise, once the detectives understood the entire story, and how Patti was possibly a part of the first lady's death and a lot of other chaos ongoing, they agreed with him that his friend had been taken against her will. On that much, everyone agreed, and the physical evidence in the apartment confirmed it. Harm knew which cab company Patti used whenever she needed one, and a check with their dispatcher confirmed that when the driver arrived to take her to the airport, she never came to the door. When it came to the matter of who had taken her, however, and where she was, there was wide disagreement.

"I'm telling you," Harm had insisted, digging in his heels and forcing the officers to hear him out, "Reynolds and Rawlings are mixed up in this. I would swear my life on it."

"Careful, fellow," one of the Secret Service cautioned him. "When you start making accusations against the vice president, I have to take notice and take action."

"But I tell you, both those men are in collusion. They're in this somehow. I can feel it in my gut."

"Does that gut of yours also have evidence, irrefutable evidence? Can you prove what you're alleging?" The agent punched Harm in the chest. "Because without ironclad evidence, buddy, I can't even think about what you're charging, never mind act on it."

Harm had known when he was beaten, and said as much. "But I think you'll be eating crow by the time this is over."

"Maybe. Maybe not. But I'd rather eat crow than bring unsubstantiated charges against the Vice President of the United States. And in the meantime, if you go around shooting off your mouth, you will find yourself in big trouble."

That had been the day before, and it was now shortly before noon. Harm was changing clothes, getting ready to head to the airport to collect Patti's parents when his phone rang.

"Hello."

"This is Deputy Sheriff Harold Watkins of the Randolph County Virginia Sheriff's office. I'm trying to reach Harmon Bostwick." Harm was immediately trying to place exactly where the county was. He assumed the call had something to do with an article he'd written in a recent issue, where he'd shined an unflattering light on small town law enforcement operations, and how much illegal activity occurred in some of them.

He said, not hesitating to bend the truth a little, "I'm sorry, but I'm up against a deadline. If you'll call me back tomorrow, I'll be glad to talk to you." He was about to end the call when he heard the man's voice say, "Do you know a Patti Hobgood?"

*Patti! This man knows something about her.*

"Patti Hobgood. Yes, I know her well."

"Are you family?"

The question about being a family member set off an uneasy stirring in his stomach. "Look," he said, totally ignoring the man's question, "Patti has been missing for almost a week, and both D.C. Police and the Secret Service are searching for her." Then, before he could lose his nerve, he posed the question that, in his mind, anyway, could only be answered one way. "You're not calling to tell me she's dead. Please say you're not."

"Sounds to me," the deputy said, "like I'd better speak to someone in the Metro Police. Thank you, Mr. Bostwick."

"Tell me, please," he begged. "Please tell me she's alive."

"I'm sorry, Mr. Bostwick, but protocol dictates that we not release that information."

As the call was about to end, Harm grabbed the last straw available. "Detective Sergeant Wilcox, Deputy Watkins. Speak to Detective Wilcox. He's heading up the Metro's investigation."

"Thank you, Mr. Bostwick." The call ended, but not before Harm realized that the deputy hadn't given any indication that he would actually ask for the proper person.

He hesitated only a moment, before he placed his own call to Detective Wilcox, and still, Harm had to endure delays and uncooperative interference before finally he heard the sound that was the sweetest music. "Detective Wilcox here."

"This is Harm Bostwick." He quickly related the gist of the conversation he'd just had with the Virginia sheriff's deputy. "He asked me, specifically, if I knew Patti Hobgood. But when I made the mistake of telling him that Patti was high profile and missing, he wouldn't tell me anything. He wouldn't even tell me if she was alive."

"I'll call him myself. Stay close to your phone."

Harm checked the clock and realized if he was going to meet Patti's parents he needed to get on his way to the airport. As he navigated the nightmare D.C. traffic, the question foremost in his mind was whether he should share with his soon-to-be passengers that there had been word of Patti. And by the time he helped them claim their luggage, and they were making their way to the short-term parking, he was still struggling with what to say and when to say it.

As he fought his way out of the airport complex, his phone rang again. He recognized Detective Wilcox's number, and struggled to answer while still negotiating the bumper to bumper traffic.

"Yes, what did you find out?"

Their conversation was short, but fruitful, and when he arrived at the expressway, rather than heading back into the city, he turned instead to the right. It was, he estimated, about sixty miles to the hospital where Patti had been taken.

"I have news for you," he said to his passengers. Mr. Hobgood was in the front passenger seat and his wife was in the back seat behind the driver. While they'd been polite when he connected with them in the airport, very little conversation had happened since.

"News?" Mr. Hobgood asked. "About Patti?" they said in unison.

"She's been found, and we're headed there now."

"She is alive?" Mr. Hobgood asked, and Harm could hear the hesitancy in his voice."

"She is alive," he said, and before he could continue, Mrs. Hobgood said, "Thank God. My prayers have been answered."

Harm heard the woman quietly praying in the back seat, and he waited until he heard the whispered "Amen," before he told them the rest of the news.

"Patti is alive, but she's in pretty rough shape."

"But she'll recover. Right?" The question was from her dad, and Harm could feel the agony in his voice.

"She should recover, but it won't be overnight. She's badly dehydrated, she has a broken ankle that's going to take reconstructive surgery. She has cuts and bruises and is just generally in very poor condition."

"But what happened to her? And why is she in a hospital here in Virginia?"

"We still don't have a lot of answers. What we do know is that she was found mid-morning today on a very rural road that's rarely traveled. She was unconscious and badly sunburned and in shock."

"Dear God," Mr. Hobgood said. "However did she end up there? And why was she abducted in the first place?"

"We simply don't know," Harm told his passenger. "Hopefully, Patti can fill in a bunch of the blanks for us."

"Is she conscious? Is she going to know us?" The question was posed in almost a whisper from the little woman in the back seat. Harm felt her grief, and wished there was something he could do to alleviate her pain.

It would be better not to get their hopes up, so he said, "I don't know exactly what her status is. We'll just have to wait and see." It was, he reasoned, better for them to expect the worst, and be pleasantly surprised, rather than the other way around. These two people were already hurting. He didn't want to add to their agony.

The drive dragged on for what seemed forever, before he finally spotted the first of several directional signs routing traffic to the regional hospital and trauma center. On the one hand, it was such a relief to know that Patti had been taken to a medical center equipped to treat her multiple injuries. At the same time, it was troubling that her injuries were so critical that she needed this level of trauma care.

He found his way into the hospital parking garage, and quickly located a vacant spot. As the trio headed into the hospital, Harm's phone rang. Again, it was a number he didn't recognize, but again he answered. "Hold on just a second," he told his unknown caller. He said to Patti's parents, "Follow those red lines in the floor, and according to the signs, you should end up in the ER. Someone there can direct you to Patti." He held up his phone. "I need to take this call, and I'll join you in a few minutes." Aside from the call, he felt like the couple might like some time alone with their daughter.

"Yes, this is Harmon Bostwick. Who am I talking to, please?"

"This is Lee Stanton, Patti Hobgood's fiancé. I can't find Patti, and I'm wondering if you might know where she is?" As he heard

249

the man's smooth patter, the hair on the back of his neck stood at attention. He tried to tell himself that he disliked the other man because he'd proven himself to be a jerk so many different times.

"I really need to talk to her, like this morning. I've left her four voicemails, but she hasn't called me back."

*If the shoe was on the other foot, and I didn't know where my fiancée was, I wouldn't appreciate somebody keeping that information from me.* Then it hit him. Patti had given her engagement ring to the arresting officer, who had passed it along to Lee while he was in jail.

The feeling of unease was growing, and he decided to err on the side of caution.

"Patti's in Kansas visiting her parents," he told Lee, and felt not the first bit of guilt over his blatant lie. "She left about a week ago, and I'm not sure when she plans to be back."

"Oh, I didn't know."

This guy was working with an agenda, and Harm had no intention of helping him. Perhaps one more lie was in order? "What do you mean you didn't know? I was sitting with Patti when she called to tell you she was going."

Patti had specifically told him she wasn't letting Lee know she was leaving town. But Lee didn't need to know that. If his reaction was any indication, that last statement had freaked him out.

"She what? I didn't talk to her. I didn't know anything about her going to Kansas." His words were playing leapfrog over each other. "I tell you, I never talked to her."

Harm knew it was time to end the conversation, if for no other reason than the guy made him sick. "If I see Patti before you do, I'll tell her to call you." Then he pushed the button to terminate.

As he hurried toward the ER, two very troubling thoughts invaded his mind almost simultaneously. *Lee said he'd left four voicemails that morning. Yet Patti's phone had been non-functioning for several days. There's no way he could have left any messages. And how in the heck did he get my cell number, because I know Patti didn't give it to him.* Suddenly, he was more troubled than ever.

When a nurse showed him to the trauma room where Mr. and Mrs. Hobgood stood together beside their daughter's bed, his already heightened perception of trouble ramped up even farther. The couple was a picture of distress, and he could hear Mrs. Hobgood crying softly. He stepped up to the bed next to them, and when he saw Patti, he couldn't keep his tongue from saying what he thought.

"Holy crap," he muttered, then was immediately ashamed. "I'm sorry," he said to the couple next to him. But the patient in the bed was so horribly disfigured, if he hadn't been told that it was Patti, he might never have recognized her.

"No apology necessary," her dad replied. "I said a lot worse than that."

Had his friend not been so badly injured, Harm would have taken comfort that his words hadn't been offensive. But as it was...

"Have they told you anything?" Harm asked. "Have you been able to talk to a doctor?"

"Nothing," Mrs. Hobgood said. "The nurse opened the door,

251

showed us in, and left. We don't know anything more than we did when we got here."

"I'm going to see what I can find out," he said, as he clinched his right hand into a fist and slammed it into his left hand. "We need to know something. For the moment, never mind how she got here. We need to know what her prognosis is." He left the room attempting to tamp down the anger that threatened to consume him, leaving behind a confused and distraught set of parents, who were so far removed from the life their daughter lived as east was from west. Somehow, he knew they had become his responsibility, as least temporarily. And he was going to do for them what he would want someone to do for his parents, if they were still alive.

*As ridiculous as it sounds, I still believe that Reynolds and Rawlings had a hand in all of this.*

His search led him back to the nurses' station, where despite his pleas, no one would tell him anything, except to repeat the term HIPPA several times as justification for their closed-mouth attitude. Finally, one nurse did offer the information that the doctor would be in to talk with Patti's parents within the next thirty minutes, as soon as he finished with the surgery he was on.

"So are you telling me she's going to have to have surgery?"

"You'll have to have that conversation with the doctor," she replied, all of her goodwill and cooperation suddenly evaporating.

"Thank you," he said, feeling that some expression of gratitude was necessary. "I'll go back and tell her parents." Before he could get out of the waiting area, Harm heard a man's voice calling.

252

"Mr. Bostwick... Mr. Bostwick."

He turned and caught sight of Deputy Wilcox. Another uniformed man, a stranger to him, was with the D.C. officer." He stopped to wait on them.

"Mr. Bostwick," Deputy Wilcox said, as the two men reached him. "Have you seen her yet?"

"I've seen her," Harm said, "although if they hadn't told me who she was, I would never have recognized her."

"She's been through an ordeal, all right," the other man said. "Mr. Bostwick, I'm Deputy Watkins; we spoke earlier today." He put out his hand, as he said, "I'm sorry I couldn't tell you anything. Obviously, you're one of the good guys, but I couldn't take a chance."

Harm wanted to tell the deputy not to worry about his hostile attitude of cooperation, but he realized that he was still pissed, so instead he said, "So do we know who the bad guys are?"

The deputy removed his hat and ran his fingers through his hair. "No sir, we don't. We're hoping Ms. Hobgood can at least point us in the right direction." His fingers ruffled his hair again. "There was absolutely nothing on her person or even around her that would give us the first clue. And as badly injured as she appeared, we didn't waste time trying to get answers to all our questions."

*Thank goodness!*

"So how did you know to call me?"

"In the pocket of her slacks, there was a business card from a home maintenance service. On the back, she'd written her name and "Call Harmon Bostwick" and your phone number."

While the deputy's explanation answered one question, it caused at least two other queries to germinate.

*Patti must have been in great fear for her life to have left that message, knowing the chances were good that her captors probably wouldn't search her pockets.*

There was, Harm knew, much more to this story than they knew. More than they would ever know, unless Patti could fill in the many blanks. Question was, would she, or would she die, forever leaving the individuals who were responsible to escape punishment by default.

# CHAPTER THIRTEEN

"Let me tell you how we found her," Deputy Watkins said.

"Please do, but hold your story just a second, and come with me. Patti's parents from Kansas are here, and they need to hear this too."

He led the men back to the room, where he made quick introductions. "Deputy Watkins is going to tell us how they found Patti." The room became strangely silent, save for the sound of the machines around the bed.

"Yes," Mr. Hobgood said, "we need to know, and we'll be forever grateful if you'll help us understand what happened."

"Very well," Deputy Watkins said, "while we can't tell you how she got to the place where we found her, I can tell you what we do know."

Over the next five minutes, he painted a picture that only brought more pain to the three individuals there for whom Patti was special. It seemed that she had been found unconscious on the side of a small, rural road in the middle of a large landholding that ended in a dead end. The road itself was an access road to a storage barn where farm equipment was kept.

"That's the miraculous thing about all of this," the deputy said. "There are days at a time when no one uses this road. Even the open end is gated and locked because of the value of the equipment. However, a piece of equipment had broken down, and one of the farm hands was on his way to get another backhoe, when he spotted her lying on the side of the road."

"Did you say 'lying on the side of the road?'" Mrs. Hobgood asked. Harm marveled again at the soft hesitancy in her voice, while he also zeroed in on the pain in her heart.

"Yes ma'am," the deputy said. "Lying crumpled on the side of the road, looking pretty much the same as she looks now."

"And she was unconscious? You weren't able to get any information from her?" The question was from Mr. Hobgood.

"No, sir," as far as we know, she's been totally out of it, and basically unable to speak since she was found. Mr. Ellis, the farm employee who found her, tried to revive her, but was unsuccessful. He immediately called nine-one-one, and stayed with her until paramedics got there. Law enforcement was close behind."

"Here's what you don't know," Harm volunteered, unable to keep silent any longer. "Patti was on her way to Kansas," he said, and indicated her parents. "She'd been the target of some hostility here in DC, and the powers that be at the newspaper thought she would be better off out of town for a few days. She wanted to surprise you folks, so she didn't call you."

"That was when?" her dad asked.

"A week ago today" Harm said. "Only she never boarded that plane."

"So it stands to reason that she's been missing since this time last week, only nobody realized it because everybody thought she was elsewhere."

"Exactly," Detective Wilcox said. "And given that her packed luggage and plane boarding materials are still sitting in her foyer, it's a safe guess that whatever happened, occurred shortly before she was ready to leave for the airport."

"That's backed up by the taxi driver who arrived within just minutes of the pick-up time she'd requested, but couldn't find anyone at home."

"You make it sound like a kidnapping or something," Mr. Hobgood said.

Detective Wilcox said, "Because that's exactly what we think this was."

"So how do you explain where she was found and her injuries?" Patti's mother asked.

Deputy Watkins held up one finger. "There's little doubt she was taken against her will. Either her captors beat her and then dumped her with those injuries expecting that she would die shortly, or somehow, she managed to escape and who knows what she endured to get to that roadside."

Mrs. Hobgood swayed on her feet, and had Harm not reached for her, would have collapsed in the floor. He and Mr. Hobgood guided her to a nearby chair, and her husband remained by her side, as she sobbed softly into her hands that concealed her face.

"I'm more inclined to believe that she escaped," her father said. He gestured toward the bed. "And this, this heartbreaking sight we see here, is the price she paid for freedom."

"We would agree with you," Deputy Wilcox said.

"You know," Harm said, "she was…"

The door opened from the hallway to admit a medical person in green scrubs, and a white coat who interrupted him. "Good afternoon," the man said, "I'm Dr. Bogart. I hope some of you are this young woman's family." His words were delivered with a smile, but Harm was quick to note none of that smile reached the man's eyes.

"We're her parents," Mr. Hobgood said, as he moved to take the doctor's outstretched hand. "Jim Hobgood, and this is my wife, Mary Lou."

"Then we need to talk," Dr. Bogart said. He glanced at the other three in the room and said, "If you folks could step out in the hall for a few minutes."

"Nonsense," Jim Hobgood insisted. "If it weren't for these people, our daughter would still be missing. They can stay. As a matter of fact, they are staying." His attitude clearly demonstrated the length of his remaining patience with the whole situation. "So get on with what you have to say."

"Very well." The doctor moved to the bed, checked the patient's vitals, and looked her over carefully. "The good news is, as bad as your daughter looks right now, most of that is cosmetic, if you will. Surface injury and bruising, along with some minor cuts and abrasions."

"But why can't she talk to us?" Mrs. Hobgood pleaded. "If I could just hear her talk to me and know that she can hear me."

The doctor consulted an electronic tablet which he'd removed from one of the large pockets in the lab coat. "Don't be alarmed, Ma'am. We've got her heavily sedated for the pain. If she were awake, she'd be able to talk. But she does have…"

The ringing of Harm's phone interrupted, and Harm grabbed for it quickly to decline the call and silence the ringing. But when he saw that it was the same number that Lee Stanton had called from earlier, his gut told him he needed to answer. "Excuse me" he said, already halfway to the door. What could this scumbag be calling about now?

"Hello?"

"This is Lee Stanton again. I really have to talk with Patti. Like it's life or death." The thing that made no sense was the degree of panic Harm heard in the other man's voice. "Can you give me her parents' number in Kansas, so I can call her there? I've left two more messages since I talked to you earlier, and she's just not calling me back. I guess she's mad with me."

*Duh, do you think? She gave you back your ring, doofus. What can't you understand?*

"You don't have her parents' phone number?"

"No, dude, I don't. I don't even know their names so I could search for the number."

*You were engaged to Patti, and you don't even know her parents' names or their phone number. Obviously you couldn't be invested enough in the woman you were going to marry to even learn who her parents are. What is wrong with this picture?*

However, it wasn't his job to educate Lee Stanton, and if it were up to him, he'd banish the guy to somewhere outside the country. Permanently.

"Look, Lee. I'm in the middle of something that I can't miss. And I don't have her parents' phone number, but seems like I heard somewhere that her dad's name is Jim. You might try that." Then without waiting for an answer, he keyed off the call and returned to the hospital room. The words he heard as he rejoined the group plunged his heart into dread.

"We'll be prepping her for surgery shortly," Dr. Bogart was saying. "We'll fix that ankle. It's a pretty bad break. About as bad as a break could be and her still keep the foot." He consulted the iPad again. "There's not much we can do for the ribs. Time is the great healer. And she has a mild concussion, but I don't see any long-lasting effects there. She'll have a headache for several days, but the pain in her ankle ought to keep her mind off of the pain in her head."

Harm had to ask, because he didn't know what he'd missed. "But she's going to pull through." He didn't phrase it as a question. "There won't be any permanent disability."

Dr. Bogart who was already on his way out of the room stopped, turned, and said, "She's young, she's strong, although she's exhausted from the ordeal she's been through. You won't see her back to normal this week, or even next week. Maybe not for several weeks. So be patient."

The doctor's retreating back was the signal for conversation to begin anew, and for the next few minutes, Harm and the Hobgoods peppered the two officers with questions, and answered as many of their questions as either Harm or her parents could.

"Has anyone talked with Herb Martin at **The Washington Times**, where Patti worked?" It had just struck Harm that the editor needed to be brought into the loop. But it had to be done so very carefully, because, as Harm considered all they had learned, Patti should have been dead. And he realized as well that Lee Stanton was lying through his teeth. There was no way he could have left two more voicemails in the last hour.

The two officers looked at each other, and each shook his head. "I didn't even know about him," Detective Wilcox said.

"Then with your permission," Harm said, "I'm going to step outside and put in a call to him."

Needing no further consent, Harm retreated outside the hospital, to an area where he felt he could say anything without being overheard. When he was finished a few minutes later, he and Herb had an understanding.

"So you really think all of this is related to the first lady's death and then Hal Warren's?"

"I do, Mr. Martin. Too many of the puzzle pieces fit. Try it any other way, and they don't."

"So you're suggesting that for the moment, anyway, we don't publicize the fact that Patti is badly injured and receiving care in a hospital in Virginia?"

"If the people who took her get even a hint that she's where they might get their hands on her again, her life isn't worth a plug nickel. I know you can smell one hell of a news story here, and I can as well. But for her sake, you've got to keep up the pretense that she's visiting out of state, and will return shortly."

"We can do that," Herb agreed. "Plus, if this is as big as you say it is, I want Hobgood here to write the story."

"That's the way to look at it," Harm said. "And if I'm right, that story will unleash an earthquake on Capitol Hill like nothing any of us have ever seen before. It'll make Watergate look like a minor snafu."

Having secured Herb Martin's cooperation, he returned to Patti's room. Very shortly, nurses came to prep for surgery, and the five of them were escorted to a large if not totally comfortable waiting area on the other end of that floor.

"We're going to go," Deputy Watkins informed them on the way down the hall. "We can't do anything else here until we can question Ms. Hobgood, and the doctor says that won't be before sometime tomorrow, at the earliest."

The doctor had suggested that Harm and Patti's parents return home, until such time as they could see the patient again, but all three had declined. Not only was the only home any of them had well over an hour away in good traffic, none of them wanted to be parted from Patti any more than was necessary.

It was almost four hours and three phone calls from surgery later, before the doctor appeared in the doorway. "Good news," he said, and Harm noted that this time, there was a twinkle in the man's eyes. "She came through with flying colors, but the next three to four days are going to be rough. In addition to the ankle, she's going to be hurting in places she doesn't even know she has."

"My baby," Mrs. Hobgood moaned.

"That's why we're going to keep her pretty heavily sedated, so don't expect her to be sitting up in bed tomorrow carrying on a conversation."

Harm hated to inflict any unnecessary pain on Patti's parents, but he knew things they didn't. "Dr. Bogart, I can't go into great detail, but if Patti can shed any light on what happened to her, the authorities need that help ASAP. This is not just a run-of-the-mill abduction."

"Hmmmm. I hear what you're saying, Mr. Bostwick. But my first allegiance and my first responsibility is to my patient." He appeared to be studying the situation. "I'm not sure she's even going to be responsive enough to answer questions for another three, maybe four days."

"But Dr. Bo..."

Jim Hobgood who had been quiet thus far, stood and began to walk the waiting area. Finally, he said, "You would have to know our daughter, Doctor. She is a very dedicated investigative journalist. I truly believe if she could talk to us right now, she would say that given all the pain she's already endured, she could stand a few more minutes. Especially, if it meant she could help the authorities begin to round up the animals that did this to her."

Most surprising to Harm, it was Mrs. Hobgood who said, "I'll fight to give her the chance to tell what she knows as quickly as she's awake, never mind how much pain she's in."

"Very well," Dr. Bogart said, as he turned to leave the room. "We'll play it your way, but I insist on personally asking her if she prefers something to knock her out, or if she wants to talk with the authorities first."

"Fair enough," Jim Hobgood said. "But if I know my little girl like I think I do, you don't need to be preparing that needle full of sedation just yet."

"Then will you contact the law enforcement and tell them...." He glanced at the clock on the wall. "They should be able to talk with her about eleven o'clock in the morning."

Harm grabbed his phone and placed the call immediately to Detective Wilcox, who agreed to the plan, and agreed to bring the Secret Service into the loop. "And before you question her, so you know what questions to ask, which will make it easier on her, you and I need to put our heads together."

"I'll talk to you in the morning," the officer said.

The parents and Harm spent the next few hours, now that the uncertainty and not-knowing had been lifted off of them, visiting and getting to know each other. But try as they might, Harm refused to speculate on what had happened with Patti. In part, because if he was even half right, the story that would emerge would be overwhelming.

When the nurse summoned them, Mr. and Mrs. Hobgood went into ICU first and visited with their daughter who, they told Harm when they came out, simply lay there, unconscious, and no matter how they spoke to her or rubbed her hands, she didn't respond.

They insisted that he be allowed to see their daughter as well, and as he stood by the bed of his friend and colleague, he took small pleasure that she looked so much more at peace than she had earlier. But he also understood, perhaps more than her parents did, that rough days still lay ahead. Perhaps in more ways than one.

"I promise you, Patti. I refuse to stop until the animals that did this to you are made to answer for their deeds. And I want us to be able to write the story together."

He leaned down and kissed her on her forehead, confident that she would never know. And he would never tell.

At the Hobgoods' suggestion, he drove the three of them back to town. They detoured by the airport and Mr. Hobgood rented a car. He led them to Patti's apartment, and made certain they were settled in before he left. They had stopped in eastern Virginia, out from Falls Church, to grab a bite to eat.

"We're here, and we thank you," Jim Hobgood said, extending his hand to Harm. "I know you didn't sign on for all this when you offered to meet our plane, but I'm mighty glad you did. How can we ever repay you?" He reached for his wallet, and Harm said quickly, "I don't want your money, Mr. Hobgood. Patti is my friend, and a top-notch journalist. I just want to see all of this made right."

He was already out the door, and had heard the lock being thrown behind him, when a troubling thought struck him. He turned around and retraced his steps. As he rapped on the door, he said, "It's Harm. I just remembered something."

Jim Hobgood opened the door. "Well come on back in. What's so important?"

Harm wrestled with what to tell them, and how much to tell them. In the end, he opted for full disclosure, with minimal facts.

"Before you unpack, I'm wondering if we don't need to take you folks to my apartment. I'm concerned for your safety."

"We'll be fine," Jim assured him. "We're not afraid to stay here."

"But I'm afraid for you here. Come on, let's load you back up and we'll go to my apartment. At least for tonight."

"You have two beds in your apartment, young man?" The question was posed by Mary Lou.

"Uh, no ma'am. Not exactly. But I sleep on the couch a lot of nights."

"Well you're not sleeping on the couch tonight, for us."

"Something's got you spooked, son. Why don't you spill it?" Patti had told him once that her dad was very blunt, very matter of fact, and he'd reflected that he understood why his daughter was the way she was.

"Somebody abducted Patti out of this very apartment. Trust me when I say that your daughter's disappearance could be tied to the highest levels of national security. Somebody could be watching this apartment." He thought of Lee Stanton, but didn't say it aloud. "If they want in, they can get in. And you might find yourselves hostages as well, and in a way that could hurt Patti." Another thought struck him. "The official story is that Patti's visiting you in Kansas. So how could you be here in her apartment?"

"I don't know you all that well, Harmon. But what I know, I like. I don't pretend to understand, but if you feel that we could put Patti in further danger, then by all means, we'll not stay here tonight."

Harm reached for their luggage. "Great. Then let's get you out of here."

"But not to your apartment, as much as we appreciate the invitation." Mary Lou took him by the arm, squeezed it, and said, "Take us to a decent hotel. We'll stay there."

Once they had the suitcases loaded, Harm made a couple of calls, then led the couple about six blocks away, and waited while they checked in. Then he escorted them to their room.

Mary Lou said, "I don't know what our daughter did to deserve a friend like you, but I give thanks that she has you in her corner."

"I told you, ma'am. Patti is a fine journalist, a colleague and a friend. I'm the one lucky enough to call her friend."

Back at his apartment, Harm piled down on the couch, very thankful that he wasn't going to be forced to pass the night there. He'd pulled a beer and some potato chips from the kitchen, and as he slowly drained the bottle and watched the bottom of the sack get closer and closer, he reviewed everything he knew. Everything he suspected. And everything that could blow up in all their faces.

Before he turned off the light that night, he made a couple of phone calls, and the answers he received only further convinced him of the truth and the depth of what had happened with his friend.

*You may think you've gotten away with murder, but guess again.* He turned out the light, and too weary to move, passed the night on the couch after all.

\* \* \* \* \*

"Ms. Hobgood. I'm Dr. Bogart."

The doctor stood beside Patti's bed, holding her hand, as he felt for her pulse. "Are you hurting?"

Patti didn't answer, but simply nodded her head.

"On a scale of one to ten, with ten being the worst, how bad is the pain?"

"Twelve," she mumbled, and scrunched up her face, as if to emphasize her answer.

"Then you need to listen to me. Listen very carefully."

Patti opened her eyes wider, then grimaced again. There was no doubt that the painkillers she had after surgery had worn off.

"I'm prepared right now to give you a massive dose of pain medicine that will knock you out of all this pain until sometime tomorrow." He felt of her hand. "In fact, that's what I prefer to do."

"Patti, you..."

The look the doctor shot Harm was pure venom. "Mr. Bostwick, this is my show. Do we understand each other?"

Harm buttoned his lip and nodded.

The doctor bent back to his patient. "Ms. Hobgood, there are law enforcement authorities here who would like to talk to you, to find out what you can tell them." His eyes roved the room, as he seemed to challenge any of them to interrupt. "I'm not in favor of this, but your parents seem to feel that you would endure pain, at least for a short while, rather than ask these investigators to wait."

Harm could see Patti's eyes moving, and could almost see the cogs in her head turning.

"What's your choice, Ms. Hobgood? A shot right now? Or talk now and a shot a little later?"

"Talk," she said, although her voice was raspy and sounded terrible. Talk. Shot."

"All right. They've got no more than thirty minutes, then I'm going to be back in here and I'm going to put the medicine into your IV line myself and these people are going to leave."

The look on his face clearly conveyed the message that he would brook no interference.

The Hobgoods' and Harm had driven in separate vehicles that morning, and when they arrived at the hospital, Detective Wilcox, Deputy Watkins, and a third man, introduced only as a Secret Service agent, were waiting for them. Harm had spoken with Detective Wilcox before he left Washington that morning, and a very succinct list of questions had been developed. The officer wasted no time beginning the interrogation. He had with him a voice recorder, and he turned it on, then began.

"Can you tell us who abducted you from your apartment?"

It was clear that speaking was difficult, but finally Patti managed to form the words, "Lee Stanton."

"Lee Stanton?" Mary Lou exclaimed. "Your fiancé kidnapped you?"

Officer Wilcox flashed her a cautionary glance, and the older woman said no more.

"Lee Stanton is your fiancé. Right?"

"Was," Patti mumbled. "Gave ring back."

"And this is who kidnapped you?"

"Yessh," Patti answered. Harm noted she was having trouble forming her words, and he ached to help her answer.

"Was Lee the only one?"

"Others," Patti mumbled. "Strangers."

"Where did he take you?"

"Cabin," she said, finally. "Woods. Don't know where."

"Did they beat you? Did they feed you?"

"Mc... McDonald. Didn't beat."

"Then why are you so badly injured? How did you get hurt?"

"Tricked. Got away. Ran and ran."

"Just one more question, Ms. Hobgood. For now, anyway. And then you can get the sleep and rest your body needs and desperately deserves."

Patti was very restless in the bed, and it was obvious to all that it was taking everything she could do to cooperate. Before the officer could ask his last question, she said in a high and querulous voice, "Harm? Harm?"

"I'm here, Patti." He stepped to the bed and took the hand

272

that didn't have an IV line attached.

"Harm. Story. Write it."

"I will," he promised her. "But you need to finish answering the officer's questions, so you can get some relief. "I'll take care of everything."

"Ms. Hobgood," Officer Wilcox asked, "Do you know why you were kidnapped? Did you learn anything from your captors that would help us?"

During the days she was held captive, as Lee had shown up to bring food at least one of the two runs every day, she had peppered him with questions. Knowing that in his mind, at least, that Patti would never leave that cabin alive, Lee had gotten cocky. He'd talked, and she'd learned as much from all that he said, as she had from the unsaid.

All the time she was on the run through the dark woods, Lee's words had run in an audio loop in her head. One of the things that had kept her pushing was her refusal to allow what she knew to die with her. Between what he had said, as well as the unsaid, Patti had managed to put together a most horrifying scenario that could not go unpunished.

She motioned the officer closer to her mouth, and when, finally, she spoke, it was with great difficulty. "Reynolds. Rawlings. First lady blackmailing. Lee with them." Then, she collapsed, and the machine behind her began to beep.

Even Harm, who'd already figured out the basics and educated Detective Wilcox, felt totally bowled over when he heard her words.

The door swung open, and Dr. Bogart dashed in. Meanwhile, Mary Lou Hobgood was shaking her daughter, screaming, "No. Nooo. You can't die. You can't."

Dr. Bogart literally pushed the woman out of the way, and bent over the patient. When he straightened, his face was one of pure fury. "I was against this, and here's why." He gestured at the bed.

"Is she dead?" Jim Hobgood asked, as Harm found himself unable to even entertain the possibility.

"She's not dead. No thanks to any of you. But she is absolutely exhausted." As he spoke, he placed a filled syringe into the port on the IV line, and pushed the plunger. "Now all of you get out of here, and do not come back until I call you. Do I make myself clear?"

To their credit, no one, not even Patti's parents, spoke one word. They simply left the room, and adjourned to the waiting area at the end of the hall.

It was Jim Hobgood who broke the silence and asked the question that had to be asked. "Did I understand her to say that our own vice president and a Senator Rawlings are somehow a part of all of this?" His face mirrored his amazement. "Is that even possible?"

It was then that the Secret Service man who had been silent up to that point answered. "It is possible," he said, and there was no missing the seriousness of his reply. "It would have been better if none of you in this room had heard that information. But now that you know, I must insist that what you know does not leave here." He swung around to look at each of them, before he said, "I cannot stress how much keeping this under wraps until the proper investigation can be mounted, is absolutely essential. This must not get out until the administration is ready to release the information."

He looked straight at Harm, as if to further emphasize his words.

"Trust me," Harm said, "I know how explosive this is. Patti and I want that byline, but we don't intend to jeopardize our government to get it."

"What happens next?" Jim Hobgood asked. "Somebody has to do something."

"We're on our way now to begin the process of picking Lee Stanton up as a "person of interest" in the abduction of Ms. Hobgood," Detective Wilcox said.

Over the next few minutes, the group slowly dispersed. All three law enforcement officers left, and after Patti's parents got consent to see their daughter for just a minute, they joined Harm and left the hospital.

"She was sleeping so peacefully," Mary Lou shared with Harm. "I hated to leave her, but she needs deep sleep and rest right now. Later, she'll need Mama's love and nursing, and that's when I'll be here."

Harm didn't doubt that she would.

They parted ways in the parking lot, but before he climbed behind the wheel of the rental car, Jim Hobgood told Harm, "Given what we know now, and needing to keep everyone in the dark about what happened to Patti and where she is, we're going to go back to the motel tonight."

"I think that's best, Mr. Hobgood. Never mind Patti at this point, you could put yourself and Mrs. Hobgood in danger if you go back to the apartment."

"Please, son. We're just Jim and Mary Lou. It would please us if you would think of us that way." Harm thought he saw a tear at the corner of the man's eye. "If you hadn't sounded the alarm when you did, she might still be lying out there on the side of the road. More than likely dead."

Harm found himself overcome, but finally managed to say, "I'm just glad she was found and that she's safe. Mr.... 'er, Jim."

\* \* \* \* \*

Lee Stanton's hands shook so badly, it was all he could do to grab underwear and socks from his dresser and shove them into the open suitcase on his bed. It was barely daylight, but since he hadn't slept at all, it was no big deal to go ahead and roll out. In fact, the sooner he got a few things together, and was gone, the safer he would feel.

According to the clock across from his bed, it had been at three-thirty-seven, during the darkest part of the night, that he'd realized that if he had any chance to continuing to breathe, he had to get as far away from Washington as possible. The question was, where could he drop off the face of the earth? How could he manage to go off the grid?

*I know too much, and those who have entangled me in this mess are going to throw me under the bus. There's a target on my back, and I can literally feel it.*

By the time he finished packing everything he could cram into one piece of luggage, and looked around one last time, he had a plan in place. How good that plan was, only time would tell. On the table beside his bed, was the picture of Patti showing off her engagement ring. He couldn't bear to leave it behind, but to take it with him would be a constant reminder of how she had brought him to this point. He wasn't sure where she was, because for certain she wasn't in Kansas. And she hadn't returned to the cabin. He couldn't be lucky enough that she was dead. If she was alive and able to talk, hopefully she couldn't finger him until he had time to get past the D.C. borders.

He'd already determined to leave his car in its accustomed space. And he needed money. Outside his door, he grabbed a local transit bus and got off at the nearest branch of his bank. So nervous he could barely complete the withdrawal slip, he got all of the money in his account, except for one hundred dollars. He couldn't afford to use a debit card for funds. Better he carried everything he had on his hip.

He hopped back on a transit bus and a little later, he transferred to one of the trains that traveled between official Washington and the adjacent counties. He rode the train to the end of the line in Manassas, Virginia, where he got a cab to the local Greyhound bus station. It wasn't until he was a good hundred miles outside of Washington that he allowed himself to relax.

At lunch time, he departed the bus at the Richmond depot, and caught another cab to the airport. After standing in line for longer than was comfortable, looking over his shoulder every few seconds, he managed to rent a small compact car. He'd rented the car for ten days, and listed Los Angeles, California as his destination. That should throw anybody searching for him off his trail long enough for him to reach a place of safety.

Thanks to his devoted grandmother's obsession with making sure he was never without money, he used a special credit card she'd provided when he first came to Washington. It had been for emergencies, only, his granny had insisted. So whenever he was in the mood for a more expensive meal than he could afford, the card was used to address the emergency of being hungry. He and Patti had dined on that card more than once. After all, it needed to be used, lest the credit card company close the account, he said to himself, and felt totally justified. Granny might have more money than God, but she didn't understand how the world worked today.

It was also how he'd bought Patti a much more impressive engagement ring than his salary would have normally allowed. He even chuckled to himself at the time that granny never bothered to peruse the bill. She just paid it..

But this time, it truly was an emergency. It was, he knew, a matter of life or death. And the only way he was going to avoid being killed was to establish an entirely new life. Senator Rawlings had made that abundantly clear during their last conversation, when Lee had to confess that Patti had escaped, and that there was no way of knowing where she was. And when the senator, on a bigger tirade than Lee had ever witnessed, had informed him if he had any questions for Mollie Montgomery, he would soon be able to ask her in person, Lee had gotten the message. Loudly, and way too clearly. Lee Stanton was as good as on his way to the mortuary.

*All those people he fired down through the years warned me that he would kick me to the curb when he was finished with me. I'm not only kicked to the curb, I'm lying in the gutter being pissed on.*

Lee knew better than to expect anyone in Washington to help him. He was on his own.

The next stop after the rental car agency was to a discount store where he purchased a pre-paid phone. He didn't expect to be making many calls, and where he was headed, the cell signal was guaranteed to be unreliable. When that phone's minutes were used up, he'd figure out what to do next.

The last of his errands behind him, he pointed the little car west, stopping only when he crossed the Mississippi River to toss his long-time phone into the muddy waters that silently promised to forever protect his secrets. He stopped every so often to nap, and when hunger struck, he found a fast food drive-through.

Three long, hard days later, he arrived at his destination. Blonders Pass, Wyoming wasn't more than a wide place in the road in the rugged northern end of the state. During his tortured last night in Washington, a time that now seemed eons ago, he'd remembered a small, rustic cabin that a fraternity brother owned in the wilds of Wyoming. He'd visited there with his friend once, and even knew where the key was hidden. His friend had joked that anytime Lee was in the area, he should stop and make himself at home.

Lee had gambled that the cabin was unoccupied, and that gamble had paid off. At least temporarily. The musty smell inside the small, one-room structure had assured him that no one had been there recently. Lee felt he could safely stay there indefinitely, but for sure at least for a few days. Just until he could make other plans. Until he could scout the lay of the land.

The cabin was rudimentary at best, no electricity, no running water if you didn't count the manual pump just outside the back door, and an outhouse a few feet away, supplemented by a five-gallon bucket near the bed.

He would have no TV or even newspaper, no contact with the outside world. He would also have had no groceries, had he not stopped at a general store in a settlement about thirty miles away to stock up on pre-packaged food and snacks. It would be a life far removed from the catered meals and cocktail parties he had enjoyed in Washington but, as he reassured himself, at least it would be a life.

The term on his rental car would soon be up. He would have to drive it to a branch of the rental agency at the airport about a hundred miles away and beg change in plans in order to turn it in there. Then he'd have to find a beater car he could buy for cash, the more beat up the better. Then, and only then, could he begin to feel comfortable that Stanton Lee, as he's re-branded himself, was safe.

Those not in the know might have considered all his clandestine actions overkill. But they didn't know what he knew, and now that it had all gone south, he wished he were as ignorant as the outsiders.

*If only I hadn't taken the bait when Rawlings asked me to "divert" Patti's attention from investigating the first lady's death. If only he hadn't involved me with all those other men who were committing unspeakable things. If only… if only…*

\* \* \* \* \*

For almost two weeks, nothing happened. It was, for Harm, and for Patti's parents, a seemingly endless time of agony and discomfort. The Hobgoods continued to stay at a motel, although earlier they'd moved to one within just a few blocks of the hospital. And even though she was slowly recovering, Patti was still a badly-injured young woman, and she was still semi-sedated, to the point that visiting with her was almost like visiting with a zombie. Finally, more than a week after her rescue, when Harm and her parents visited her in the private room where she'd been moved the day before, they encountered not the shell of their former friend and daughter, but a clearly conscious and talking Patti. It was like she'd turned a corner.

"Oh, baby," Jim Hobgood said through tears that were running off his cheeks. "It's so good to have you back." He hugged her as if he thought she might disappear if he released her.

Mary Lou Hobgood was equally demonstrative, giving her daughter a kiss, and standing back to take an objective observation.

When her parents had pulled back from the bed, Patti said, "Well, Harm. It's good to see you."

"Not half as good as it is to see you more like your old self than we've seen lately."

They visited for a short while, then Patti said, "Mom, Dad. I need a favor. Harm and I need to talk, and since I can't get out of this bed, yet..."

"You need us to make ourselves scarce," her father said, laughing.

"Of course you and your young man want some time alone,"

Mary Lou said, as she began moving toward the door. "Come on, Jim. Let's give these two some privacy."

Her mother's words, "you and your young man" caused the color to rise in her pale cheeks, and Patti was momentarily at a loss for words.

"No, no," she protested. "This is strictly business. Harm and I are friends and professional colleagues. Nothing more."

"Whatever you say," her father said, as he pulled the door closed behind him.

Patti colored again, but tried to not let it distract her. "I'm sorry," she muttered, not daring to look at Harm. "My mother is a hopeless romantic."

"Your mother is terribly sweet, and you're fortunate to have her. No apologies needed."

"Looks like to me that the three of you have become pretty tight."

"Your folks are good people," he told her. "And we've become tight, because someone we all care about has been in a dangerous, bad place."

Patti looked about the room, glanced down at her legs under the cover, and the huge lump that was her ankle, and said, "Hey, compared to where I was, this place is a paradise."

"So are you comfortable telling me everything you know? If it's too painful to revisit, then we can wait."

"Absolutely not," she said. "It's not too painful. I need to get it

282

out, but Mom and Dad don't ever need to know all the little details. Mom would drag me back to Kansas and chain me to the side of the house." Realization of what she'd just said, and memories of the time she spent chained to the wall in the cabin caused her words to lodge in her throat.

"What is it? What's wrong?" Harm was moving closer to the bed, the better to catch her if there was a problem.

"That comment about being chained to the house brought back some unpleasant memories," she said. "But just for the moment. No biggie." But the haunted expression in her eyes told a different story.

"They chained you up. Your captors."

"They did." Then she grinned, "But I got loose."

"Yes, you did, although I don't know how you did it."

"Then, let me tell you."

"For the next twenty minutes or so, Patti shared everything that happened, and she held nothing back. She began with opening her door expecting to see the cab driver and finding Lee Stanton instead. And while doing so, she discovered that talking about the entire ordeal was not only therapeutic, but she was already beginning to format the leads for the stories she would soon write.

"I remember stumbling out of the woods, onto that road. I've never been so glad to see pavement in my life. That's all I remember, until I woke up here hurting worse than I have ever hurt in my life, and with people working over me."

"I am totally in awe of your strength and your cunning, and

I never will be able to picture you disabling that young man so you could get away. Where did you learn how to do that?"

"I'm not really sure, but I think it was something of a cross between my Girl Scout training and a deep and abiding sense of desperation."

"Whatever it was, I'm just so thankful you could get away." He tenderly touched her injured ankle. "I'm just sorry you've had to endure so much pain."

"But the pain is good, you see. Because when I was here in the hospital, hurting so badly, I knew I was still alive, that I hadn't died."

"No, you didn't die."

"You wanna know what hurts worse than all my injuries?"

"Lee Stanton's betrayal." His answer came swift and true, without even a hint of a question mark.

Surprise registered on Patti's face, and she asked, "How did you know?"

"Because I know you. And I pegged Stanton for a first-class slime ball the first time I met him."

"Wish somebody had pointed it out to me."

"You wouldn't have believed us," Harm said, and pulled a straight chair closer to the bed, and sat down. "But speaking of Stanton, you wanna know the latest?"

"I do," Patti said, "so tell me he's been arrested, because I will never feel totally safe until he and all of those working with him are arrested."

"I wish I could tell you that, but just the opposite is true. In fact, no one knows where he is."

"He couldn't have just dropped off the face of the earth."

"But it appears that he has. His car is here, but his bank account has been drained. Apparently, he's on the run. And he's not using his phone or any of his credit cards that would allow the officials to track him."

"But where could he have gone? His parents are dead, at least that's what he told me. And he is an only child."

"Friends?"

"None that I know about." An idea pierced her consciousness. "Come to think of it, he does have a grandmother somewhere. I never even talked to her."

"Lives in New Orleans. The authorities have found her. She lives in a hoity-toity senior apartment complex and has more money than the U.S. Mint. But she says she hasn't seen him, hasn't even heard from him in several weeks. But that's a lie, because we've found the paper trail where she sent him bail money."

"Yeah, he said once she rambled and it was boring to talk to her."

"She also told them that Weejee... that's what she called him... couldn't have done anything wrong, because he was Grammy's good little boy."

"Obviously, she's willing to lie for him."

"Well, Weejee is guilty of a long list of offenses, starting with pretending he was somebody he wasn't, kidnapping, and who knows what else. Believe me," Harm said, "you should see the list of charges they've built against him, and I'm sure there will be more, once they locate him."

"Do you think they will find him? 'Cause it sure sounds like he doesn't intend to be found."

"The authorities are circulating his photo via internal means. So far, the public knows nothing, because they fear how the folks at the top might react if they knew. But every law enforcement agency in the country has his picture and instructions not to approach, but to contact the FBI if they spot him."

"I would just never have dreamed…"

"Face it, Patti. Lee Stanton is a con artist."

"Then let's hope they can soon find him, because he's the key to unraveling this whole mess." Tears welled up in her eyes. "Beginning with Mollie Montgomery, and ending right here."

They spent the rest of their time before Patti's parents returned planning for the stories they would author, just as soon as they received the go-ahead.

* * * * *

"It's boring as hell," Lee Stanton, known to the few people he'd interacted with so far as Stanton Lee, told himself, as he stood on the small porch of the mountain cabin that had become his safe house. "But it beats being on the run."

He'd successfully turned in the rental car, and by doing a little homework ahead of time, he'd found a badly used car that he'd been able to buy for only a few hundred dollars cash. He'd rented a post office box about fifty miles away, and had directed that the vehicle title be mailed to that address. Then he'd stolen a tag off of a conveniently-wrecked vehicle, and he was set. Since he didn't plan to drive down to the settlement but about once a month, there shouldn't be much chance of anyone discovering all his deceptions.

Fortunately, the general store stocked enough food to make it possible to buy what he needed. He wasn't the only man in that part of the country living the life of a hermit, off the grid, so he didn't necessarily stand out. And he'd stocked up on magazines and paperback books, but he steered clear of all newspapers, choosing to remain ignorant to what was happening back in Washington.

The only thing that worried him was that his college friend might somehow turn up, unexpectedly. Such an encounter might get very awkward. Still, he'd looked around for another place, a deserted cabin or mining shack that he might commandeer, but so far had found nothing.

*I'm just going to have to gamble and take my chances on this. After all, everything else has worked out in my favor. Why should this be any different? Lee Stanton is dead, and Stanton Lee has taken his place.*

Everything was going to work out, he told himself. If the authorities were on to him, if they were going to find him, it would already have happened.

He watched the sun set over the snow capped mountains to the west of his cleared spot of land, then went into the cabin for the night. He didn't even lock the door. Why bother? He lit a lantern and piled up on the bed to read an article in one of the magazines he'd bought about decorating mountain homes.

*Maybe I can get some ideas to spruce this place up a little. After all, looks like this is going to be my forever home.*

# CHAPTER FOURTEEN

Patti leaned with her back against the arm of her couch, her injured leg extended before her. And around her, in addition to copies of **The Washington Times**, were issues of other newspapers and magazines as well.

"I knew this would be explosive," she told Harm, who sat on the ottoman across from her, but I don't think I ever thought we'd see all the peripheral damage that we have."

"Well, how often do you remember the sitting vice president and the leading member of Congress being hauled off to jail in both handcuffs and leg-irons, charged with six dozen counts of murder, just for starters?"

"You've got a point. Still…"

She picked up an issue of **The Times**, and studied the front page that was dominated by a photo of two of Washington's once most powerful men being booked into jail. Nearby, but smaller, was a photo of Lee Stanton in his jail orange. But instead of the arrogant body language he'd displayed of late, Patti saw an attitude of total defeat and uncertainty. In his eyes, she saw no hint of the person within.

"I still can't believe how easily they captured him," Harm said. "After all of his elaborate actions to bury Lee Stanton and resurrect him as a totally different person, it's almost as if he drew them a map and sent them an engraved invitation."

It had been a joyous day when they got word that Lee was under arrest. What's more, he was spilling his gut so fast, those asking questions had to ask him to slow down. Once he'd dished on everything he knew, federal authorities wasted very little time beginning the biggest criminal round-up in the country's history. And they had started, simultaneously, with the arrests of the vice president and the dean of the senate right on the floor of the senate, while that august body was in session.

Patti felt her left ring finger where, until recently, a very pricy engagement ring had proudly ridden proclaiming her engagement. That joint still felt naked. Not that she wanted either it nor Lee back. Any feelings she might have had for Lee Stanton had been totally dashed when she read how he'd explained her abduction to investigators.

He had confirmed her worse fears, when he explained that had she not managed to escape, Patti Hobgood would definitely be dead. Senator Rawlings, it seemed, had promised him a position in the vice president's office, once Rawlings obtained the title, if Patti didn't queer Rawlings' chances of becoming vice president. Rawlings, Lee said, had explained that dead people didn't talk. He had, Lee had explained, people who could easily make death happen.

*"It was either her or me, and I chose me,"* Lee had stated very matter of factly.

Patti had shuddered just thinking how close she'd come to dying twice. *Yeah, Lee, you chose yourself, just like you always did. How could I have been so stupid and blind?*

"Read that part again about how the federal agents found Lee. I still can't believe how that one went down."

Patti found that place in the article, and began to read.

*"Stanton, who had simply reversed his first and last names, was apprehended without issue at about three o'clock in the morning. SWAT agents were surprised to find his door unlocked, and the man they sought sound asleep in the bed a few feet inside the door.*

*"'We woke him up out of a sound sleep,' an unidentified agent reported. 'He was so zonked out, it took a couple of minutes for him to understand that we were there to arrest him.'*

*"When asked how Stanton reacted once he was awake enough to understand that the jig was up, the agent said, 'He just sort of wilted, and then it was almost like he was relieved that it was all over.'"*

"Man," Harm said. "Imagine waking up to a nightmare of that magnitude." His face took on momentary hardness. "But he deserved to be caught."

"Yeah, but he was careless." She continued reading.

*"Stanton's mistake that tipped authorities to his whereabouts was made a few days earlier at the general store in the settlement closest to the cabin where he was basically living as a squatter. When the clerk gave him the change from his purchase, she accidentally shorted him ten dollars. He realized her error, and got hostile even though she apologized and quickly made things right.*

*"That might have been the end of it, were it not for the fact*

that the clerk also worked part-time in dispatch for the local sheriff's office. Stanton made such an impression on her, that when she saw his picture the next day, she knew exactly who her difficult customer was, and where he was living. 'If he hadn't picked that fight with me,' the clerk told authorities,'"I doubt I would ever have connected him with that photo in the sheriff's office. But while he was shouting at me, I got a really good look at his face.'

"While people living off the grid aren't uncommon in that area of the state, new people moving in is uncommon, so it hadn't taken long for Stanton's sparsely-spread neighbors to know where he lived.

"Federal authorities were notified, surveillance was set up, and once they had visual confirmation that he was their man, officers moved in during the middle of the night when opportunities for injury or his possible escape were minimal.

"Stanton was taken by armored convoy to Jackson Hole, Wyoming, where private federal aircraft was waiting to fly him back to Washington. A laundry list of charges await him, but sources in the know, who asked to remain anonymous, believe that while Stanton did not have any hand in the murders of first lady Mollie Montgomery and Hal Warren, he does have knowledge of those who are responsible, and that he is cooperating fully with the authorities.

"Rumor has it that the information he has will reach into the highest echelons of U.S. government."

"I'm getting my information third-hand," Harm said, "but from what I hear, the web of lies and deceit all of this has exposed goes all the way to Eastern Europe and back. This is much more of a story than either you or I ever envisioned."

"Yeah," Patti groused, and Harm could hear the anger in her voice. "And here I am, sidelined, and can't get out there and do my job."

"It doesn't matter. Herb is still giving you totally free rein to bring the story to the public from right here in your own little apartment." He grinned. "Now tell me honestly, you are glad to be home, aren't you?"

"Oh, yes, no doubt about that. But I don't like not being able to put any weight on my foot for another four or five weeks. I wanna get out and do."

"All things in good time," Harm cautioned her. "And think about poor Lee. Even though he had no direct connection with Mollie and Hal, he's still going to serve a good many years for everything else that he did. At least in a few more weeks you'll be free as a bird."

"Can you believe how deep and how involved this whole mess became? I could never have imagined the size of this web of deceit and murder." She grabbed another newspaper, flipped it, and then found what she wanted. "This article tells it even better than our article does." Herb and Harm's employer had agreed that the two of them would co-author several of the stories to run first in **The Times**, and then be rewritten, slightly, for publication in Harm's magazine.

"That's only because it came out a day later than our article, and they had a little more information. But for writing style and quality, your article wins hands down."

"OUR article," she said, stressing the double authorship.

"But listen to this…"

*"Vice President William J. Reynolds and Texas (R) Senator Albert L. Rawlings were both taken into custody yesterday on a long list of charges, the biggest of which include the assassination of first lady Mollie Montgomery along with deaths of seventy other people on board the ill-fated presidential aircraft and Hal Wallace, CEO of The Cumberland Group. They have also been implicated in the kidnapping and torture of Patti Hobgood, a writer for **The Washington Times** newspaper, and the paper's Chief White House Reporter. It is estimated at this point that as many as eight or ten other individuals will also be indicted in this case, including foreign nationals from former Russian republics.*

*"Sources close to the investigation, which has shaken official Washington to its very knees, say the first lady had discovered several years ago that both Reynolds, while he was still a U.S. Senator, and Rawlings had conspired to sell to certain European countries massive quantities of black market arms which, through a complicated and multi-level scheme, they had stolen from the military. These countries were in dire need of arms, and had previously been refused aid by the U.S. If they were to break free from Russian rule and oppression, and gain their independence, they had to have arms to do so. This act alone, if substantiated, could carry a charge of treason with it, and is punishable by death.*

*"Mollie Montgomery, so reports go, had been quietly blackmailing both men for a number of years, and is estimated to have removed at least three million dollars from them to date, not counting votes in her husband's favor that she also extracted. There's also evidence that the men had wearied of her constant demands for money, and had determined to put a stop to the blackmail, one*

*way or another. It's believed that it took almost two years to put their scheme into place, whereby the first lady would be killed.*

*"Warren, who headed the first lady's Cumberland Group, was reportedly recruited by Reynolds and Rawlings to bring the first lady back in line, on the grounds that national security was under serious threat. When he was unable to accomplish that task, which ultimately led to the first lady's death, Warren found himself in a position from which there was no win and no out. In the end, he also was killed for his trouble.*

*"Authorities say it will take several months of investigation to discover everyone involved and to bring them under arrest. Then it will be up to the justice department to bring about convictions and ultimately a penalty for those convictions. Both Reynolds and Rawlings have been denied bail, and will remain jailed in a secure, unknown location until such time as they can be tried for their actions.*

*"The actual deed itself was achieved by recruiting a top-notch arms and ballistics expert from Bosnia. Thanks to the hands-on intervention of Vice President Reynolds, this hired gun managed to obtain contract work as a civilian company doing work for the U.S. government at various military posts around the country. When it was learned that the first lady's aircraft would overnight at Vandenberg Air Force Base while she was in California, the die was cast. In ways that are still being revealed, this man was able to gain access to the plane to plant the series of state-of-the-art explosive devices that snuffed out the lives of seventy-one people.*

*"President James Montgomery, who was already missing from many of his presidential duties as he worked through his*

*grief over the loss of his wife, is reportedly devastated by this latest development. He has given his staff instructions that he doesn't want to talk about these results with anyone. In accordance with the provisions of the Twenty-fifth Amendment, Speaker of the House, Clarence Cartwright, is acting president. In the meantime, Congress has called an emergency recess, as members struggle to find their footing and chart a path forward.*

*"'I've been in Washington for more than thirty years,' Speaker Cartwright said. 'Never have I seen this body, this government in such a precarious state. God help us.'"*

"I'm in agreement with the Speaker," Harm said. "If ever there was a time when we need a strong person in the presidency, that time is now." He shook his head as if he didn't know what to make of the situation. "But it doesn't look like the President we have is that man."

With Lee Stanton and Reynolds and Rawlings all in jail, all of the major players, except for the hired weapons specialist, who had mysteriously disappeared, were behind bars. Agents throughout Europe were searching for him.

"I can't believe security and background check agencies were so lax that this man was able to simply walk onto the base and deal democracy such a blow," Patti said.

"Look at it this way. When the Vice President himself, especially when he has such a domineering, dictatorial personality, makes a phone call, the person on the other end is really in a bind. It's easier to just say 'yes,' and ninety-nine percent of the time, there's no problem."

"But this time, there was."

"Yep. This time there was a problem, and what a problem it's turned out to be."

Later that day, the problem grew in gigantic proportions. During one of the afternoon audience talk shows, the network interrupted with a breaking news bulletin. Vice President Reynolds, who was being held in a special area of the jail, away from the general inmate population, had committed suicide by grabbing a guard's gun and shooting himself in the head. "The Vice President was pronounced dead on site at five-eleven this afternoon. Death was instantaneous," the anchor announced.

Patti's parents had returned to her apartment to prepare the evening meal, before heading back to their motel. They were planning to return to Kansas by the end of the week, feeling that any danger to their daughter was now past. They insisted they needed to get back to their normal routines.

"You know," Jim Hobgood said, "this is as freaky as back in 1963, when Lee Harvey Oswald supposedly killed President Kennedy, and then Oswald was killed a couple of days later by Jack Ruby." He rubbed his chin, then said, "And to this day, some people still don't believe the whole truth has ever been disclosed. I hope this doesn't become another Oswald-Ruby debacle."

Over the next few days, the media was filled with stories about the vice president, dating back to when he first ran for a school board seat in Texas. There were photos of his grief-stricken wife, and while Patti felt some degree of sympathy for her, she found it most distasteful that Mrs. Reynolds persisted in sanctifying the man who had beaten her black and blue too many times to count.

299

Because the vice president had been charged with treason and multiple other felonies, there was no move to allow his body to lie in state in the Capitol rotunda. There would only be a very private, close family service at a small church back in Texas. Washington was washing its hands of the disgraced VP as quickly as it could.

Over the next couple of weeks, as news circulated and re-circulated and rumor ran rampant, Patti chafed at the restrictions her slowly healing ankle was imposing. She struggled to do her work solely by phone, but there were days that it was an overwhelming task. Information forthcoming from the White House Press Office was spasmodic and disjointed. A news release at ten a.m. would later be contradicted by a revised release at one p.m. And the entire time, President Montgomery was nowhere to be seen. If the grapevine could be believed, he not only had holed up in his bedroom, but he wasn't concerned with grooming. Reports were that he hadn't shaved since the day of Mollie's funeral.

When Harm told her about the rumor that James Montgomery now had a beard, he added with a chuckle, "For all we know, he could be out walking among us and we just don't recognize him."

But all of it was very frustrating for her, compounded by her inability to walk into the Press Room and speak face to face with her sources. Being unable to network was really putting a crimp on her productivity. And just to be blunt, as she confided in Harm, she missed being with people and was about to go nuts confined to her house.

*I will never, ever again take walking on two healthy feet for granted.*

When the dam broke, it did so in several ways.

When she saw the doctor at the five week mark, her cast was exchanged for a walking boot. With it and a set of crutches, she was finally able to become somewhat mobile again. It was awkward, it took longer to cover the distance, but she vowed not to complain. For the first time in almost two months, she was back at her desk at the newspaper. It was like a homecoming celebration.

That afternoon, too late to make the deadline for that day, suddenly, and with no advance notice, President James Montgomery surfaced in a big way. In a most unusual way.

The President's penchant for a Big Mac® burger was common knowledge. Equally well known had been his wife's disdain for that same burger, and as a result, his enjoyment of that brand of cuisine was spasmodic at best.

But that afternoon about three-thirty, James Montgomery was seated at a table in a downtown set of golden arches ringed by Secret Service agents, as he chowed down on his favorite comfort food. While his face was gaunt and lean, and his eyes were sunk back in his face, if indeed he had gone weeks without shaving, his bare cheeks made lie of that rumor. As Patti watched the drama unfolding on TV from the comfort of her living room couch, she did believe that there was more silver in his hair, which was also neatly groomed.

*I'm surprised he's not totally white headed!*

Word had spread faster than a California wildfire, and by the time the President finished his burger, news media had begun gathering and jockeying for a position. TV stations began breaking into their regular programming to document the President's return to civilization.

But what came next made his sudden re-appearance take a back seat. As he made his way across the parking lot to the unmarked black GMC that had brought him the seven blocks from the White House, a man that Patti didn't immediately recognize was escorted to the President's side. She wracked her brain trying to place the man, and was coming up blank.

Her phone rang. Harm's face popped up. She answered and confirmed that she was watching the President's outing. "What's happening, Harm? Has the President finally gone over the edge?"

"I don't know," he answered. "I guess we have to wait for him to tell us." He confessed that he had no clue who the mystery man was.

The presidential motorcade left headed back to the White House, and the press hustled to follow. Patti knew she couldn't cover this event from her couch. She called for a cab, and was waiting on the curb, balancing on her crutches, when the car pulled up beside her. Once underway to the White House, she called Cindy Lewis and managed to actually speak with her.

"The President's going to make comments in about thirty minutes. On the South Lawn."

"I'm on my way."

Patti concentrated on deciding how she could get from the security gate to the South Lawn. It wouldn't be easy, but somehow, she would be front and center. It was time to get back to work.

When she presented herself and showed her credentials, one of the longtime guards who recognized her, offered to give her a ride on a small, four-wheeled vehicle. She accepted, and was soon gathered with the rest of the media. The President, and his mystery visitor approached the podium and microphone that had been hastily erected for his use.

"Good afternoon," he said into the microphone. There was a smile on his face, but Patti could still see the depth of the sadness in the man's eyes. First of all, let me tell you how much I enjoyed my outing and my mid-afternoon snack a few minutes ago. In fact, I can think of no better way to re-enter life again than by eating a food that I truly enjoy. Thanks to the news I received this morning, I realized that I was craving a Big Mac®. I knew then that it was time to get on with living."

He paused, pulled a handkerchief from his pocket and wiped his eyes. "It's been a hell of a few weeks since I lost the love of my life. I will never forget the woman who made me what I am, but grieving for her will not bring her back. I'm not the first man to lose his wife, and I won't be the last. But I am the first president in a long time to have his wife so cruelly taken from him."

Again, he struggled. "However, it's time that I rejoined the world. Our country has suffered a massive blow, and I need to do the job that I was elected to do. So this afternoon, I have two major announcements. First of all, thanks to investigators working around the clock in this country and overseas, we have apprehended Sergio Zhynzi who actually built and planted the bombs that robbed Mollie of her life. He was taken alive, and will receive the justice that he and all of those associated with him deserve. In addition, he has identified more than two dozen other people who had some sort of hand in this travesty, some of them high placed in government here and around the globe." He went on to share that Mr. Zhynzi was

303

already enroute to Washington to face charges, and indicated that in the days to come, others on the list would be taken into custody."

He wiped his eyes again, and the next words he spoke were low and husky. "I pledged to you standing in this very spot on the afternoon that changed this country forever, that I would not rest until the people who perpetrated this massacre were brought to justice. I'm proud to say that I have now achieved that goal. I can get back to running the country."

In a rare show of support, the media gathered before him applauded.

"Thank you," he said, and Patti heard the sincerity in his voice. "Now, for my second announcement." He indicated the man next to him, and motioned for him to step forward. "This country's founding documents call for a president and a vice president. It's a good plan, and we've seen in the last few weeks how vital the office of the vice president is." He went quiet for a moment, licked his lips, and continued. "For the past few weeks, your President has been MIA – missing in action. You simply haven't had a president. And for reasons I couldn't identify at the time, I was unable to bring myself to formally ask the sitting vice president to step into my shoes. As it turns out, thank goodness I listened to my gut."

Several hands went up in the air. "Just a minute," the President said. "Just let me finish, and I'll be glad to answer all your questions."

The crowd got quiet, a first for that group, Patti knew. "In a first step back to normalcy, we need a new vice president. A partner for me, a team player who can actively participate in the running of our government. Someone the President can rely on, and the

Constitution gives me the authority to appoint a placeholder, when the office of the vice presidency becomes vacant. It is now vacant, and in accordance with law, I'm about to fill that vacancy."

He brought the man that Patti estimated to be in his early forties to the podium. "I'd like to have you meet Brian Robertson, currently the governor of Mississippi, who has pledged to me that not only does he want to help me stabilize and rebuild this country, but he's anxious to join me on the campaign trail, as we secure another four years to bring this country up to its potential."

The media corps went wild, jostling to get their chance to ask questions.

"One more thing," the President said, shouting over the press. "Governor Robertson will, of course, have to be confirmed by the Senate, but I am asking all one hundred three members, it used to be one hundred four members, to put partisan issues aside and give me the governing partner I need. Let's give this country the vice president and normalcy it deserves."

Then he stood aside, and allowed the press to question the newly nominated VP candidate to its heart content.

* * * * *

Four weeks later, Patti's walking boot and crutches had been exchanged for a cane and physical therapy. Brian Robertson's nomination had been taken up by a newly-convened Senate body that gave him only token resistance. Sergio Zhynzi had arrived in the U.S. and was incarcerated in a maximum security facility, where he was visually overseen by multiple armed guards every minute of every day. There was never a second that he was alone. His court date was rapidly approaching, along with the trials of numerous other participants in what the media had begun to call the crime of the century. And gossip out of The Cumberland Group painted a picture of absolute chaos within the organization. The ship was totally lacking in purpose and direction.

Lee Stanton had twice attempted suicide, and had twice been rescued from his need for self-destruction. Legal pundits predicted that he would receive a life sentence without the possibility of parole, and when he learned this disturbing fact, he suffered a third unsuccessful try to take his own life. Disgraced Senator Rawlings remained defiant and any time he got a chance to speak his mind, his diatribes were venom-laced at best. He refused to acknowledge that he'd done anything wrong, and insisted that he was as big a victim as any of the people who'd lost their lives.

His ex-wife, who hadn't been seen in Washington in many years, returned from Wyoming where she'd lived in self-imposed exile and cleaned out the Senator's house and bank accounts. Turned out, he'd never divorced her, because he didn't want to give her half of everything he had. In the end, she got it all, and held a press conference to gloat. The next morning, while shaving for a court appearance, the Senator's razor went rogue, and he bled out before the guards around his cell could do anything.

Patti sat at the desk in her cubicle, feeling like she'd come home. But at the same time, it felt like she'd somehow outgrown not just her desk, but the niche in which she'd been so comfortable. Perhaps, just perhaps, she'd grown too comfortable. Perhaps all that she'd been through for more than three months had changed her.

The question was, what should she do? Where could she go?

After closely cheating death not once but twice, she was not only leery of stepping out into the unknown, but was hesitant to even consider the possibility. After all, she should have died with the first lady. And were it not for the grace of God, she would have died on the side of that deserted Virginia road. It was like she was alive by default.

It wasn't, she assured herself, a decision that had to be made that day. Or maybe not even the next day. But soon.

Her phone rang as she was unlocking her apartment door, and she struggled to get inside before she answered. It was a White House exchange, and she assumed it was Cindy Lewis checking in on her.

"Hello."

"Ms. Hobgood?"

It was a woman's voice she didn't recognize. "This is she."

"Hold please," the woman on the other end said, "for the President."

*The President! Of the United States?*

"Ms. Hobgood?"

Oh, my gosh! It is the President. What can he want?

"Yes, Mr. President?"

"I'm wondering if you might have time in the next few days to meet with me here at the White House?"

"Well, yes sir, I'm sure I can. When would you like me to be there?"

"How about ten-thirty tomorrow?"

"That will work," she told him. She wanted badly to ask what the meeting was about, but simply couldn't force the words from her lips. The prospect of knowing was too intimidating.

If he sensed any hesitancy on her part, the President didn't address it. "You know, Ms. Hobgood, my sweet wife thought so much of you."

"I admired her as well," she confessed. "In fact, I wish I could tell her that knowing how she fought her way up has given me courage more than once to help me succeed when I probably should have failed."

"I'm glad to hear you say that, Ms. Hobgood. Because I think I may have a way that you can demonstrate your appreciation."

*Where is he going with this?*

"I know you're familiar with The Cumberland Group. It's in trouble, you know."

"Yes sir, I've heard."

"Well, it was my wife's own creation and she put all of herself into forming and shaping it. Perhaps tomorrow, you and I can talk about how you might plug in to the group and help save it."

"The Cumberland Group? Me?"

"See you tomorrow, Ms. Hobgood."

# Coming in 2023-2024

## Cruisin' for a Crook
### Another Slop Bucket Mystery

Mags Gordon, real estate maven and owner of Mountain Magic Realty by Mags has finally given in to pressure to take time off. To go on a cruise along with her office manager, friend, and partner in their unofficial, unsanctioned, unlicensed private investigation agency. Making the trip doesn't feel right to Mags, and when a body is found back in Crabapple Cove that's linked to her agency, Mags takes little pleasure in saying "I told you so." Instead, she must find a way from thousands of miles away, in the middle of a big ocean, to solve the crime before nemesis Doogie, aka the sheriff, can do a number on both her business and her reputation.

## Blessings and Conflict

Victims of domestic violence and abuse are affected for life. This is a sad fact that Margaret Haywood embraced early on in the pages of **Hear My Cry**, **Paths of Judgment**, and **Lift up Mine Eyes**. As she fought her way out of the aftermath of the violence that marred and destroyed their entire family unit, she and each of her children, Brian, Sally and Jason, acted and reacted in drastically different ways. How have the scars of what each experienced affected and directed where each of these four people are today? In the pages of **Blessings and Conflict**, catch up with these captivating individuals that readers bonded with over thirteen years ago. See where each of them is today, and how the specter of violence has colored each of their lives.

## Jaynesville

In 1904, a young mother died from complications of childbirth, leaving behind a grieving husband and several minor children. Her demise wasn't that uncommon in that era in south-central Mississippi. "Yesterday morning, hardly before the day was begun," her obituary read, "the bright and happy hearthstone of one of Magee's pleasantest families was visited by cruel and relentless death, when Mary Magee Shivers closed her eyes in an everlasting sleep, and was borne across that river from which no traveler ever returns." The heart-rending details of her departure from this life were indelibly etched in my head following first hearing this story about my paternal great-grandmother. And from that beginning more than sixty years ago, **Jaynesville**, was conceived and finally, a novel set against a historically-accurate timeline inspired by the story capsuled in that obituary was delivered.

## Serving Freedom for Life

Kathryn McCormick has been paroled from federal prison, after serving fourteen years for a massive Ponzi scheme conviction. She feels she's more than paid her debt to society, but her victims, their families, and even many of her closest family members feel otherwise. She's ready to pick up the pieces of her life and go forward, but is shocked to learn that saying and doing are two different things. She actually craves to be back behind bars, where she could always depend on what was, and credits her faith in God for getting her through those long, lonely years. She believes He has forgiven her. But it isn't until she begins trying to function in a world totally without structure, when she's trying to forgive all those who refuse to forgive her, that she begins to truly find God, and to understand how utterly lost and adrift her soul is.

## Hysterical Preservation

Joell Jenkins doesn't fit the mold of carpenter extraordinaire, known as much for her tightly-fitting mitered molding corners as her Pepto-Bismol® pink hair. Hers is a reputation nurtured in large part because of her regionally syndicated DIY TV show, "Hammerin' It Home." The show's producers have ambitiously created an entire season around the renovation and restoration of a local antebellum home. But when murder comes calling, Joell finds herself tasked with salvaging the project, and saving her own reputation and that of her assistant who's charged with that murder. To obtain justice for the dead man, Joell must circumvent tunnel-visioned investigators to uncover the real reason for the killing, as well as the guilty party.

## Kissin' Kin for Christmas
### 2023 Christmas Collector Book

As soon as Christmas is over, Alex Greeson can get his life back on track and begin dreading the next yuletide season that's a year away. It's been that way since he spent his last Christmas with Nanny Bishop, his mother's mother, when he was only five. That was thirteen years ago, and he never saw her again after the child welfare authorities seized him and placed him in a foster home. Now, he's aged out of the foster care system, is alone and adrift. All he can think about is finding Nanny again, the one person he knows can make everything right. He decides to tempt Santa Claus and God, and in doing so, encounters people who would bar his search, as well as those who champion his cause. How he finds the true meaning of Christmas is revealed in the outcome of his search.

*To receive notices on upcoming book releases,*
email to:  jswriter@bellsouth.net
Check out my web site:  www.jshiverswriter.com
Like me on Facebook:  JShivers Wordweaver

# About the Author

John Shivers began writing for his hometown newspaper when he was only fourteen years old. As a lifelong wordsmith – some have called him a wordweaver – his byline has appeared in over forty Christian and secular publications, winning him seventeen professional awards.

**Hear My Cry**, his first novel, was published in 2004, and a dream of forty-four years was realized. **Alive by Default** is his twenty-fourth book. Eighteen of those books are Christian fiction, four are mysteries, and two are mainstream novels. Additional titles in all three genres are in the planning stage.

John and his wife, Elizabeth, and Callum and Rosie, their beloved four-legged children, divide their time between Calhoun, Georgia and Magee, Mississippi, where his Shivers' roots are almost 200 years planted. He is a Certified Lay Minister in the United Methodist Church and has, since the summer of 2020, served as pastor of Farmville United Methodist Church and Plainville United Methodist Church in Gordon County, Georgia.

When their schedule permits, John loves to slip away to the northeast Georgia mountains. It's there, and at their rural retreat in Mississippi, where he hears music of the heart and inspiration for much of his writing.